Death
at
Beresford
Hall

BOOKS BY EMMA DAVIES

EMMA DAVIES

Death
at
Beresford
Hall

THE ADAM AND EVE MYSTERY SERIES 4

Bookouture

Published by Bookouture in 2022

An imprint of Storyfire Ltd.
Carmelite House
50 Victoria Embankment
London EC4Y 0DZ

www.bookouture.com

ISBN: 978-1-80314-422-1
eBook ISBN: 978-1-80314-421-4

For Holly, Dylan, Ethan and Angharad

1

Miranda Appleby was the nation's darling. As the face of one of TV's best-loved cookery shows she was admired by millions – the string of best-selling cookery books and shelf full of awards was proof enough. She had the world at her feet. From her trademark tumbling golden locks to the voluminous skirts of the fifties-inspired outfits she always wore, every inch of her said 'starlet', yet with a kind word for everyone and generous to a fault she was loved as much for her personality as she was for her looks.

Today, they were filming for the new series of *Country Cooks Cook*. It was the Christmas edition, too, which always made it that bit extra special and soon she would be back on set ready to judge the first day's competition. Would it be Christine who triumphed, despite her rather ropey start? Or would it be Vinny – cool, calm and collected – who would impress her? Viewers would love Pea, this year's mother hen, and Tony, too, who would score for his old-fashioned charm. Jenny would perhaps appeal to the younger audience with her passion for vegan cookery, although Miranda wasn't at all sure she would pull it off. Which only left Fran, of course, who'd stood in at the last minute after that little bit of unpleasantness, but she was a safe pair of hands and shouldn't give them any problems. It would be interesting to see how everyone fared over the course of the week, it always was.

Miranda rose from the opulent seating area that spanned one end of her deluxe trailer and settled herself in front of her dressing table. A perfunctory knock sounded at the door and she turned slightly as it opened, ready with a smile of greeting.

Oh... Now that was a surprise. It was also a problem, because she was due back on set quite soon, yet, try as she might, she couldn't rise from her chair or shout out. Let alone pull out the cake slice that had been thrust into her chest with such force. She had no time to ponder whether it had been a lucky strike or skilful placement from someone who knew what they were doing because her severed aorta was already beginning to take its toll.

And that really was a problem, because seventy-two seconds later Miranda's heart stopped. Miranda Appleby, the nation's darling, was dead. And it was all Fran's fault.

2

ONE DAY EARLIER

Fran contemplated the crowd of people scurrying back and forth, and tried hard to quash her instinctive feeling to run. Everything would be fine, everything *was* fine, but it was hard to feel relaxed when those around her had faces fixed with harried intent. What she wouldn't give to be back at home in her kitchen, icing cupcakes for a christening or putting the finishing touches on a wedding cake. Anything but what she was about to do.

'Don't say it,' she warned as Adam grinned at her, his dark eyes twinkling in the sunshine. 'This is not in the slightest bit cool. I'm frankly terrified.' She looked around, wondering where they should go.

'Yes, but you're getting to meet Miranda Appleby,' replied Adam. '*The* Miranda Appleby. The woman who inspired you to train as a chef in the first place. The woman whose books line the shelves in your kitchen. The woman who—'

'Adam, you're not making this any easier,' said Fran, putting down her suitcase for a moment. 'I'm nervous enough as it is. She's also the woman who has been receiving some really nasty "presents" and now I'm here to investigate, while pretending to be a writer penning a fly-on-the-wall book about Miranda and the show that made her famous, which I haven't the foggiest idea how to do.' She stopped, frowning at Adam's smiling face. 'What?' she asked.

'Fran,' he said, still grinning, 'breathe... you know, that thing where you inhale and exhale. It's supposed to be calming—' He broke off. 'Everything's going to be all right. You do know that, don't you?' He pulled his beanie hat down even further over his ears and adjusted the weight of his backpack.

But Fran couldn't answer. Adam looked just as nervous as she was and it was usually *her* reassuring *him*, not the other way around.

'Come on,' she said, grasping the handle of her suitcase. 'Let's find out where we should be.'

Beresford Hall didn't open to the public very often and Fran had only been to the stately home twice before. On both those occasions it had been busy but this morning it was unrecognisable. Not only was the large forecourt in front of the house full, but the area to the side of the hall as well, where open-air theatre performances took place during the summer. Now, two huge trailers all but filled the space, looking over a swathe of green lawn on the far side, while another, much smaller, campervan stood a little distance away. Everywhere she looked, people scurried to and fro, ant-like in purpose.

Fran was about to ask someone for directions when a slight woman carrying a clipboard approached them, broadening her smile.

'You must be Francesca,' she said as she reached them. 'Or, rather, Fran...' She checked her notes. 'Have I got that right? And Adam?'

Fran nodded, wondering what it was about herself which gave away her identity. Lack of height? Unruly, short dark hair which was resolutely tucked behind her ears? Freckles which ganged up over her nose? Or the look of abject terror on her face?

'I'm Midge,' said the woman. 'Miranda's PA. Welcome to the set of *Country Cooks Cook*. Isn't it beautiful here?' She looked around her as if inviting Fran to do the same. 'Would you like to come with me? I'll show you where you're staying first of all, but you'll have plenty of free time today to wander around and get your bearings.'

With a quick look at Adam, Fran fell into step beside Midge. The young woman wore a fixed smile, which gave Fran the impression she was permanently harassed but desperate to show she wasn't. A limp ponytail hung over one shoulder of her navy-blue trouser suit, not the best colour to hide the dog hairs which clung to it, but, nonetheless, the outfit suited her petite frame. Her face was lit up by a pair of startling-blue eyes which transformed her otherwise pale complexion.

Despite the bright autumnal sunshine, the morning was still pretty chilly. Fran was glad of her coat but Midge clearly moved too fast to ever get cold. Fran lengthened her stride and endeavoured to keep up.

'The contestants are all staying in the guest wing of the house,' said Midge, 'so we've put you and Adam there too, if that's okay?' She led them across the front of the impressive main building, neatly sidestepping another woman whose arms were full of foliage. 'There's an orientation meeting for everyone later this afternoon and an icebreaker this evening, which will be huge fun, they always are. I thought if you came along to both of those it would give you a good opportunity to meet everyone and see how we do things. Folks think you're researching a book so I don't suppose anyone will question why you're there.'

Fran nodded, trying to take in everything she had been told. The details she'd been given were very thin on the ground which, given the lateness of the arrangements, wasn't surprising, but it wasn't helping her nerves. She *had* been told, however, that Midge was the fount of all knowledge.

'This is some set-up,' remarked Fran. 'I didn't imagine there'd be quite so many people here.'

'Everyone says that,' replied Midge, smiling. 'Given that there are only six contestants on the show, it doesn't seem possible, does it? But that's TV for you. The fact that it's the Christmas edition makes a difference too. It's a huge draw as far as the ratings are concerned and everything has to look really festive, even though it's only September. There are seven florists here this morning alone.'

Fran flashed a look at Adam: that wasn't entirely good news. With so many people around it would be very difficult to keep an eye on things, or work out what was happening. She scuttled after Midge, resolving to have a proper look around as soon as they could.

The side entrance of the house, albeit with a much smaller portico than the front, still retained an air of grandeur. A flight of stone steps rose to an impressive oak door studded with ironwork, flagged on either side by two huge urns. Each held a miniature Christmas tree topped with an elaborate red bow. Fran had to resist the urge to give a low whistle.

'We thought they might help get people in the festive mood,' said Midge, pushing open the door.

A waft of rather oppressive heat greeted them as they followed her into an equally impressive hallway which opened onto a central space lined with oak panelling. A fireplace was merrily ablaze and a huge Christmas tree twinkled from a corner. Three enormous sofas had been arranged around the fire, while matching armchairs filled another two corners.

'Your rooms are just through here,' said Midge, indicating another hallway. 'This is yours, Fran,' she added, turning to her left. 'And Adam, you're on the right.' She was about to say something further when her phone trilled from where she held it clamped against the side of her clipboard. Swapping hands, she mouthed an apology and answered the call.

'Yes, I'm just with them now,' she said, nodding. 'Uh-huh, ten minutes... no, I told her to leave it with Miranda... yes, I'll go and check.' She paused, listening for a moment. 'Okay, but they promised me they'd be out by twelve at the latest... I know... yes, I know... right, bye then.' She disconnected the call with a smile. 'No rest for the wicked,' she said. 'That was Harrison – he's the show's director and producer, you'll meet him later. Lovely, lovely man...' She gave Fran a bright smile and pushed open the door to her room. 'I hope everything is okay for you, but you must let me know if there's anything else you need and I'll have a word with Betty. She's the housekeeper here – heart of gold – and will be looking after everyone this week.'

Fran nodded, adding Betty's name to those she'd already been given. The housekeeper could be a useful person to talk to, she may well know a lot about goings-on.

Midge was hovering. 'Shall I let you get your things unpacked? Then perhaps you'd like to have a look around? On your own is fine... I can come back for you later. I've put some information on the desk there about timings and so on. You might want to have a little read.' Midge very evidently had to be elsewhere.

'Of course,' said Fran. 'Thank you, that's very kind. I'm sure we can sort ourselves out from here.'

Adam nodded agreement, a slightly dazed smile on his face. Fran knew exactly how he felt.

'Excellent... I'll get out of your way then,' added Midge with another smile. She was halfway across the hallway before Fran could even reply.

Fran raised her eyebrows at Adam. 'Shall we meet back up in fifteen minutes or so?' she asked. 'Will that give you enough time to unpack?'

Adam eyed his bag, which was roughly half the size of hers.

'Make it ten,' he said, grinning. 'I want to explore, this place is incredible.'

'Ten it is,' she replied, turning to wheel her suitcase inside. She closed the door behind her, smiling at the sight which met her eyes. The room was beautiful, full of lovely antique furniture, the warm colours of which were replicated in the soft furnishings. Sinking down on the bed, Fran took a very deep breath. Since Friday, which was only three short days ago, she'd hardly had time to catch her breath and she was rather dismayed at the level to which her life had descended into chaos again. You'd think she'd have got used to it by now.

She had got up on Friday, to all intents and purposes a normal day, fully expecting to spend it making a buffet for a corporate party, when she'd received a panicked and near-hysterical phone call from one of her clients. A client who was expecting to get married the following weekend but who was now in a Swiss hospital with a broken arm and leg. Honestly, who on earth goes skiing a week before their wedding?

The result had been postponed nuptials and Fran out of a very lucrative and very lavish wedding to cater for. It had also left a gaping hole in her diary during what would otherwise have been a busy week. Plus, to accommodate the elaborate preparations, Fran had turned down several bookings, bookings which she then would have been very grateful for. With a heavy heart she had turned her attention back to the buffet in hand. She hadn't got very far, however, before the phone rang again and that time it had been Nell, Detective Chief Inspector Helen Bradley. Which was why, two days later, she and Adam were about to install themselves at Beresford Hall.

The *Country Cooks Cook Christmas Special* was something Fran had watched every year for the past five or six, ever since it had been running. The main edition of the show aired in the summer, when twelve contestants battled it out for the title of 'Best Country Cook'. The Christmas edition, however, was a shortened version with only six competitors and a little more emphasis on Miranda Appleby than the competition. As the show's star host, it was an opportunity for her to showcase her culinary prowess and pass on a few tips to make the season's festivities ultra-successful.

But this year Miranda had a problem. Since the filming of the summer show back in April, some not very nice person had been sending her nasty little surprises: a bunch of dead roses, a sympathy card consoling her for the loss of her youth and, most recently, a tube of Polyfilla with a caustic label attached making reference to her wrinkles. All of which had sent her running to the wife of the district police commissioner who was a dear friend of hers. Responding to his wife's demands that something be done, the district police commissioner had been keen to reassure Miranda that it was more than likely just some silly prankster but, given who she was, he had also simultaneously tasked Nell with the job of getting to the bottom of whatever was going on. Crippled by several complicated investigations and a nasty bout of flu which had been doing the rounds of her workforce, Nell had turned to Fran and Adam for a little helping hand.

'Oh, come on, Fran,' Nell had said. 'You couldn't get a person more suited to working undercover on a cooking show.'

Adam had been far too excited when Fran had told him the news. He'd been desperate to become an official police consultant ever since their last case when they'd helped to solve a murder that no one even suspected was a murder. Fran, however, wasn't quite so happy about the situation. Being undercover was tantamount to lying and she never felt comfortable with that, even if it was justified under the circumstances. Plus, she hated being away from home, and although her husband, Jack, had never minded parenting single-handed, it didn't feel right being so far away from her daughter, Martha, either. And at such short notice too.

Ever since she and Adam had solved their first case, she'd tried to play down her subsequent sleuthing activities but Jack wasn't daft. He was worried about her and she only hoped her promises that nothing dangerous would be going on held true. At least the accommodation would be worth it, the place was gorgeous!

Fran was hanging up the last of her clothes in the room's capacious wardrobe when a soft tap sounded at the door. Adam was still smiling as she opened it.

'Has your room got a—' He broke off, pointing at the rather ornate bed frame. Not quite the full four-poster, but the two by the headboard it did include were still draped with an expanse of expensive-looking fabric. 'If this is a guest room, then what do you reckon the main house is like?'

Fran gave him a pointed look. 'Off limits,' she said firmly. 'So, your exploring isn't to include any of the private residence.'

Adam pulled a face but then smiled benignly up at her from under his dark curls which, as usual, were peeping out from his colourful beanie hat. 'Okay, boss,' he replied.

That didn't fool her one little bit. Adam was... hard to describe in some respects. Almost half her age, they had met about eighteen months ago when his mum, Sara, had become the prime suspect in a murder investigation. One of Sara's friends had died in mysterious circumstances following Sara's birthday party, a party where Fran had been the caterer. With no one else to turn to, Adam had come to her for help in clearing his mum's name. They had not only done so, but also uncovered the real killer's identity and since then seemed to have an uncanny knack of being in the wrong place at the wrong time where murder was concerned. Or, as Adam liked to put it, the right place at the right time. Adam was very good at solving puzzles but his methods could be a little unorthodox at times, actually borderline illegal some of the time, a fact which irritated Nell no end. His natural curiosity and whip-smart brain, however, were a very useful combination and the perfect accompaniment to Fran's observational and people skills, as recent months had proven. It was an unlikely friendship, but somehow it worked.

'So, what do we do now?' asked Fran. 'We need to have a look at the information Midge left, but I'm keen to make contact with Miranda too. The sooner we get a handle on what's been going on here, the better. We also need to know if anyone apart from Midge knows the real reason we're here. We could easily give ourselves away with a slight slip of the tongue if we're not careful.'

Adam nodded. 'So, who are our suspects then? Presumably not the other contestants?'

Fran wrinkled her nose. 'Never say never. As you know, each series of shows is filmed in a different county, with contestants from the local area, but the fact that the so-called gifts only started appearing in April has to be significant. They were filming the summer series then, which could suggest a contestant from that show was responsible, but then the Polyfilla with its rather unpleasant note only arrived last week, which seems to contradict that theory. I think the culprit is more likely to be someone who has access to Miranda, so possibly someone who works on the show, but I'm also wondering when the contestants for the Christmas show found out they'd got a place. It could be one of them.'

'So, it might be like a stalker then?'

'Perhaps. Although I think it's more likely to be someone she knows. There must be any number of staff in her entourage: make-up people, cameramen, sound engineers. Who knows? It could be a pretty long list.' She paused. 'It could also be Midge,' she added. 'We need to be mindful of that.'

'Then let's go see who we can find,' said Adam. 'Before everything gets really busy.'

. . .

Retracing their steps, Fran and Adam made their way around to the front of the main house, walking towards the vehicles they had first seen when they arrived.

'Those big trailers must be where the crew are based,' said Adam, pointing to the far-left side of the house. 'Maybe even Miranda herself.'

'Then we need to check for certain because, if that's the case, plenty of people could have access to her. It's not exactly private, is it?'

Adam shook his head. 'Anyone walking this way could easily be seen.'

While that was true, Fran wondered just how much anyone was paying attention. Everyone she could see seemed pretty intent on what they were doing, moving purposefully, and at speed too. 'Let's see what's around there,' she said, noticing that most people seemed to be moving away from them, towards the rear of the building.

She'd only gone a couple of steps, however, when a voice came from behind. It was Midge.

'I'm glad I've caught you,' she said, taking Fran's arm and all but spinning her around. 'Miranda's asked me to fetch you and I was on my way when Harrison needed a word. Again.' She smiled, but it didn't reach anywhere near her eyes. 'We'd better go now before he spots us, I'm not sure he's altogether in favour of someone writing a book about Miranda and the show.' She gave Fran a complicit look. 'It's nothing to do with him, obviously, Miranda is her own boss, but they've worked together a long time and he can be very protective of her.'

Fran flashed a look at Adam. Harrison obviously wasn't aware of the real reason they were there.

Walking at speed again, Fran was about to ask if Harrison even knew about Miranda's strange 'gifts' when Midge suddenly stopped.

'You will find out who's doing these awful things, won't

you?' she said. 'Miranda's lovely, really lovely, but she's understandably a little more stressed than usual and...' Anxiety was written across Midge's pale face, and Fran could sense her predicament – how to say what she needed to without being in any way derogatory about her boss.

Fran gave Midge a warm smile. 'Don't worry, we will. As soon as we can.'

Midge nodded, her composure fully back in place. 'Great, just let me know if you need anything. Right, here we are.'

She had led them across the driveway to the two trailers, so Adam's assumption had been right. 'This first one belongs to Harrison,' said Midge. 'While Miranda's is the one bordering the gardens. I'll just give her a quick knock.' She started up the steps and then turned as she reached the top. 'Oh, you don't mind dogs, do you?'

Fran shook her head, looking at Adam who did likewise.

'Great, they're Miranda's pride and joy, you see. She never goes anywhere without them.'

Midge tapped softly on the door. 'Miranda...? It's only Midge. I've brought Francesca and Adam to see you.' She pulled open the door, beckoning for them to join her.

Fran took a deep breath. She wasn't at all prepared to meet Miranda Appleby and was bound to say something toe-curlingly embarrassing. But what *did* you say to one of the country's best-loved celebrity cooks? Somehow she didn't think swapping recipes for Victoria sponge would go down all that well.

Midge moved aside when Fran reached the top of the steps. 'Go on through,' she said.

The trailer could give most five-star hotel rooms a run for their money. Fran had imagined a smart caravan-like interior but that was about as far away from reality as was possible. Thick carpet, expensive furniture, a tented ceiling for heaven's sake. It was luxury on wheels.

At the far end of the room was the woman who had taught Fran so much about her craft. Miranda Appleby was reclining on an opulent corner-seating arrangement piled high with velvet cushions. She was wearing buttery-coloured trousers and a pale-pink jumper which was undoubtedly cashmere, her trademark golden waves tumbling over her shoulders. Fran could see the shine on them from the door. Sprawled on either side of her were two tan and black spaniels, all silken ears and big brown eyes.

'Francesca! Oh, it's so good to see you.' Miranda uncurled her legs from beneath her, getting to her feet. 'I can't begin to tell you how pleased I am you're here. And they tell me you love to cook as well, my very favourite kind of person, obviously.' She beamed a warm smile, one which the camera loved. 'Come in and we can get to know one another.' She held out her hand and, taking Fran's, pulled her towards another sofa opposite. 'Now, sit there and tell me everything is going to be all right. I've been so worried.' She smiled up at Adam who was hovering nervously, beanie in hand. 'Adam... come in, come in... I don't bite, despite what they say. Come and sit here.' She patted the sofa beside her as she retook her seat. Almost immediately one of the spaniels made way for her, draping itself over Adam instead, who almost disappeared behind a cloud of fur. She looked enquiringly up at Fran, who blushed furiously.

'Um... yes, of course. Well, everything *is* going to be fine. Once we've got to the bottom of whatever's been going on... *which* I'm sure will be soon,' she finished, seeing the alarm in Miranda's eyes. 'We obviously have lots of questions, so the sooner we—' She stopped as Miranda waved an airy hand.

'You can ask Midge. She can tell you everything you need to know.'

Fran looked at Miranda's expectant face. 'That's great, but it would be helpful to run through events with you as well – to get your take on things. Would now be good time to do that?'

Miranda laid a hand on one of the dogs' heads. 'This is Pippin. Isn't he a beauty? I don't know what I'd do without my darlings. Not forgetting Bramley, of course. They're such a comfort to me. I couldn't bear it if anything happened to them.'

Fran gave her a hesitant smile. Perhaps Miranda didn't think the question had been directed at her, or maybe she simply hadn't heard it. But then Miranda turned her gaze on Midge. '*Is* now a good time? There's always so much to do, and without Midge I'm sure I'd forget my own name.'

Midge's pale skin flushed pink as her eyes darted to the clipboard in her arms. She was about to reply when Miranda leaned forward.

'Let me know how you get on, Fran, won't you? I'm sure Midge can find a window for you to go through everything, and she really is the best person to talk to about all this, I...' She trailed off. 'It's very good of you to come and help me out like this, I feel so much better knowing you're here. And it's been lovely meeting you.'

Fran frowned as Miranda's gaze drifted towards the window. Was that it? Was the meeting over? Evidently it was, because Midge was holding out an arm to indicate that they should get going. Fran scrambled to her feet, throwing a look at Adam. He slid out from under a pile of doggy limbs, looking equally bemused.

Midge offered them a warm smile as she shepherded them towards the front of the trailer, catching Fran's eye as she did so. 'I'll come find you, if that's okay?' she said quietly. 'And if not, I'll catch up with you at the orientation. Maybe you'd like to have a look at the stable in the meantime? Just follow the driveway around to the rear of the house. You can't miss it.' She paused. 'I just need to check up on a couple of things with Miranda...'

Fran nodded. 'Oh, absolutely, don't worry. Thanks, Midge.'

And then she was walking back down the steps with Adam, feeling rather bemused.

She was almost at Harrison's trailer when she realised she hadn't checked the one thing she really needed to. Asking Adam to wait a moment, she doubled back and was poised ready to knock on the trailer door when she became aware of raised voices inside.

'For God's sake, Midge, take them back to the cottage, there's fur everywhere!'

'Yes, they're dogs, Miranda, that tends to happen.'

'You can't have been brushing them. Not properly. Oh, look at me, I'm such a mess, I'll have to change.'

'No, if you'll just let me— Pippin, get down! Look, Miranda, I'll come back, okay? Let me take them back to the cottage and then I can sort out your clothes. I can't do it while they're here.' There was a pause, followed by a dog barking excitedly. 'Come on, boys, this way, that's it.'

Fran shot back down the trailer steps and hurried to where Adam was standing, pulling him from view just as the trailer door flew open. The dogs burst through it a second later, dragging a helpless Midge behind them. Fran watched as the young woman wrestled with their leads for a moment, before eventually getting them in order. She stopped, bent down and ruffled each of the dogs' heads in turn, touching noses with them. Then she rose, and with each spaniel perfectly in control, walked across the front of the house towards the guest accommodation.

Fran stared at her retreating figure before her eye was caught by the trailer door swinging back open. Miranda was standing on the step, staring after Midge with an angry scowl on her face. 'Bloody dogs,' she muttered, and slammed the door.

3

Fran waited until they had passed the trailers and were well out of earshot before turning to Adam.

'Is it me?' she asked.

He shook his head. 'No, that was weird. *She* was weird.'

'And rude... She asked to see *us*, not the other way round, and then she can't be bothered to talk to us, even for five minutes. Or tell us any of the things we really need to know. How are we supposed to find out who's behind all the horrible things which have happened without any information? Like who might have had the opportunity, for example? Who might possibly have a grudge against her? Either Miranda's worried witless or she isn't, but surely she's aware we're not going to get anywhere without her help? As for poor Midge... I heard what came out of Miranda's mouth, but I can't help feeling as if she was belittling Midge somehow. So what if Midge carries a schedule around with her, she's obviously a very busy person.' Fran tutted. 'And what was with the dogs? Whatever Midge might have told us it certainly doesn't seem as if they're Miranda's pride and joy.'

Adam brushed several hairs from his jacket sleeve. 'I know

what I think,' he said. 'If it was a choice of the dogs or Miranda, I'd take the dogs any day.'

Fran stopped abruptly, hands on her hips. 'I know what I think too, and now I'm really miffed.' She sighed. 'I admired that woman, Adam. I thought the sun shone out of her—'

'Don't say it!' warned Adam.

Fran caught his look and smiled. That was usually her line. 'But I did, you know I did. I've spent years following her recipes, buying her books, thinking how talented she was, how brilliant she was for making ordinary everyday cookery so popular again and, now, after less than five minutes with her, I'm wondering how I could have been so stupid. How we all could have been so stupid.'

'I suspect what actually happened is the press and a damn good publicist made cookery popular again. And Miranda's was the face that fitted, the one the cameras loved. I mean, she's quite... erm...' He held up his hands in a helpless gesture.

'Fit?' offered Fran. 'Alluring?'

Adam coloured.

'And now that I've seen her in the flesh, I'm wondering if flicking hair and coy looks are all there is,' continued Fran. 'She's clearly trading on her appearance. And to think I was taken in by all that.'

'Maybe she is just very stressed, like Midge said,' offered Adam, 'and we're not seeing her good side.'

Fran narrowed her eyes. 'Hmm... we'll see.' She tutted. 'No, you're right. I'm always telling Martha to be a little more considered in her opinions, not to jump to conclusions about people so quickly. I should follow my own advice.' Fran's daughter was a teenager, it was almost in her job description to be judgemental. Fran, however, was an adult and should know better. She indicated the driveway ahead of her. 'Come on. Now that we're here, we might as well see what there is.'

They followed the wide sweep of gravel around to the rear

of the house and, almost immediately, Fran could see they were in the right place. It was certainly where all the activity seemed to be centred. A large group of people stood virtually in the centre of a wide, flagged yard, all of whom seemed to be talking at the same time. Fran pointed to the stable block. 'I think that must be where the competition is being held,' she said.

Its title didn't really do the stable block justice, given that it was evidently some while since it had housed horses. The partitions between the stalls had been removed and it was now one long, low structure, with elegant windows and doors. A row of wooden barrels had been positioned at regular intervals down its length, each holding a Christmas tree topped with the same large red bow as the one outside of the guest wing. Strings of lights were being hung along the roof line and someone else was fixing large rustic-looking stars to the wall on either side of the main door. Fran gave Adam an amused glance. They looked incongruous in the bright sunshine of an Indian summer.

As they took in their surroundings, a man came forward out of the crowd, his arm raised to attract their attention. Fran had never given much thought to what a TV executive might look like, but if she'd had to hazard a guess, the man coming towards them would be a good fit. Younger than her, tall and slim, he wore his longish, black hair swept back off his face. Boyish good looks were tempered with a pair of wire-rimmed spectacles, and the perfect white teeth and casual, yet no doubt very expensive, clothes shouted success.

He pointed two fingers towards Fran's chest almost as if he were holding a gun. 'Fran, right?' He flashed a smile. 'Which means you must be Adam? It's great to meet you guys.' The hand extended. 'I'm Harrison, the show's producer and director.'

Fran shook it, gratified that he hadn't immediately gone for the kiss to both cheeks. 'Yes, we've met Midge. She mentioned who you were.'

Harrison nodded towards the group of people he'd just left. 'Looks alarming, doesn't it? But don't worry, this lot will all be gone by tea time, and then there'll be just a select few of us left to keep the show running. Although maybe this kind of stuff is useful for your research? A behind-the-scenes look at one of the most popular shows on television.'

'Oh yes, wonderfully so.' Fran didn't trust herself to say any more, seeing that her cover story was the thing she had given the least amount of thought. Her stomach started to fizz with nerves, it was suddenly all very real. She smiled and nodded, resisting the impulse to run straight back to her room, pack up her things and leave.

'You couldn't have picked a better time to come,' Harrison added. 'The Christmas shows are my favourite. Everyone's favourite, actually. Such a wonderful atmosphere.' He beamed at Adam. 'Let me show you both the stable. You're local, I gather. Have you been here before?'

Fran managed to shake her head. 'Not the stable, no, only the main house.'

'I was going to say you won't recognise it, but come and see what the team have done, it's incredible.'

He led them through a set of double doors which had been propped open, making way as he did so for two women who were leaving. 'I'll introduce you later,' he said, as he opened his arms wide in an expansive gesture. 'We've been so incredibly lucky with the setting. Isn't it beautiful?'

Fran had to agree that it was, but despite the festive adornments, the real star of the show was the stable itself. The aged, oak timbers of a cruck frame crisscrossed the space, intersecting the walls and soaring to the rafters in a series of beams and joints. In between, the whitewashed walls were festooned with swags and wreaths of holly, ivy and mistletoe. It could have come straight from the pages of *Country Living*.

Miranda's kitchen, or rather the TV set equivalent of one,

had been set up on the far side. It never failed to amaze Fran how they could make this appear so lifelike when in reality it had more in common with a doll's house, complete with flimsy partition walls. It was here that Miranda would demonstrate some of her favourite festive recipes. There was even a Christmas tree nestled in one corner providing the perfect backdrop of twinkling lights which would sparkle over Miranda's shoulder while she cooked. Slightly further down the room was an even larger tree, reaching almost to roof height. An army of dressers were busy transforming it into a seasonal centrepiece, complete with a pile of brightly wrapped presents waiting to be placed into position. An armchair stood beside it, together with a small coffee table, and Fran realised it was the cosy sitting room where Miranda would do her pieces to the camera. Fran had seen her do it so many times before but it never occurred to her that they were not real rooms. The rest of the space was given over to a series of workstations which had been set up at regular inter-vals down the centre. Complete with sinks, hobs and numerous items of kitchen equipment, they were clearly for the competitors' use.

Following her gaze around the room, Harrison smiled and pointed to the far end, where another partition was being erected. Fran could just make out a clutch of armchairs through the gap. 'That's going to be our green room,' he said. 'For when everyone is off camera. We really do think of everything here. The catering truck will be on the yard, just outside, so it's abso-lutely ideal.'

Fran stared at him. 'There's going to be a catering truck?' The very idea struck her as hugely ironic. A catering truck on a cookery show?

But if Harrison thought it odd, he didn't show it, merely nodded. 'You'll meet Judy later. The woman's a star, she looks after us all beautifully. Amazing cook.'

Fran couldn't help but wonder what Miranda might make of that particular comment, but she let it go.

'People don't realise how much hanging around there is,' continued Harrison. 'And the crew do love their coffee... and their bacon sandwiches.' He looked at his watch. 'In fact, I must check to see where the truck is. It's usually set up by now.'

'Yes, of course,' said Fran. 'Don't let us keep you. I'm sure you have loads to do.'

Harrison smiled. 'Have a look around though, don't be shy. The crew are a great bunch and if you have any questions, fire away, they're used to being interrupted. Did Midge mention the orientation meeting at three? That would be a great opportunity for you to meet everyone.'

'She did, thanks,' replied Fran. 'Although I haven't seen sign of any contestants yet. Are they here?'

Harrison gave her an amused look. 'Oh yes, but engaged in preparation, I would imagine. There's going to be some hot competition over the next few days.' He touched a light hand to Fran's sleeve. 'I'll catch you guys later and, in the meantime, if you have any burning questions, Midge is your woman. She'll be around somewhere, she always is.' He beamed them both a bright smile and, with a wave to a woman across the room, was gone.

Fran steepled her fingers together. 'Right then, beautiful though it is, let's see if we can find Midge. All this is giving me the collywobbles.'

'Colly *what*?' asked Adam, eyebrows raised in amusement.

'Wobbles,' replied Fran. 'Nerves, anxiety, or, in my case, sheer terror... I'm sure people are going to see straight through me. What do writers even look like? Anyway, let's keep our eyes open, one of the people here might be responsible for Miranda's little "gifts".'

They threaded their way back through the yard and around

to the front of the house, automatically looking to their right at the two trailers belonging to Harrison and Miranda.

'I wonder where Midge is. Do you suppose she's still removing all those pesky dog hairs from Miranda?' asked Fran. 'Because I'd rather not disturb *her* if we don't have to.'

Adam looked around. 'Midge walked off with the dogs in that direction,' he said, pointing left towards the guest wing. 'We could try over there.'

Fran eyed Miranda's trailer. 'Let's do that. I don't fancy the alternative.'

It soon became evident that even if Midge wasn't around, the dogs certainly were. As they passed the guest wing door excited yips filled the air and it sounded very much like the dogs were enjoying themselves. It hadn't even occurred to Fran that they might be loose but, as they rounded the corner, a spaniel came flying, ears flapping, a tennis ball in its mouth.

Midge gave a sharp whistle. 'Pippin, no! This way, boy.' The dog skidded to a halt and trotted calmly back towards her. 'Sorry,' she called. 'They get a bit excited.'

Fran raised an arm in greeting. 'No problem. They look like they're having a great time.'

If Fran had got her bearings right they were now on the other side of the stable block, in an orchard and what looked as if it was once a kitchen garden. It was now an area of rough grass with a path running straight down the middle, on which Midge was standing, ball in hand.

'The owners of the house have been great,' she said. 'There's not really anywhere else I can let the boys run and I daren't let them near the formal gardens. Can you imagine the havoc they could reap?' She pointed towards the other end of the path and a snug little building which sat there. 'I'm staying in the old gardener's cottage so it's absolutely ideal.'

'They're beautiful dogs,' said Adam. 'And that was some whistle.'

Midge pulled a face. 'They're good boys, but this is no place for them, really. There aren't enough hours in the day to look after them the way they ought to be, but...' She trailed off, brightening her face. 'How's everything going? Are you finding your way around okay?'

Fran nodded. 'It's all lovely,' she replied. 'Terrifying, but lovely.' She paused a moment. 'We could do with a chat to you, though, about the real reason we're here. Sorry, I know you're very busy.'

Midge whistled at the dogs. 'Let me loose these boys back in the cottage, and I'll be right with you. Bramley, put that down, sweetheart. I can't let you take sticks in the house.'

Fran watched as Midge walked down the path away from them. It was clear she doted on the spaniels, and they on her, but it didn't seem right for her to be taking responsibility for animals that didn't even belong to her.

'Do you get the feeling that whatever she's being paid, it's nowhere near enough?' said Adam, as if reading Fran's mind.

'The woman deserves a bloody medal,' she muttered.

Midge reappeared a couple of minutes later, carrying her clipboard as she hurried towards them. 'Your detective inspector asked Miranda for the names of people who work with her, so I've put together a list.'

Fran was about to tell Midge they didn't actually work for Nell, but something made her stop. It wouldn't really be a bad idea if that's what Midge thought.

Midge fished under the top sheet on her clipboard and pulled out a piece of paper, handing it to Fran. 'It's just the regulars, people like me who travel around and work on all the shows. If I listed everyone involved, *I'd* have written a book by the time I'd finished.'

Fran looked at the neatly typed spreadsheet she'd been given, showing everyone's name, position, the date from which they'd started work with Miranda, as well as myriad other bits of information which Midge evidently thought might prove relevant. It was concise, clear and extremely helpful.

'I made two copies so you could have one each,' said Midge. 'But you'll see there are a few things missing, some of it I just don't know. I could probably find out, but I didn't have long to put this together, so—'

'No, it's brilliant,' replied Fran. 'Really.' She handed a copy of the list to Adam. 'Commit that to memory,' she said, smiling.

Adam studied the names. 'So, assuming that whoever left these little "gifts" for Miranda is one of her regular staff, who could it have been?'

Midge frowned. 'All of them,' she replied. But then her brow furrowed. 'Sorry, are you asking me who might have done it? Or who could have done it? They're very different things.'

Fran shot Adam a quick glance. He would most definitely approve of the way Midge's brain worked. Her clarification of language reminded Fran of her primary school teacher. She was a stickler for grammar. *Yes, you* can *have a banana*, she used to say, *in that there is a bowl of them over there and with two hands you are perfectly capable of picking one up to eat it. Whether you may have a banana is an altogether different question.*

'Let's just stick to the *could* have done it, for now,' replied Fran, smiling at the young woman's intelligence. 'I don't want to put you in an awkward position.'

'In that case, my answer stands,' replied Midge. 'Everyone on that list had opportunity. You've seen the set-up here, and it's generally no different wherever we are – a main building where we film the competition, an area where the competitors are housed, another for the crew or regular staff, including myself, then Harrison and Miranda's trailers. Miranda usually has them placed a little aside from everything, says it affords her a bit more privacy, but people often pop in and out and the trailers aren't locked during the day, it wouldn't be practical. So, in theory, anyone could have accessed them. Once filming is underway it's very busy. People concentrate on their own jobs, and you don't necessarily have time to notice what everyone else is up to.'

'You do though,' remarked Adam. He indicated her clipboard. 'Sorry, I couldn't help noticing. You seem to have a list of everything going on.'

Midge coloured slightly. 'True, but I have to know what's happening at any given time. It's part of my job to ensure everything stays on track. Delays can very easily mount up and, before you know it, the filming schedule has gone completely out the window.' She raised her eyebrows. 'I generally only get to hear when someone is in the wrong place or hasn't appeared when they should have. Mind you, I often think a clone would come in handy, then I could be in more than one place at a time.'

'It's a very useful point to make, though,' remarked Fran. 'Because you're right, I can see how easy it would be for someone to slip away unnoticed when the focus wasn't on them.' She looked down at Midge's list. 'Would you be able to point out some of these people to us?' she asked. 'We need to get a handle on who's who as soon as possible.'

Midge checked the time on her phone. 'I can do better than that,' she said. 'It's nearly two o'clock and the orientation meeting is in just over an hour. It's mainly for the competitors' benefit but the staff go along as well so they can introduce themselves. After today it will be a closed set, pretty much, and you'll get to know everyone quite well over the course of the week.' She indicated that they should walk on ahead. 'If we go back to the guest wing, I'll show you where the kitchen is. Betty won't be far away, she tends to hover in case anyone needs anything and she seems to have the kettle almost permanently on the boil. Why don't you have a cup of tea while you wait? You can go through the list I've given you. I've also written down everything I can about the incidents themselves. I found one of the "presents" Miranda received – the dead roses – but she found everything else, so what happened on those occasions is mostly a recount of what she told me. I thought it might help you to start with.'

Fran's face lit up. 'That's brilliant, thank you. I was about to ask when would be a good time to go through everything. Miranda doesn't seem all that keen on helping us.' She paused. 'Which seems a bit odd under the circumstances.'

Midge met her look. 'I know she gives that impression, but...' She cast about for what to say. 'It's not that she isn't keen on helping, more that she's become so stressed by the whole thing she's pushing it away so she doesn't get upset. She has a show to film and I think she's a little worried how she'll look.' Her glance flicked away momentarily. 'That might sound silly, but it can't do for Miranda to appear on camera with puffy eyes and have anyone comment on how tired she looks. We have a fabulous make-up artist, but even she can't work miracles. People talk and... I'm sure you understand. Besides, I probably *do* know as much about what's been happening as Miranda, so I'm sure you'll find my notes helpful.' She gave a tight smile.

The fire was still burning brightly in the sitting-room grate when they arrived back at the guest wing. Their day seemed to have been going at ninety miles an hour so far, and Fran would have rather liked to sink into one of the cosy armchairs. Instead, she touched a hand to Midge's jacket. 'Can I ask you something else before we go any further?' She dropped her voice. 'Who knows about us? The real reason we're here. Only we could make a very silly mistake if we assume.'

'Oh God, of course.' Midge looked contrite. 'I should have said, sorry. The only people who know are Miranda and myself. She was adamant. She really doesn't want anyone to know about this.'

'Isn't that going to make it a little hard for us to figure out who's guilty? If we can't ask questions, how are we going to get anywhere?'

Midge's gaze sunk to the floor and Fran relented.

'Sorry, Midge, I know none of this is your fault. But you do see how difficult this makes things?'

'I do, but I very much doubt I can change it. I'll do all I can to help, but...' She gave a slight smile and hurried off down the hallway, passing Fran and Adam's rooms before turning left. 'Here we are...' She pushed open a door. 'Ah, Betty... Can I introduce you to someone? This is Fran, and Adam, who's her assistant. Fran's a writer and is here to research material for a behind-the-scenes book on Miranda and the show. I wondered if you might be able to find them some tea before the orientation meeting?'

Betty was tiny, even shorter than Fran, and thin as a rake. Her long grey hair was pinned up in a very elaborate bun and her rosy cheeks grew even rosier as she smiled a welcome. 'Of course I can, that's what I'm here for. But for goodness' sake, girl, look at you. Stop and have a cup of tea before you fall down.'

'Honestly, Betty, that's very kind, but I'm fine, really, and I have to dash.'

Betty rolled her eyes. 'Later then. Sneak back and I'll find you a piece of cake.' She tutted loudly as Midge left, waving a goodbye. 'That girl works far too hard, you know. I keep telling her, but she never listens. Mind you, I don't suppose she can, can she? Not when she's got Miss High and Mighty Miranda on her tail. Now, you two sit down. The kettle's not long boiled and I'll get a pot of tea going.'

Fran smiled. 'How long have the TV people been here?' she asked. 'Has it taken them long to set up?'

Betty thought a moment. 'Two days.' She frowned and turned away to busy herself with the teapot. 'It seems longer somehow...'

Fran gave Adam a pointed look, wondering whether he'd spotted how quickly Betty had sussed out the lie of the land. His eyes crinkled in reply and he turned away to hide the smirk on his face.

'Right then, here we are,' said Betty, moments later. 'Tea, and a plate of biscuits too.' She put down a large pot, two mugs and the plate. 'Sugar and milk are already on the table, help yourselves. Now, I'll leave you to it, but shout if you want anything.'

Fran thanked her and sat down, waiting until she'd gone before leaning forward to whisper. 'Is it me, or is Betty one of those people who just appear as if by magic?'

Adam grinned. 'Almost certainly,' he said, eyeing the biscuits. 'Not that I'm complaining.'

Fran poured them both a cup of tea and nabbed a biscuit before Adam ate them all. 'This is incredible,' she said, spreading out the information Midge had given them.

Adam simply nodded, already reading and halfway through his first biscuit. Fran settled herself and began to do likewise. She hadn't even reached the end, however, when she became aware that Adam's stance had changed.

'What are you thinking?' she asked. 'You've been sitting staring into space for the last few minutes. Something is ticking away in that brain of yours.'

Adam frowned. 'Hmm... I suspect you're not going to like it very much.'

Fran raised her eyebrows.

'This is really helpful.' He indicated the information Midge had given them. 'We've got a list of everything we need to know about everyone here, plus a comprehensive rundown of what happened on each of the occasions Miranda found one of the "presents".'

'I know, isn't it great?' Fran narrowed her eyes, noticing Adam's hesitation. 'What, it isn't great?'

'No, it is,' he said. 'Only… isn't it all just a little too pat? It doesn't leave room for any questions, does it? Instead, we're presented with a fait accompli – this is *what* happened, and this is *how* it happened. It's too black and white.'

'Yes, but if that's what did happen, then I can't see—'

'But that's just it. It doesn't leave room for any *thinking*… for any speculation. Instead, if we're not careful we're going to accept Midge's account as gospel truth without considering that any of the detail on here could be wrong. When people receive a written report, and that's essentially what this is, they instinctively take what they read as the truth because it's seen as factual more often than not.'

Fran frowned. 'I see what you mean, but I think Midge was just trying to be helpful. She's obviously very busy, I doubt she even has time to catch her breath.'

Adam nodded. 'I know, that's very obvious, and on the one hand this information is perfect.'

'And on the other?'

'What if Midge is the guilty party?' He paused a moment, fidgeting slightly. 'All I'm saying is that it's far easier to spot a lie or a misdirection when it's given verbally. There's nuance of expression, subtle changes in delivery and body language that just aren't there when the recount of events is written down. If Midge wanted to hide her involvement in all of this, what we have here would be a very good way of doing it. Midge is Miranda's right-hand woman, the person she trusts, the person she depends on for everything. Following that line of thinking to its logical conclusion, I doubt Miranda's even checked what Midge has written. So, in fact, not one word of this might be true.'

4

Fran stared at Adam, a warm flush spreading up her neck as she realised just how true his comment might be.

'Sorry,' he said again, seeing her reaction. 'I know that goes against our first impressions.'

'Maybe it does, but you're absolutely right. We shouldn't take anything at face value. This is TV, remember, most of what viewers see on their screens isn't a true record of events. An edit here, a cut there, clips shown out of sequence. Everything is manipulated to fit with expectation. Why should anyone's behaviour be any different?'

Adam dipped his head in acknowledgement.

'So, we should stick to our guns,' added Fran. 'Midge was the one who drew the distinction between who *could* have left the "presents" for Miranda and who *might* have. We never asked her that last question, but I think we should. At least that way we'll get a verbal recount of events.' She glanced at her watch. 'And we should get going, it's nearly time for the orientation.'

Despite being ten minutes early, the front half of the stable was already massed with people, gathered loosely around

Harrison and Miranda, who were standing in front of the large Christmas tree. Elsewhere in the room, work was continuing apace. Fran scanned the faces of those she could see, although as they had arrived later than everyone else, most people had their backs to her.

'It probably would have been helpful to have been sent the names of the competitors beforehand,' she said. 'Then at least we could have found out a little bit about them. Coming in cold like this is going to make our job much harder.'

'Speaking of which, there's always the icebreaker later,' said Adam with a grimace.

Fran knew that a room full of people he didn't know was his worst nightmare.

'It might be interesting though,' he continued, 'to see how everyone plays it, I mean. Harrison might not want people to be too pally to start with or there'll be no competitive spirit. That's before everyone starts bonding, of course.'

Fran nodded. She had watched countless episodes of the show, she knew how it worked. Curious as she was about the competitors, she was still far more inclined to believe that one of the crew was responsible for what had been happening.

From the corner of her eye, she saw Midge circumnavigating the crowd, clipboard in hand and pen poised. She was obviously conducting a head count. Once finished, she moved forwards to speak to Harrison. The murmurings of conversation began to trail away of their own accord and, after a moment or two more, Harrison raised a hand and an expectant hush fell.

'Welcome, welcome,' he began. 'Hello, everyone.' He pointed to the tree. 'And Happy Christmas! If you haven't already realised that the festive season is upon on us, then you soon will. By the end of the week we'll have eaten so many mince pies, you'll be begging for mercy.' He grinned, at length and sparing no one.

Fran had to stop her eyes from rolling. It wasn't that funny, the shops were already beginning to groan with Christmas products.

'So, without further ado,' continued Harrison, 'I'd like to welcome you all to the very special Christmas edition of *Country Cooks Cook* – for a lot of people, the highlight of the year, just in case you didn't think it would be pressured enough. And, of course, it wouldn't be *Country Cooks Cook* if we didn't have the star of the show with us, Miranda Appleby!' He paused for the statutory round of applause which followed. 'Miranda, have you got some welcoming words of wisdom for everyone?'

Miranda had changed from when they'd last seen her. She'd swapped the trousers and jumper for a pale-pink Bardot top and voluminous flowery skirt. There wasn't a dog hair in sight. She smiled demurely at everyone.

'Oh, you lovely people! Thank you, thank you... but please save the applause for yourselves, you're the real stars of the show.' She beamed at the faces around her. 'And thank you, Harrison. As to whether my words are wise, who knows, but I would like to welcome you all to our *Country Cooks* family. Without you, the show wouldn't go ahead and, I won't lie, you have a hard week ahead of you, but I also know it's going to be such tremendous fun. You'll leave having had the time of your lives, with a bunch of people who truly will feel like family by the end. Plus, it's Christmas, so what could be nicer? I can't wait to get to know you all.' She paused, looking at the expectant faces around her. 'And, importantly, taste the array of incredible food I know you're going to be cooking. I'm going to hand back to Harrison now, who will run through some logistics of how the week will work, but I wish you all the very best of luck.'

There was another round of applause as Miranda returned to stand beside the tree, handing the limelight back to Harrison.

'Thank you, Miranda. Now, in case anyone doesn't know, my name's Harrison. I'm the show's director and producer and

one of the people you can turn to for information. The other is
Michelle – Midge – who I think you've already met. Midge
keeps an up-to-date schedule of what happens when, and
where, so if you're in any way uncertain, she's the person to
find.

'As I know you're also aware, the Christmas edition of
Country Cooks Cook is unusual in that its format is slightly
different from our regular shows. There are fewer of you, of
course, which means that we have room for segments show-
casing some of Miranda's amazing seasonal fare. It also allows
for more interview time, both singly and with all of you in a
group. Christmas is such a special time for family and friends
and we want to get across the social aspect while also learning
about you and your favourite Christmas traditions. We believe
it's this mix of cookery competition, plus fly-on-the-wall docu-
mentary, which has made these shows so successful.

'You will always know when the cameras are rolling, but I'd
just like to take this opportunity to remind everyone that we are
a family show. So, when the heat rises, which it will, the more
times we have to stop to edit out swearing, the longer everything
will take. We do also have to shoot sections out of sequence
from time to time, or retake scenes, so on occasion we will be
working late into the evening. Fortunately, we have an exceptionally good make-up artist who will ensure that no one looks
too knackered.

'Finally, I want to thank you all in advance for your efforts
this week. As Miranda said, we really couldn't do it without
you. Now, to get started, I need to introduce a few of our family
members before Midge outlines what each day will look like.
You'll be seeing these people a lot during the week, and
although it looks busy here today, from tomorrow we'll be quite
a cosy, self-contained group. Judy, would you like to be first to
come forward and say hello?'

Fran gave Adam's elbow a nudge. Judy Mulligan was the first on the list of names Midge had given them.

Smiling confidently, a tall, lithe redhead came forward out of the crowd, her hair coiled upwards into a messy bun. She was dressed in jeans and a bright-green Puffa jacket, done up to the neck.

'Thanks, Harrison. It's so lovely to be back with you all for another series. My name's Judy and I'm the catering manager on set.' She held up a hand, smiling broadly. 'And I know that sounds weird but there's an awful lot of food on this show and it doesn't appear by magic. My role is to source all the raw ingredients you'll be using throughout the week, and to make sure that everything is exactly where it should be. If you have a particular problem as we go along, therefore, be sure to let me know. I can't always promise to resolve things, but I'll do my best. My truck will be in the courtyard, outside the stable, from later this evening, and you can always come to me any time you need a chat. I also keep the crew supplied with drinks, bacon sandwiches, and anything sweet, usually doughnuts, so if you fancy anything, do come and knock on the door.'

Harrison smiled. 'Thank you, Judy!' He raised his hands to lead another round of applause. 'Now, let's have Sam and Woody, please?' He paused, looking expectantly left and right. 'Sam Ellis is our very talented cameraman, guaranteed to get you from just the right angle, and his partner in crime, Stuart Woodham, or Woody as he's always known, is our sound man. Give everyone a wave, lads.'

It was evident why both men had the roles they did. Wearing regulation black jeans and tee shirts, they stood awkwardly in front of everyone, clearly preferring to leave the limelight to other people.

'And finally, Hope, if you'd like to come forward,' said Harrison. 'Hope is the aforementioned make-up artist, and definitely someone to make friends with unless you like looking haggard and ten years older than you really are.'

Fran had to stand almost on tiptoe to make out the woman who came forward, and even then she could only see glimpses of her face around other people's shoulders. It was enough to reveal how extraordinarily pretty she was though. Gamine features and a short, dark pixie cut.

'Hello, everyone, I'm Hope and I'm... well, Harrison has said it really. I'm the make-up artist on set, so I'll be seeing you all at some point or other. Hot kitchens and stress can wreak havoc with the way you look, and although we have to preserve an element of realism, we still want you all to look your best. That's what I'm here for.'

There was a pause of several seconds before Harrison realised Hope wasn't about to say anything further. He flashed another smile. 'Great. Thanks, Hope.' He frowned, scratching his head. 'I always think I've forgotten someone but I think that's all the people you need to know. Midge, do you want to take it from here?'

Midge was busy checking her phone, and at the sound of her name looked up, startled. She coloured slightly and rushed forward to stand beside Hope, who gave her a warm smile. 'Thanks, Harrison. Most of what I want to say is actually in the information packs I gave each of you when you arrived, so do make sure you read those. They'll tell you when regular things will happen, such as meal breaks, as well as outline the schedule for each day. One of the most important things, however, is the meeting we have every morning to finetune those arrangements and tell you about any changes which may have become necessary. It's at eight thirty, so pretty early, but if everyone can come to that meeting it makes life a lot easier.

'There won't be a great deal of free time, I'm afraid, but during what there is you're welcome to explore the grounds. The house itself, though, is off limits, apart from the guest wing where the sitting room and kitchen are open to you at any time. Oh, and if you haven't already met Betty, the housekeeper, do go and say hello. She's such a lovely lady and is also the one to let know if you have a problem with your room or need any extra blankets or pillows, for example. She'll also be providing your evening meal.' Midge looked about her. 'Um, I think that's it for now... Oh, no, there are two other people to tell you about. We're very lucky to have a writer with us this week, and her assistant. Fran and Adam, do you want to give everyone a wave? They're here researching a behind-the-scenes book on the show, but don't worry, they know you've got lots to concentrate on this week, so won't need to speak to any of you at length. You'll see them around quite a bit, that's all.' She inhaled a deep breath. 'Right, there are teas, coffees and mince pies on the tables just behind us, so help yourselves to those and have a mingle. And if everyone can be back here for six o'clock we'll get the icebreaker started. Miranda will be present, but I need to stress that it isn't part of the competition. It really is just an opportunity to get to know one another better and eat lots of lovely food, of course.'

Fran frowned and looked at Adam. 'Have I missed something?' she whispered.

'Like what?' Adam's attention was already straying to the mince pies.

'Well, that made it sound as if everyone will be cooking tonight, but I thought nothing started until tomorrow. I thought the icebreaker was just a party-type thing.'

Adam shrugged. 'Me too.'

People were already starting to drift over to the refreshments and, as Fran turned, she bumped into another woman who had done the same. She was met by an apologetic but friendly smile.

'Sorry, I'm in too much of a rush for caffeine,' said the woman. 'Don't you just hate it when people say things are absolutely not part of something, when they very obviously are?

Reminds me of interviews I've been to in the past.' The woman smiled again, her plump rosy cheeks growing even more round. 'I'm Penny, by the way, Penelope Hardy, but most people just call me Pea.'

Pea was dressed exactly how Fran would like to if she had the nerve. Mid-fifties or so, she was wearing bright-orange leggings, yellow Converse and a vibrant-pink smock top of the kind Fran favoured herself – they covered all sorts of wobbly bits and meant she didn't have to go around sucking in her stomach the whole time. Tousled, short grey hair completed Pea's look, along with large hooped earrings.

Fran grinned back at her. 'I'm Francesca, but likewise only my mother calls me that, so I'm Fran to everyone else. And this is Adam.' She paused. 'This is an incredible set-up, isn't it? I've been a fan of the show for so long, I can't believe I'm here.'

'I can't believe I'm here either,' replied Pea. 'Applying to be on the show was one of those things I did on a whim because I didn't really think I stood a chance of getting in. Then it sort of snowballed... that'll teach me.' She stretched her neck to look over Fran's shoulder. 'Are you going to get a coffee?' she asked. 'Because if you are, can we go together? Safety in numbers and all that.'

Fran nodded. 'I think Adam has his eye on the mince pies.'

Adam dipped his head and fidgeted nervously.

Pea patted her stomach. 'Oh, me too. I'm famished.'

Fran smiled, a little shy as they reached the refreshment table. The staff had disappeared in favour of leaving everyone to introduce themselves, which meant these people were all competitors. Two young women were already deep in conversation, not even looking up as they arrived, but the third, a middle-aged man, caught their eye.

'Hello, ladies... oh, and gentleman,' he added, catching sight of Adam. 'Can I pour you some coffee, or tea maybe? I'm Tony, Tony Morrison.' He gave a slight bow, colouring up a little.

Fran smiled at his rather endearing introduction, giving her own name and Adam's before pointing at the smaller of two catering flasks. 'I'll have tea, if I may? What about you, Adam?'

But Adam's attention had evidently been caught by something on the other side of the room. Fran watched the direction his eyes were travelling and was just in time to see Harrison slip into the partitioned room at the rear of the stable; the room they'd been told was designated as the set's green room.

Adam looked back, catching Fran's eye. 'Oh, yeah... tea, thanks. Back in a sec.'

Fran smiled brightly to cover his exit. 'So, how are you feeling? You must be so nervous.'

Tony nodded. 'Terrified.' He smoothed down his shirt. He was dressed casually but there was no mistaking how much care he'd taken with his neat appearance. 'But I'm trying to view it as necessary experience. I'm hoping to open my own business one day soon and I imagine that will be just as nerve-wracking.'

'So, winning *Country Cooks Cook* would be a real boost for you, wouldn't it?' said Pea with a look at Fran. 'I'll have to watch this one.'

'Sounds like it,' replied Fran, smiling. 'And what about you, Pea? What kind of food do you like to cook?'

'Very traditional,' she said, smiling. 'Dinner parties, cakes for weddings, that kind of thing. It was my daughter who convinced me I should have a go at this. *Before you get too old, Mum*, was what she actually said.' Pea's eyebrows disappeared beneath her spiky fringe.

'My mum thinks I'll be home by the end of tomorrow,' said one of the other women, smiling as she came forward to join the group. 'I think she meant it to be comforting, as in *never mind, your ordeal will all be over soon*, but I'm not quite sure how to take it.' She pushed a cloud of bushy brown hair away from her face. 'I'm Christine,' she added with a nervous smile. She looked scared witless.

'And I'm Jenny,' said the other woman, joining them.

'Jenny's very brave,' remarked Christine. 'She's a vegan. I wouldn't even know where to start.'

'Me neither,' added Pea.

'I've been a vegetarian since my teens,' Jenny replied. 'And a vegan for five years, so I'm used to it now.' A tiny diamanté stud in one side of her nose twinkled under the lights as she spoke.

'It must make things more difficult though,' said Fran. 'What about making pastry? Does it turn out okay?'

'Well, I think so, but I suspect I'll be finding out soon enough. There are ways around most things, but I prefer replacing things like pastry with something even better rather than trying to replicate it.' She pulled a face. 'That's the plan anyway.'

'I still think you're brave,' said Christine, her cup rattling slightly in its saucer.

'Is everyone here?' asked Pea, looking around. 'Aren't we missing someone?' As she spoke a man came towards them, raising a hand in greeting.

'Sorry, sorry... just chinwagging with the make-up girl. Making sure she knows how to make me look even more handsome. Only kidding! I'm Vinny, it's great to meet you all.'

Fran smiled politely, trying very hard to resist rolling her eyes. Tony's mild-mannered and unassuming introduction was far more likely to catch her eye than Vinny's designer stubble and perfect teeth.

The conversation ranged back and forth for a few more minutes, but Fran's mind was elsewhere. She was tallying the list of contestants in her head: Pea, Tony, Vinny, Jenny and Christine, a total of five altogether. So, who was the sixth contestant? There was no one else here, and yet she'd seen Midge do a headcount.

More to the point, where was Adam? He seemed to have completely disappeared.

The whereabouts of the sixth contestant became immediately apparent as Fran slipped out through the stable doors. A young woman was hunched over one of the barrels in the courtyard.

'Is everything okay?' Fran asked, hurrying to her side.

There was a low groan. 'Please, go away. I'm fine.'

Fran paused, before laying a gentle hand across one of her shoulders. 'I used to get sick in department stores all the time,' she said. 'I know how you feel. I have a tissue here, if you'd like one.' She fumbled in her pocket.

Slowly, the woman straightened, closing her eyes briefly before taking the tissue to dab at her mouth. 'Thank you...' She groaned again. 'Sorry, I couldn't stand it in there any longer. It was so hot, I thought I was going to pass out.'

'It is rather stuffy,' agreed Fran. 'Take a few deep breaths. Now you're out in the fresh air I'm sure you'll begin to feel better.'

The woman grimaced. 'I doubt it, but thank you.' She gave a rueful smile. 'Are you one of the contestants too?'

Fran shook her head. 'No, and don't worry, everyone else is filling their faces with mince pies, no one's going to see you. Besides, they're all just as nervous, I'm sure they'd understand.'

'Maybe, but they're not the ones throwing up in a flowerpot, are they?' She looked up at Fran. 'God, what a start.' She shook her head. 'I don't think I can do this.'

Mindful that someone could come out at any minute and add to the poor woman's embarrassment, Fran touched her arm. 'Would you like to go back to the house? Maybe you'll feel better once you've had a sit down.' Fran was anxious the young woman shouldn't make any rash decisions. She wasn't sure how the show worked, but having one of the contestants pull out couldn't be good. 'I'm Fran, by the way.'

There was a small smile. 'Emily,' she replied, looking back towards the stable. 'I can't go back in there,' she said.

'Come on then,' said Fran. 'A sit down and a cup of tea might be just the thing.'

'I think I'd be better off packing. I don't know why I thought this was a good idea.'

Fran took her arm. 'I'm sure you'll feel better soon.'

5

Adam had always been an avid people-watcher, on the rare occasions when he actually left his room, that is, before he met Fran. He'd been something of a recluse until then, naturally shy and never quite finding his place in a world where people tended to baffle and confuse him. As a gifted maths and science scholar, in his world things were usually black and white, whereas people never were. He couldn't quite understand why they did things which were totally at odds with what they said, or said things which were totally at odds with what they did. So when he saw Harrison acting in a way which could only be described as furtive, his interest was well and truly piqued.

According to what Harrison had told them earlier, the partitioned area at the rear of the stable was for the contestants' use between filming, so quite why Harrison needed to slip inside in such a clandestine manner was beyond him. Although, the fact that Judy had done so only moments earlier was perhaps a clue.

Adam sidled closer, pulling out his phone. If anyone spotted him he could say he was taking photos of the stable. That way he'd at least have a legitimate reason for being at this end of the room when everyone else was busy up the front scoffing mince pies and drinking tea. His stomach rumbled; there'd better be some left for him.

He halted as the sound of tinkling laughter reached him. Definitely not Harrison's, it had to belong to Judy, unless someone else was in there too. He supposed they could be discussing the catering for the show, but somehow he didn't think so.

About to creep closer for a spot of eavesdropping, he started as he caught sight of Miranda walking at speed down the length of the stable. Dropping to a crouch, he waddled behind one of the kitchen stations and pretended to tie his shoelace. Fortunately, Miranda seemed so intent on her quarry she didn't spot him, but he wasn't sure he dared move any closer.

Almost immediately, Judy appeared from behind the partition, red-faced, but whether from embarrassment or anger, Adam couldn't tell. The description *scalded cat* popped into his head. Making no attempt to engage with anyone in the room, Judy left the stable as quickly as she could, which happy fact meant that Miranda and Harrison were now alone. Certain that furious whispering was about to start, Adam was surprised when Miranda's voice floated out the partition door, crystal clear.

'Ah, Harrison, there you are. Well, this is all looking fabulous, isn't it? Sorry to be such a bore, I know you've got a million and one things to do, but I wondered if I might have a quick word with you? Shall we pop to my trailer? I've got something I need to show you too.'

Adam ducked his head as, a split second later, Miranda appeared with Harrison by her side. They walked leisurely up the room, Miranda wearing a bright smile, gesturing at the decoration in the room as she went. Adam frowned. Something didn't quite stack up here and he slipped out behind them in pursuit.

With so many people still milling about, it was easy for

Adam to keep Harrison and Miranda in sight while still appearing to be engaged in his own business. Several other people were walking in a similar direction, why shouldn't he? Once he cornered the house, however, and crossed the drive towards the trailers, it was a little more difficult. Happily, the gardens provided a perfect viewpoint from which to take a photo of the handsome main building and, under this pretence, it was easy to scoot behind the trailer and work his way around the side which was hidden from general view.

Adam had wondered earlier why Miranda chose to have the trailers parked in such an exposed position, particularly as Midge had already told them she liked her privacy. In light of recent events, it didn't seem prudent to be so easily accessible, but now, as he crouched at the trailer's rear, he realised that the 'gifts' might be exactly why she had chosen this spot. Sure, you could creep up behind as he had, but there was only one door into the trailer and it was in full view of anyone in the vicinity. It would be very difficult to sneak in without being seen.

Keeping his head low, Adam worked his way forward until he was able to crouch beneath one of the long side windows. It faced the garden, but the other, directly opposite, would give the trailer's occupants a good view of anyone approaching. Neither window was open, but hopefully Miranda's voice would carry sufficiently for him to hear what was being said. He needn't have worried. From the minute Harrison closed the trailer door behind him, Miranda's voice rang out loud and clear.

'For God's sake, we've only been on set a minute and you're back to your old tricks. Judy this time, is it? Whatever's going on between you, keep it out of my face and everyone else's for that matter. You know how the crew pick up on things. Besides, people aren't stupid, and there's a very fine line between friendly and creepy, Harrison, just remember that. The last thing we need is someone shouting harassment.'

'I don't see how my relationship with Judy is any of your business, given that we're both very happy with the situation. Perhaps you just like shouting at me and asserting your so-called authority.'

There was a noise which Adam couldn't quite make out, but which may well have been Miranda's anger venting itself.

'I'd like you to go find Midge,' she replied. 'Who will be with Emily whatserface, the contestant who, not two minutes ago, threw up in one of the potted Christmas trees outside the stable, and is in grave danger of not competing at all. That writer woman found her and alerted Midge, who is over in the house now trying to convince Emily that nerves are normal et cetera, et cetera. Although it pains me to say it, what I need is for you to work your charm on *her* otherwise we might as well kiss this whole show goodbye.'

'Oh, so when it suits you it seems I do have my uses after all. Or is it perhaps that if you went to speak to her yourself, you'd probably send her running for the hills? Despite the fact that it's your show, and so it really ought to be you who has the chat, could it be that you're actually not that good with people?'

'Don't push your bloody luck, Harrison,' grumbled Miranda. 'This is a problem of your making. You're responsible for vetting the show's applicants, so I'd like to know how she got this far in proceedings without anyone noticing she was as flaky as—' Miranda halted abruptly. 'I thought we'd agreed that after the last near-miss disaster with a contestant, we would make sure we had the *right* people for the show, regardless of their culinary abilities.'

Adam swallowed. That didn't sound good. Furthermore, it wasn't something he would be happy sharing with Fran. As an avid fan of the show, she'd hate knowing the contest wasn't what she thought it was.

'Emily Williamson *is* the right person for the show,' argued Harrison. 'For exactly the reason you've so accurately described. She might have a slightly flaky side, but audiences will empathise with her, and we can't have everyone being as nice as pie and jolly hockey sticks. It doesn't make for good ratings. Besides which, I'm not the one making things even more difficult by having some bloody writer on set, poking her nose into everything. That's all we need. I don't even know why she's here, apart from to massage your ego.'

'I told you, it's a smart business move. The public have cookery books galore but what they don't have is a companion volume to their best-loved show. Something that goes behind the scenes and reveals what the camera doesn't see.'

'And that's supposed to convince them, is it?' replied Harrison. 'That you're actually a pussy cat to work with, one of the nicest people in showbiz? If I were at all cynical, I'd say it was a very well-timed attempt to ameliorate the rumblings of rumours to the contrary.'

There was a lengthy pause and Adam could only imagine the looks the pair were giving one another.

'And I know full well the idea will have come from your publicist. You don't have a head for business, Miranda, you never have had. You're just here to pout and simper and look good.'

'Just get this competition up and running. And in case you need reminding of the fact – people tune in to see *me*. You might think you can make your mark on the show, but how do you think you're going to do that without me?' Adam almost missed what Miranda said next as her voice dropped to a menacing snarl. 'So, forget it. You will never get control of this show, Harrison, not while I live and breathe. Now run along and see to Emily, I have to get ready for this evening.'

Seconds later, the trailer door slammed. Peeping around the corner, Adam could see Harrison striding towards the front of the main house, presumably heading for the guest wing. But there was little point in following him now. Besides, Adam was quite keen to tell Fran what he had learned. Was there anyone who actually liked Miranda?

Fran had left Emily having a chat with Harrison. He was charm itself but, she suspected, would get nowhere – Emily was adamant she was leaving the show. With nothing more she could do to help, Fran had hurried back to the stable only to find that the gathering was on the point of breaking up. Jenny professed a need for a freshen-up before the icebreaker, Pea wanted to ring her daughter, and Vinny had some emails to answer. Despite what Midge had said they were all of the general opinion that tonight's event wasn't about getting to know one another at all but, instead, was very much a part of the competition. Fran was pretty certain people were sloping off to prepare in some way, although quite how they would do that she had no idea.

She stared at the empty cups and discarded plates the gathering had left behind. Most of the mince pies lay untouched as well. There were still people bobbing about the room, straightening decorations, bringing in last-minute bits of equipment, but no one seemed the slightest bit concerned by the mess. She wondered whose responsibility it was to clear it all away, not only out of an instinctive desire to help, but because experience had taught her that where finding out information was concerned, it was always best to ask the 'invisible' people. Without cleaners, receptionists and waitstaff, places simply would not function, and yet their views were often overlooked. Not only did they regularly see and hear everything that went on, they usually had an opinion about it too, and Fran was very keen to meet them.

Seeing no one who seemed to fall into that category, Fran was about to leave when she saw Midge run through the door. She skidded to a halt, eyes raking the room and then turned on her heel, disappearing as fast as she had arrived. Alerted by the panicked expression on her face, Fran hurried after her. Midge was still in the courtyard when Fran caught her up, but only just.

'Midge, wait!'

The young woman turned at the sound of Fran's voice, almost immediately breaking into the fixed smile which Fran was getting quite used to seeing. Midge hadn't quite been quick enough, however, to hide the look of fear on her face.

'Is everything all right?' asked Fran.

Midge's smile grew brighter. 'Yes, of course. How can I help you?'

'I'm fine, but *you* look very flustered. Can I help with anything? I can clear away the refreshments perhaps or...'

Midge's eyes grew round. 'Damn, I'd forgotten about those.' She dropped her gaze to her clipboard, tutting at what she read there. 'I'm looking for Miranda, actually. I don't suppose you've seen her, have you?'

Fran shook her head. 'What's wrong? Is it Emily?'

For a moment Midge looked as if she was about to deny everything, but then she touched Fran's sleeve. 'Walk with me,' she said. 'Miranda must have already gone back to her trailer. Damn.'

She said nothing further until they were clear of the court-yard and well out into open space. 'Emily's pulled out,' she said. 'I can't believe it. We've had a few wobbles before, that often happens, but not someone actually packing to leave. She's adamant she's going home. Even Harrison can't charm her round and he's usually very good at it.' She swore under her breath. 'Sorry... Miranda's not going to be happy, let's put it that way.'

'No, I don't suppose she is.'

Midge grimaced. 'Emily's been quite nervous through all the preliminaries, bless her, but she's only young. We know it can be very overwhelming, but we're used to that – it's one of the reasons we have the icebreaker on the first day. People always seem far more relaxed afterwards. Plus, it gets people cooking, doing something they love, and they can also see that everyone else is just as nervous as they are. Once we get into the swing of things folks usually settle down quite quickly.' She stopped a moment, staring at Miranda's trailer. 'Oh God, what am I going to tell her?'

Fran hated the look of something approaching panic on Midge's face. 'Do you want me to come with you? Safety in numbers and all that,' she added, repeating Pea's words of earlier.

Again, Midge was about to refuse, but then she sighed. 'Actually, would you? Maybe Miranda won't be quite so angry if I've got someone else with me.'

'Of course I will, but what's she got to be angry about? It's nobody's fault Emily can't face the competition. The poor woman was beside herself, I bet she feels awful.'

'Oh, she does. Not that it will make any difference. Miranda will still be angry because she gets angry with anyone who threatens the show, especially if it's something which might bring it into disrepute. She can be a little touchy about that sort of thing.'

Fran was pretty certain that 'a little touchy' was a massive understatement. There was something about the way Midge had said it too. 'Why?' she asked. 'Have there been other issues?' She could see immediately she was right and gave Midge an encouraging smile. 'Come on, Midge, you know why I'm here. If something's been going on I should probably know about it. I'm sure that whoever has been playing silly buggers with Miranda is just being spiteful, having a joke at her expense, but it's still not very nice, is it? What if it got out of hand?'

Midge sighed, eyes downcast. 'Okay, I'll tell you, but you'd better not let on I've said a word. I need this job, Fran, and what I said to you earlier was true – most of the time I love what I do. Only Miranda can be a bit spiky at times. It's a very high-pressured environment and when you care deeply about something, I guess we're all capable of being hot-headed. Trouble is, this is a very high-profile show and people love to gossip. There've been a few snippets in the media recently. Nothing major, just the odd allusion to the fact that everything might not be as rosy on the good ship Miranda as everyone makes out. That's one of the reasons she got the dogs.'

'Sorry?'

'The dogs. Miranda thought it might counteract any bad press if she was seen as an animal lover. It paints her in a better light.'

Fran frowned. 'But that's no reason to become a dog owner. They're not accessories, for heaven's sake.' She was about to continue when she realised that Midge was already fully aware of the point she was trying to make. And in agreement too. 'That's quite some step to take, are things really that bad?'

Midge shook her head. 'No, I think Miranda is simply hyper-sensitive, that's all. You know what they say – the higher you go, the further you have to fall – and with each series of the show attracting more and more viewers, well... I'll let you draw your own conclusions.'

Fran was about to carry on walking when a thought suddenly popped into her head. 'Midge, you probably know Miranda as well as anyone, so given that she seems so paranoid about her reputation, do you think it's possible she might have invented what's been happening? Stage-managed a situation so that if it "accidentally" got out – how Miranda has been the victim of a cruel prankster – it might sway public opinion back in the right direction?'

But Midge's response was immediate. 'No, she's as paranoid about news of what's been happening getting out as she is of what people think of her. I see what you're getting at, but no, I'm sure it's nothing like that. Besides, I've got to know when Miranda is putting on an act and, in my opinion, she's been genuinely ruffled by events. The dead roses were the worst, they really freaked her out. She said they were spooky. Macabre.'

Fran nodded. 'Okay. Just a thought.' She indicated the trailer ahead of them. 'Sorry, I'd better let you...' She trailed off. She didn't envy Midge her job one little bit.

To give her her due, Midge didn't beat around the bush. Once inside the trailer, she calmly and clearly explained the situation to Miranda, and then stood stoically waiting for her reply. Fran didn't know how Midge did it, the silence was thoroughly unnerving.

After a few more moments during which the tension seemed to tighten even further, Miranda drew in a deep breath, letting it out almost immediately in a lengthy sigh. 'And where is Harrison now?' she asked.

'Still with Emily,' replied Midge. 'But I don't think he'll be able to change her mind. Nothing he said seemed to make any difference at all, and he's very good at these things, as you know. Emily's already packed her bag and called a taxi.' She checked her phone. 'About ten minutes ago now. It should be here in another five.'

'I see...' Miranda's eyes narrowed. 'Then let her go. I can see no point in making the idiot girl stay if she really doesn't want to. It's unfortunate, but there we are. Just make sure you have a signed NDA before she goes. She talks to no one and I want a watertight assurance of that fact.'

Midge bobbed her head. 'But—'

'And as for your next question, which is undoubtedly what do we do now, it's really very simple. Fran, you'll have to take part.'

'What...?' Fran stared at her in horror. 'I can't do that.'

'Why ever not? You can cook, can't you? You must be able, surely, a woman of your age?'

Fran didn't know which of the implications in Miranda's statement offended her the most. She was about to reply when she realised Miranda hadn't finished.

'You don't need to be anything special. As long as you can peel potatoes, weigh out stuff, mix things, look like you're going through the motions, we'll get an assistant to do the actual cooking, or Judy can. The point is that Joe Public believes you're taking part, and we can make that happen.'

'But that's... surely that's illegal?' spluttered Fran. 'Okay, maybe not illegal, but certainly against the spirit of the show.'

'The spirit of the show? Fran, darling, it's TV. And, in case you haven't realised, there will be *no* show unless we have a sixth contestant to take part. It simply doesn't work with an odd number and, besides, viewers are used to seeing that number of contestants on the Christmas show. If there're less, they'll think something is wrong, and I can't allow that. No, you'll just have to take Emily's place.' Miranda's gaze was cool, her eyebrows raised. 'Is there a problem?'

'Yes, there's a problem.' Fran couldn't believe the expression on Miranda's face. She was clearly not used to having anyone argue with her. 'I didn't come here to take part in the competition, I came here to find out who's been leaving delightful little gifts for you. How can I do that if I'm cooking all day?'

But Miranda was undeterred. 'I believe you have an assistant with you, yes? So, he'll just have to fill in for you doing the detective work. One of the contestants could just as easily be responsible and if that's the case then you'll be in the perfect position to flush them out, won't you? In fact, the more I think about it, the more I think that could be the case. Harrison has so obviously ballsed up the application process with this series, what's to say we didn't get Miss Psychopath as well as Miss Flaky?'

Fran stared at her. How could she be so rude?

'I hardly think that's any way to talk about people who have applied to be on the show in good faith, who believe in—'

'Fran, listen...' Miranda's face softened. 'I'm sorry if you think this is all a little underhand but, with respect, you do your job and I'll do mine. We start filming tomorrow. The series has been months in the preparation. The people you've seen here today have all been working towards the single goal of getting us operational by the morning. I shouldn't have to mention the countless man hours which have already been spent, or the costs involved in putting on a production like this. There's simply no way we can pull the show now. So we *will* be filming tomorrow, have no doubt about that, and all I need is for you to do what you've been asked. That way everyone's happy – the production company, our backers, the accountants, not to mention the thousands of viewers for whom the *Country Cooks Cook Christmas Special* is the highlight of the season. You do see that, don't you?'

Fran swallowed, feeling a little of her anger recede. Put like that she could see the position they were all in. But even so... She glanced at Midge, who gave her the briefest of nods. She drew in a deep breath.

'Okay,' she said. 'I *will* take part, and Adam and I will still do all we can to investigate the matter which originally brought us here. What I will not do, however, is cheat, so I won't need the help of your assistant, thank you all the same.'

Miranda stared at Fran, a slight smile playing around her lips. 'Very well,' she said, 'if that's the way you want it. Perhaps you might like to leave Midge and I alone now so that we can have a chat about a few other matters which need attention.' She smiled sweetly. 'And I'm very grateful, Fran, obviously. Don't think that I'm not.' She dipped her head. 'Bonne chance.'

Fran had evidently been dismissed. Again. Which was fine, she really had no wish to stay in the trailer any longer than was necessary. She was halfway down the steps when Miranda's voice floated out after her.

'Well... problem solved, Midge, wouldn't you say? It just needed some lateral thinking, that's all. Although I must say she has quite a high opinion of herself. Not sure who she thinks she is.'

'Oh, Miranda. I do wish that every now and again you would actually read some of the information I give you. It's all on the sheet I put together when the police got in touch.' Midge's voice was thick with sarcasm. 'She's a bloody caterer, Miranda, that's who she is.'

6

'Oh God, what have I let myself in for?' muttered Fran some ten minutes later when she had found Adam. They were sitting in her room – she on the bed with her head in her hands, and he cross-legged on the floor.

'I'm not really sure what choice you had,' he replied. 'Miranda put you right on the spot.' His words might have done slightly more to comfort her, had he not been grinning from ear to ear.

'You think this is a great idea, don't you?' she said. 'You're about to tell me it's cool, I can tell. You're as bad as Jack.'

'Why? What did he say?'

'That he's always thought I'd be gagging to do something like this. That it was only a question of time. I don't know whoever gave him that idea, because it certainly wasn't me.'

Adam softened his grin, just a little. 'But, Fran, you could win. And I'm not just saying that 'cause you pretty much feed me cake on demand. You could end up a mega-star, with book deals of your own, TV shows even and—' He stopped abruptly. 'Sorry, that's not helping, is it?'

'Not really, no. I don't want to win, my life doesn't need that kind of publicity. And just the thought of being on television makes me feel sick. Apart from anything else my body is not the right shape. I need to be at least a foot-and-a-half taller to be in any kind of proportion.' She pursed her lips and took a deep breath, pushing aside her thoughts. 'Anyway, enough about the pickle I seem to have got myself in. Where did you disappear to? You missed all the mince pies.'

'I know, it's a very sorry state of affairs. I did, however, manage to get a bit of gossip. I saw Judy sidle off into the green room at the back of the stable and then, moments later, Harrison ambled along. I say ambled... he was doing that nonchalant *you don't need to take any notice of me* thing, but he really didn't want to be seen. I couldn't hear what he and Judy were saying, but there was a giggle.' He nodded his head as if to underline his last comment.

'A giggle?'

'Yes, a very loud giggle,' said Adam. 'A very pronounced "look at me, I'm a giggle" giggle.'

Fran raised her eyebrows. 'Do I even know what one of those is?'

Adam tutted. 'It was you who taught me about them,' he replied, shaking his head in amusement. 'Those giggles which are a little forced, the kind you want other people to notice. The sort that Judy wanted Harrison to notice...'

'Ah,' said Fran, finally getting what Adam was driving at. 'So you think they might be in a relationship?'

'No doubt about it. Particularly because, seconds later, Miranda strode in and Judy left almost immediately, looking like a scalded cat. Miranda wasn't happy with Harrison either.'

'Why, what did she say?'

'She didn't say anything immediately, she made out there was nothing wrong, but when I followed them back to her trailer, she implied Harrison was some kind of Lothario. She definitely wasn't happy about their relationship. That's not all though, she also had a go at him because Emily has decided to pull out. She said it was his fault for not vetting the applicants properly.' He paused for a moment. 'Then Harrison said a few more things about the contestants and, let's just say I don't think this show is quite what we thought it was, Fran.'

'Tell me about it,' she muttered. 'So Miranda's relationship with Harrison isn't all that fond either. That's interesting.'

'It is. Especially when she then went on to say something about him never getting control of the show. "Not while I live and breathe" was how she phrased it.'

Fran's eyes widened. She was about to ask how Harrison replied when there was a tap at the door. It was Midge, looking pained and very apologetic. She hurried inside and closed the door firmly behind her.

'God, Fran, I'm so sorry, I really didn't see that coming. Miranda's right, though, unfortunately – pulling the show just isn't an option. Especially not the Christmas edition.'

Fran nodded. 'I know. And at least I am a caterer. I have a feeling Miranda would have had me standing in even if I were an electrician or a ballet dancer.'

She could see from the expression on Midge's face that her assessment was entirely accurate.

Midge gave her a sheepish smile and lifted something from the front of her clipboard. 'I brought you this,' she said. 'I thought it might help. It's the information pack all the contestants receive once they're confirmed on the show. It explains the way we work and what's expected. The rules, too, and which elements of the competition they're allowed to practise at home beforehand.' She pulled a face. 'Elements which you won't have had a chance to even think about, let alone practise. Needless to say, I'll do all I can to help you.'

'And I will,' put in Adam. 'I've helped you before, lots of times.'

'Thanks, Adam, but I rather think you might be busy elsewhere. We do still have the problem of Miranda's gifts to get to the bottom of.' She gave Midge a wry smile. 'Is now a good time to ask if you have an opinion as to who might be responsible? As opposed to who it could be?'

'I'm not sure it can be one of the contestants,' Midge replied. 'Because none of them have been on the show before. We were in Oxford for the last series, which is when Miranda started receiving the gifts, and obviously they weren't on set then, so...'

'What about the gifts themselves? In your notes you said they'd been left in her trailer – apart from the flowers and the card, which arrived through the post. Would the current contestants have known they'd be on the show at that point? I'm wondering if one of them could somehow have got on set? Perhaps if they were friends with one of the staff? Or a relative even?'

Midge pulled a face. 'Again, not really possible. The current contestants would have found out they definitely had a place in January, but despite what has just happened, we do have quite stringent vetting procedures. No one with any kind of connection to a staff member is allowed to take part. And we do check what people put on their application forms, we don't take them at face value. I can't see how any of them could be responsible.'

'Okay, so it's more likely to be one of the staff then. More likely, but not definite?'

Midge nodded. 'I guess.'

'So who would your money be on?'

'Me probably,' replied Midge, rolling her eyes. 'Seriously though, I can't see who would want to do those things to Miranda. It's quite a stable crew, most folks have worked on the series for years and they don't usually see Miranda the way I do;

they only ever see her nicer side. I know she can be difficult on occasion, but she lets fly at me because, maybe with the exception of Harrison, I'm the closest person to her. It's natural she'd vent on me. It's a compliment, in a way, that she trusts me enough to let her guard down.'

Fran wasn't so sure. 'You mentioned Harrison, and Miranda seems just as hard on him. Adam heard them having words a little while ago. Could he be responsible?'

'Possibly... He'd have access. But why would he? Miranda is the goose that lays the golden egg. That's the trouble – we all depend on her for our livelihoods, so playing tricks on her would be counterproductive.' She glanced down at her phone. 'Oh my God, is that the time? I haven't even cleaned up the refreshments yet and there's a hundred and one things still to check. Sorry, Fran, can I leave you to read through the information pack for now? Just turn up for the icebreaker and I'll help where I can. It really won't be anything too difficult, I promise.'

'I am so not ready for this,' remarked Fran. 'I don't even know what to wear.'

'Well, that's easy at least – whatever you want. We won't be filming, so you just need to be comfortable.' She cocked her head. 'Something festive might be nice, if you have it. I know it's odd, given that it's not actually Christmas, but it kind of helps to get the right vibe going.' She moved to the door. 'You'll be brilliant, Fran. I can't thank you enough.'

Fran stared at the ceiling, holding a palm against each cheek. They felt as if they were on fire. 'Something festive? It feels more like Halloween than Christmas.' She blew out a puff of air. 'So, what do you think?'

Adam wrinkled his nose. 'Oh, lovely,' he replied, brows raised. 'It's all lovely, isn't it? She's lovely, he's lovely, the crew are lovely, the competitors are lovely, the setting, the decoration, the atmosphere, is all lovely.'

Fran smirked. 'I'm being serious. Apart from what you overheard earlier, did you spot anything else which might be useful?'

'I'm being serious too. There's no way all these people can be so lovely,' he replied. 'In fact, we know they're not. Because, despite what they want us to believe, and how they appear on the surface, someone here has been doing some not very lovely things.'

'Hmm... and I wonder who?'

'Hold that thought,' said Adam. 'Because in less than an hour you're going to be in the very best place to find out.'

Fran felt sick. How on earth was she going to make any food, let alone eat it? Small comfort that all the other competitors looked every shade of nervous too, they hadn't just had appearing in a TV show dropped on them from a great height.

'Good evening, everyone,' said Harrison. 'And, once again, welcome to *Country Cooks Cook*. I don't need to tell you how wonderful the Christmas special is – you're all fans of the show – so, above all, whatever happens this week, remember to enjoy yourselves. That's the thing which will really translate as far as the cameras are concerned. There will be plenty of ups and plenty of downs too, but those are the times when being a part of this wonderful family comes into its own.' He paused to flash them all a perfect smile, the overhead lights glinting off the edge of his glasses. 'So, shall we get this party started?'

There were murmurs of agreement but no one was brave enough to actually speak. Fran sneaked a look at Pea who was standing beside her, her rosy cheeks even rosier than before. The heat was definitely rising in the room. Fran plucked at the neck of the jersey top she was wearing and faced the front.

Harrison scratched his head. 'Oh, one more thing before we move on to the practicalities of this evening. I would like to mention a small change to the line-up of contestants. Our youngest competitor, Emily, has been taken rather ill, sadly, and despite desperately wanting to go ahead, has reluctantly agreed with our doctor's advice that she pull out from the competition. We didn't really get the chance to know her at all, but obviously hope she has a speedy recovery.' He beamed another smile. 'As I'm sure you can imagine, these things do happen from time to time, which is why we always plan for just such eventualities. We're very fortunate, therefore, that Francesca Eve, who was already on set in another capacity, has agreed to step up and fill Emily's place. And the TV gods were definitely smiling on us today because, as luck would have it, Francesca is also a keen cook. Well done, Francesca!'

'It's Fran,' she muttered under her breath, as all eyes turned on her.

Pea gave Fran's arm a squeeze, a bright smile on her face which seemed to be replicated by everyone else. All except for Vinny, she noticed, who eyed her a little suspiciously.

'Right then,' continued Harrison, moving swiftly on. 'To the arrangements... I'm sure you're all seasoned Christmas-party-goers, and therefore will know that the food is of utmost importance. And with you folks in attendance, the food is going to be amazing. What we'd like you to do is split into pairs, just with whomever you're next to...' He waited while everyone worked out what he wanted and shuffled slightly closer to their partner to show they had. 'Great stuff. Now we'd like each couple to make one sweet offering and one savoury. These should be buffet-style appetisers, so no huge cakes or pies please, and enough to feed all of you, plus the crew, so about fifteen portions all told. As for ingredients...' He took a step to one side. 'On the tables behind me are all manner of things, three sets of each, so no problem if each couple wants to use the same thing, and you may use as little or as much of these ingredients as you like. Be creative, play it safe, or push the boundaries a little, the choice is up to you.' He repositioned his glasses. 'Now, does anyone have any questions?'

A hand was nervously raised a little way down the line. It was Jenny, the vegan cook. 'How long do we have?'

Harrison's hand banged against his forehead in exaggerated fashion. 'Glad someone's paying attention. Thanks, Jenny. We reckoned two hours would be enough, which will give you plenty of time to work up an appetite and still leave room for partying afterwards.'

Fran eyed his boyish grin with alarm. For him maybe, not for her. She turned to Pea, who was her partner. 'Are you as terrified as I am?'

Pea's head nodded up and down several times. 'Can't even face the thought of eating anything, which is unheard of for me.'

'Oh, and one more thing before I let you all get started,' added Harrison. 'And that's to stress that the purpose of this evening is to break the ice and get you all feeling more relaxed and less daunted by what's ahead of you. There really will be no judging of food this evening, I can't stress that enough. So, if you're all ready... Country cooks, cook!'

Fran had heard the familiar refrain so many times before, and had always loved how, by the end of the series, the remaining contestants would all join in to chant it before the day's competition commenced. Never in her wildest dreams had she thought she'd ever be a part of it. And now that she was, her quiet and peaceful kitchen back home felt a million miles away.

Pea was eyeing her expectantly. 'Are you okay? Talk about being thrown in at the deep end.'

Fran nodded. 'Just about. Although I have a sudden empathy for small furry animals and approaching cars right now.'

'Lucky you like cooking though,' remarked Pea. 'Imagine how you'd feel if you didn't.'

Fran offered a wry smile, wondering if Pea's comment was meant to be sarcastic. From the look on her face it didn't appear to be, so perhaps it was just Fran who felt as if she had the word 'imposter' tattooed on her forehead. 'Even so, my mind's gone a complete blank. I'm sorry, Pea, I'm not sure how much help I'm going to be. Have you any thoughts?' She stared at the table nervously. 'How about we keep it simple?' she offered. 'Ease ourselves in gently.'

'Sounds good to me,' replied Pea. 'There's no point piling on the stress when we don't need to and although I'm not adverse to being adventurous, in my experience most folks are happier with things they know and like. I've done far too many experiments where the end result was that most of the food went uneaten. Besides, who says traditional is wrong? I mean, it's virtually what Miranda's career has been built upon.'

Fran nodded. 'That's true, actually. My daughter is my benchmark,' she replied. 'She's always been a good eater, right from when she was tiny. There isn't anything she really dislikes, but if I'm trying something new and she says it sounds weird, I usually scrap it and think again. If she doesn't like it, chances are no one else will either.'

The tables had been set up in identical fashion and Fran had to wonder where on earth all the food had come from. There was no sign of the refreshments from earlier, and everything was beautifully presented, laid out in dishes and on trays, presented in jars and bottles. Was this all down to Midge too, or had Judy had a hand in it? Either way, they were spoilt for choice.

True to Harrison's word, the crowd of people milling about earlier had also disappeared, leaving behind a set worthy of a winter wonderland. It was all extremely tasteful, with decoration of the kind Fran often aspired to, but rarely managed. The artfully arrayed foliage on the, albeit fake, mantelpiece had been intertwined with candles and sparkling lights. In Fran's hands they'd simply look like a collection of odd things thrown together. Still, perhaps there was something a little more honest about the way she dressed her living room at Christmas, with a gaudily decorated tree and ornaments which had seen better days.

She turned her attention back to the task in hand. 'What about some sort of crostini?' she asked Pea. 'They've always been popular when I've made them before. There's smoked salmon, look – I could make it into a butter so it's a little more special. My husband likes it with capers, fried with herbs, and I could top them with... some sort of greenery. Hopefully, it'll come to me.'

Pea nodded. 'Perfect. And how about macarons for the sweet element? Filled with...' Her gaze drifted along the table. 'Raspberry cream, maybe honey and cinnamon...'

'Yes!' Fran's eyes lit up. 'God, I love those. Have we got time?'

Pea grinned. 'Piece of cake,' she replied.

Twenty minutes later, all thoughts had gone out the window beyond the food they were preparing. Fran had to remind herself that while this was what she did for a living, none of the others, particularly Pea, should be able to tell. Given that she was currently all fingers and thumbs that wouldn't be difficult, but it was something she would have to keep in mind. She renewed her concentration and added a teeny bit more lemon to the butter she was making.

'Can you see what everyone else is doing?' whispered Pea, a few minutes later. She had her back to the others whereas Fran was facing them.

Fran looked up, furtively sweeping her eyes up and down the room. 'Hard to tell,' she murmured. 'Meringues, I'd say, and judging by the smell, caramel is on its way somewhere too. Not sure about the savoury dishes, but at least one lot of pastry is being rolled out.'

'Is what we're doing okay, do you think?'

'Well, I'd eat it,' said Fran. 'And you would too, so that's two happy customers. As for the rest – who knows? – but I think so. It's not part of the competition though, so it doesn't really matter.'

Pea gave her a pointed look. 'I don't believe that for a minute,' she said. 'I know what Harrison said, and he can stress it all he wants, but Miranda strikes me as the sort who knows what she likes and what she doesn't like. You can tell by the set-up here. It might not be an official judging, but I think Miranda will still form a very solid opinion of us, one that will be hard to shake off further down the line. Screw up now and we'll be playing catch-up the whole way along.'

Fran stared at the bowl in front of her. 'Oh God,' she said.

'Not that we *are* screwing up,' added Pea hastily. 'I think we've played it just right. And those are going to be gorgeous,' she said, pointing to the row of ciabatta slices which Fran had just cut.

'I hope so... and who can resist a macaron? They're going to look so pretty and anything flavoured with raspberry automatically gets my vote.'

The remaining hour and a half allotted for their cooking sped by. Fran and Pea finished easily within the timeframe, something which caused them both to feel even more anxious, as if they'd oversimplified things or hadn't done enough. But, as Fran looked around at what the other contestants had been doing, she could see that one of the other couples was in the same position. The third pairing, however, had obviously suffered a few issues and were now panic-stricken, plating up things at speed and with very little finesse. At one point Fran had seen Christine leave the room and had thought she'd simply popped out to the loo, but now she wondered whether the stress of the situation had become too much for her. Fran had experienced that same feeling on plenty of occasions and she felt for them. It was awful when you believed you hadn't been able to deliver your best.

A few moments later, Miranda swept into the room on a cloud of flowery perfume and the atmosphere changed instantly. Wearing impossibly high heels (for Fran anyway), and a stunning shimmery-blue dress with a wide skirt, she went from table to table, dipping her head as she checked out what was on offer. She reminded Fran of a tiny bird, or maybe that should be a crow...

Fran's heart was thumping uncomfortably by the time Miranda finally reached her and Pea. With a bright smile, Miranda popped one of Pea's macarons in her mouth whole and then moved away to take up centre stage in front of the Christmas tree. With a jubilant look at Pea, Fran let out the breath she'd been holding.

Miranda held up her hands to signify she was about to start speaking.

'Good evening, everyone! You know, every year we do these Christmas specials and I think we can't possibly top what has gone before, and yet every year we do. I already can't believe what I've seen, and if this is the standard you're going to set, we're in for a cracker of a competition.' She gazed around at everyone in the room. 'I think you should give yourselves a round of applause.'

It was evidently the cue for the rest of the staff to file into the room and soon there was a small crowd gathered. Fran watched as Judy took up position next to Harrison, leaning gently into his side, while the make-up lady, whose name Fran remembered was Hope, came in with Midge, both laughing about something or other. There were a couple of new faces too, as well as the cameraman and sound engineer.

'Would everyone like to bring their food up to the top table here,' said Harrison. 'And then I really think it's time we got this

party started. Come on, up you come, and please help yourselves to drinks as well as all these incredible nibbles.'

It soon became evident who hadn't had such a good start to
the evening. Christine and Tony apologised profusely for their
mini pecan pies – the caramel had been burned, Christine's
fault apparently, and that was even after three goes at it. She
couldn't understand what had gone wrong, she normally made
it perfectly. Fran was pleased to see that everyone ate the
tartlets anyway. They were bitter and a little grainy, but
perfectly edible and, at this stage of the week, the show of soli-
darity was far more important than how the food tasted.

Fran took a glass of mulled wine and felt herself beginning
to relax a little. It was nearly nine o'clock and for someone
whom Fran's husband liked to joke only went out that late at
night to put out the bins, she would normally be winding down
her evening, not winding it up. But the conversation was
flowing as well as the drinks and Fran happily joined in, pleased
that her crostini had been polished off in short order.

'Fran, I'm so sorry to interrupt.' It was Midge, giving Vinny
an apologetic smile as she pulled Fran to one side. 'Can we
just...' She indicated that they should walk on a little way.

'Is everything all right?' asked Fran, although she could see
by the look on Midge's face that it wasn't.

'Not exactly, no.' She looked back down the room as they
reached the door. 'Have you noticed anyone leaving?' she asked.
'Or not here in the first place?'

Fran frowned. 'I don't think so. Well, only Miranda, of
course. And you... Oh, and Judy popped out to get another
bottle opener. But she was only gone about a minute and then
came back again. What's happened?'

'Perhaps I'd better show you,' replied Midge. 'Come
with me.'

Fran already had an idea where they might be going and,

sure enough, as they left the courtyard, Midge led her out across the open space towards the two trailers.

'Miranda has been in here, alone, since we spoke with her earlier. It's obviously dark outside, but she hasn't seen anyone, or heard anything either. She got ready for the icebreaker and then, when I called for her, we went directly to the stable. I'm not sure how long we were there, maybe only half an hour or so, but when she got back... She's been left another "gift", Fran, only this time it's even worse than the last one.'

'And you didn't see anyone when you returned to the trailer?'

'I didn't go straight there,' Midge replied. 'I went to check on the dogs quickly. But I went over as soon as Miranda called me. She's in a dreadful state. It isn't very pleasant...' She put her hand to her mouth. 'You'll see what I mean in a minute. And there was no one in sight when I arrived. I only stayed long enough to see what had happened and then I came to fetch you.'

Miranda was standing outside the trailer, a thick jacket pulled around her shoulders. She was still wearing her heels, hopping from foot to foot as the women approached. She was either anxious or cold, Fran wasn't sure which.

'Would someone please tell me what on earth is going on?' she demanded when she caught sight of Fran. 'This is getting beyond a joke now. In fact, it's seriously unfunny. And I want something done about it. Now!'

Fran nodded. 'I'm sorry, Miranda. What's happened?'

But Miranda didn't reply, she merely pointed up the trailer steps to the door, clutching the lapels of her jacket tighter.

Fran looked at Midge, who stepped forward to lead the way. 'I don't understand it,' said Midge. 'Why is someone doing this? It isn't funny at all. In fact, it's sick.'

Fran climbed the steps to stand beside her, looking around

the trailer for the source of the upset. Nose wrinkling, she immediately saw what the matter was.

On the coffee table in front of the sofa where Miranda had been reclining earlier was a lump of raw meat, a steak if Fran wasn't mistaken. She didn't need the evidence of her eyes to know what was wrong though, the smell was enough of a giveaway.

The meat was putrid, stinking and, as Fran watched in horror, a maggot wriggled its way across the table.

7

Fran immediately pulled out her phone to call Adam, asking him to come straight to Miranda's trailer. She looked around. 'Would you have a carrier bag? Or something we could...' She trailed off, looking at Midge. It was evident from the look on her face that Fran would be the one to deal with the revolting mess.

'Sorry,' said Midge. 'I'm not very good with things like this. I'm a vegetarian apart from anything.'

Fran nodded. She may well become one herself after this. There was no way she was touching anything with her bare hands. She kept one eye on the maggot while Midge rummaged in a cupboard under the trailer's tiny sink.

'Here, will this do?' Midge asked, before plucking out something else. 'And these?'

Fran took the bag and washing-up gloves with a grimace. Breathing through her mouth, she sidled nearer. She probably ought to check if whoever had left the rotten meat had also left any clues, but it was very hard to think with both the awful smell assailing her and the possibility that the single maggot she could see wasn't alone.

Opening the bag wide so there was no chance of fumbling

with it, Fran placed it on the table, then, gritting her teeth, scooped up the disgusting mess and dumped it inside. Once she'd apprehended the maggot as well, thankfully the only one, she tied the top of the bag tighter than tight and inhaled a cautious breath. It could have been her imagination but the smell did seem a little less pungent. She straightened up just as Adam came through the door, stopping dead as he did so.

'Oh God, that's, that's... what *is* that?' He looked at the bright-orange carrier bag with deep suspicion, almost gagging at the smell.

'Don't, whatever you do, open that,' said Fran. 'Because I may resort to physical violence if you do.'

Adam's eyebrows shot upwards. 'Whatever you say, Fran. Although if the contents of that bag are what's making this awful stench, then you've no worries.'

'Someone left a piece of meat in here,' Fran explained. 'Some very bad meat...'

Adam held a hand over his mouth. 'I'm really not good with yucky stuff.'

Midge grimaced. 'I'll see if I can get one of the cleaners. Maybe Betty might—'

'No!' hissed Miranda, coming into the trailer. 'No one is to come in here. No one is to see this. I will *not* be talked about, do you understand?'

'It's okay,' said Fran. 'If someone can get me some antibacterial spray and a cloth, I'll clean it up.' She held Midge's look. 'Although I'm not sure what state the table is going to be in.' It looked like mahogany to Fran's eye.

'Like I give a damn about the stupid table,' said Miranda with a glare at Midge.

'I'll get some cleaning stuff,' Midge replied, hurrying off.

'I suppose I should be grateful everyone else is still filling themselves with booze,' said Miranda. 'The last thing I need is people getting wind of this. The gossip columns would have a field day. Can you imagine?'

Fran didn't have the heart to tell her the meat had probably been left when it had precisely because people were otherwise engaged. She made a non-committal noise. 'Well, neither Adam nor I will say anything, obviously, and Midge won't.'

Miranda stared at her. 'So where am I to sleep?' she asked. 'I can't stay here, not with the place stinking to high heaven.'

'We could open the windows?' suggested Adam.

Fran nodded. 'Once we take the meat away, the smell will go quite quickly, especially once the table has been cleaned.'

'But what about fingerprints?' asked Miranda.

Fran stared at her. 'What about them?'

'Well, aren't you going to take any?'

Fran glanced at Adam. 'Miranda, I'm sorry, but Adam and I are not police officers, we can't do that.' Not that she wouldn't put it past Adam to have all the appropriate equipment, it was just the kind of thing he would have. 'I'm also pretty sure that you can't take prints from something like that. I was wearing gloves when I bagged it up, though, so I can certainly find out if that's a possibility.'

She paused, wondering how to put her next sentence in a way that would prevent Miranda from exploding. 'There's also the question of whether the police would even see this as a crime. There's obviously the fact that someone entered your trailer, but it wasn't locked, and people come and go from here all the time, by your own admission. I know what's happened isn't very pleasant, but no actual harm has been done.' She quailed under Miranda's glare.

'Well, what exactly would you call this then?' Her voice was icy. 'I hope you're not suggesting this kind of behaviour is in any way normal? That we should just ignore it and carry on our merry way.'

'No, of course not. But the police have to be certain that a crime has been committed and—'

'Of course one's bloody well been committed. This isn't a joke. It's threatening – sinister even.' Her hand wandered to her heart as if in shock.

Adam cleared his throat. 'Actually, Miranda, no threat's been made, either now or on any of the other occasions these "gifts" have been left for you. They're very unpleasant, increasingly so, but...' He trailed off at the look on Miranda's face.

'So what happens next then?' she demanded. 'What can possibly top this lovely gift? A horse's head in my bed, perhaps?'

Fran winced. 'I think that's just in the movies. You don't own a prize horse and, as far as I know, the mafia aren't particularly active in Shropshire.'

Miranda's gaze sliced into her. '*That* is entirely beside the point. I want to know what's going to happen now. And if you can't tell me then I'll get on the phone to—'

Fran was quite sure she knew how that sentence was going to end. It would involve ringing the wife of the district commissioner and that wouldn't bode at all well for Nell. And if it didn't bode well for Nell... 'Miranda, please, that really is why Adam and I are here – to get to the bottom of all this. But we only arrived a few hours ago and haven't had time yet to work out what's been going on. Plus, I'm now a competitor on the show, which isn't going to make things any easier. Adam, however, is very capable and now that we have an incident we can actually investigate in real time, rather than an event which happened in the past, I'm sure he'll be able to figure it all out. Someone on set must be responsible and, as far as I know, no one is going anywhere. We'll find who did this, Miranda, I promise you.'

For one long moment, Fran thought Miranda was going to argue further, but then she sighed and pulled her coat around her. She pointed a long pale-pink fingernail at the bag on the table. 'Do you think we can get rid of that now?' She tutted with irritation. 'Wherever has Midge got to? I could do with a drink. Something very large and very alcoholic. And while I'm drinking that perhaps you could clean up for me. I shan't be able to sleep a wink until this awful smell has gone.'

Fran waited until Miranda had turned away before raising her eyebrows at Adam. 'Just one other thing, Miranda,' she said. 'Is there anyone you can think of who might want to do these things to you? Someone who might have some kind of grudge, or...?'

'Who could possibly have a grudge?' replied Miranda, fixing Fran with a steely gaze. 'No, I can't think of a single person.'

'Okay,' said Fran lightly. 'Thanks, anyway.'

'She's hiding something,' said Fran, once they were safely back in the privacy of her room. Adam had again taken up his cross-legged position on the floor, while Midge had gone to check on how things were progressing over in the stable. Apparently, it was usual for Midge to give Judy a hand to clear away after the icebreaker, but they would have to wait until the party had broken up. There was also the small matter of the morning's competition to get ready for. Midge was in for a very late night.

'What makes you say that?' replied Adam. 'Why would Miranda be hiding anything? Surely if someone did have a grudge against her it would be in her best interests to say so.'

'You'd think so, wouldn't you?' Fran wrinkled her nose. 'It's intuition more than anything. When I asked her the question her answer seemed a little too fast for my liking. Miranda's had an almost meteoric rise to fame, and she's evidently very worried about any negative media coverage. It makes me wonder who she might have crossed in the past.'

'So, we need to start digging,' said Adam with a smile. 'Someone here must know something.'

'And despite Miranda's attempts to keep everything hidden, people love a good gossip. They might not know anything about the presents Miranda's been receiving, but if there's been any animosity between folk – jealousy, anything like that – her staff will have noticed. I'm not sure how much of a chance I'll have to speak to them once the competition starts tomorrow, but you can. Trouble is, with Miranda so adamant that no one must know what's been happening, it will be very hard to question people.'

Adam nodded. 'The first thing we need to check is where everyone was this evening. The window of opportunity seems quite tight, but someone slipped into Miranda's trailer, so who wasn't where they were supposed to be?'

'I've just had a thought,' said Fran. 'One of the contestants, Christine, popped out of the stable while we were cooking. I assumed she'd gone to the loo, but what if she hadn't? I didn't notice her slip back in, I was too busy, but she could have easily been away long enough to get to the trailer and back.'

'What about the meat, though?' asked Adam. 'Where would she, or anyone else, have got it from? It's not the sort of thing you could easily keep hidden, not smelling the way it did.'

'That's a very good point.' Fran glanced at her watch. 'Is it too late to ring Nell?' she asked.

'Probably, but I'd call her anyway. I think she needs to know about Miranda's latest pressie. And, more importantly, if we can get a list of the competitors to her, I think it's time for some background checks.'

Nell answered almost immediately, but then Fran had never known her do otherwise. 'This had better be good, I'm just about to find out who the killer is.'

'I'm sorry?' Fran stared at her phone. 'I can ring back later if it's a bad time?'

'No, I'll be asleep by then, I've only got three chapters to go. And I'm pretty sure it's the son – adoptive son, that is. Massive chip on his shoulder... Anyway, what can I do for you?'

Fran grinned as the penny dropped. 'I'm sorry it's so late but I thought you ought to know Miranda's had another special delivery – a rancid piece of meat this time, complete with maggot. The smell was incredible.'

'Woah, that's taking things up a notch,' replied Nell.

'That's what I thought.'

'But no message with it? No threat or warning?'

'No. Same as before, nothing. Or at least nothing Miranda would admit to. It's not long happened.'

'And who found it?'

'Miranda did. Who called Midge, who then called Adam and me. We were all at the welcome party when it must have happened, including Miranda and the crew. But she hadn't long joined the party and didn't stay more than half an hour or so, so the timing is quite tight.'

'Anyone noticeably absent?'

'I can't be certain, but I did spot one of the competitors popping out of the room for a few minutes. I think that was a little earlier though. Trouble is, Miranda's still adamant no one finds out what's been happening, so it's going to be a little difficult asking where everyone was without telling them why we want to know.'

'I'm beginning to dislike this woman,' replied Nell. 'I don't care if her Victoria sponges are the dog's doodahs.' Nell never suffered fools gladly. 'She wants us to investigate but then ties our hands at the same time. So, what's your thinking here, Fran? I don't like the sound of this latest development.'

'No, me neither. On the face of it, it seems more likely that the person responsible is one of the regular staff – if for no other reason than they had more opportunity for access. But I wondered if that might not necessarily be the case. It could be someone who holds a grudge against Miranda, perhaps from some time in the past when their paths might have crossed.'

'You're right.' There was an audible sigh. 'I was hoping we could resolve this on the quiet, but it's looking increasingly like that's not going to be the case. I'll get one of my team to start running checks in the morning. Can you get me a list of all the crew? Plus, the contestants and anyone else on site you think I should know about.'

Fran nodded even though she knew Nell couldn't see her. 'There is one other thing.'

'Go on...'

'One of the competitors has pulled out, so guess who's been roped in? Miranda demanded it – the show must go on, apparently.'

'Ah.' Nell paused a moment. 'And is that good news or bad news?'

'That all depends on whether I survive the first round,' Fran replied. 'Or make a complete prat of myself. Personally, I'll settle for coming through it with my dignity intact and camera angles that don't make my backside look like the rear end of a bus.' She rolled her eyes at Adam. 'It's obviously going to take up quite a chunk of my time, though. It will be good for me to be on the inside of things, but Adam is going to be up against it.'

'It might work to your advantage,' replied Nell, 'but duly noted. Now, if there's nothing else, may I please get back to my murder?' Only Nell could say something like that, whether it was referring to a novel she was reading or a real-life case she was working on.

Fran smiled as she hung up, promising to send Nell the details as soon as she could. Adam looked at her expectantly. 'What I can't understand is why somebody would leave these little "gifts" for Miranda in the first place,' said Fran. 'What's the point of them? They're obviously meant to send some kind of message, but without any notes, or clues as to what that message might be, why bother sending them at all?'

'Unless the gifts themselves are enough,' suggested Adam. 'Maybe they *do* mean something to Miranda?'

Fran nodded. 'Or maybe she's lying and *has* received messages, just not told us about them. They might relate to a secret she'd rather not admit to.'

'Either way, it means she's keeping something from us, and why do that when we're here to help? It's in her best interests to tell us everything she knows.'

'You'd think so, wouldn't you? Well, one thing's for certain, we need to find out. And soon.'

8

Adam's stomach was still rumbling even though he'd had the most marvellous breakfast. Everyone was talking about food, and his hollow legs, which were obviously connected to his stomach, could only respond in one way. The emptiness of his legs was one of the first things Fran had ever said about him, an expression he'd never come across before, but it did seem to explain his almost constant hunger. And the fact that she regularly fed him quantities of cake and biscuits was one of the best things about working with Fran, apart from investigating murders, of course. He probably ought not to admit he really rather enjoyed doing that. Not the murder part itself, that would be weird, but the challenge of figuring out whodunnit, putting together the pieces of the jigsaw and adding up all the clues to work out what happened, that's if you could spot them in the first place. And now, while they might not be investigating a murder, there was food everywhere you looked. It was the perfect combination.

He was sitting in Judy's trailer with Fran while she tried to decide what she was going to cook that day. Stepping into the competition at the last minute meant she hadn't had any time to think about what she would make for the first challenge and panic was setting in. All the other competitors had known the theme for weeks and been allowed to practise at home. They'd been able to bring with them any special equipment they'd wanted, and Judy had already sourced all their ingredients. Fran was starting from scratch.

She nodded as Judy explained the theme for the day.

'As you might expect, the challenges get harder as we go through the competition, so today we're starting with a simple festive family get-together. We're asking everyone to make two things: a savoury centrepiece which is suitable for sharing, a baked Camembert with bread, that kind of thing, and then a trifle with a twist, your own take on the classic. We start at eleven, so I can give you a little time to have a think, but not much, I'm afraid. You'll have make-up to go to and a short piece to film to camera before then, and it's gone nine now. You'll get three hours for the first challenge, an hour's break, and then we start again at four when the quick-fire challenge takes place. That's where each contestant is given the same set of ingredients and asked to make something as inventive as possible. If you've seen the show, you'll know the kind of thing.'

Fran swallowed. 'It's the worst bit,' she said. 'Having to think on your feet.'

Judy smiled, brushing a few hairs off her sleeve. 'I'm afraid you'll have to do *all* your thinking on your feet.'

She was about to add something further, when Midge's head appeared around the door.

'Sorry, Judy, Miranda's just about to come on set. Could I get the hot chocolate from you, please?' She glanced at her clipboard. 'And shortbread stars are what was agreed.'

Judy got to her feet, giving Fran an apologetic smile at the interruption. 'No problem, it should be cool enough by now. Won't make that mistake again,' she added, pulling a face. Turning, she reached for a jug sitting on the counter and brought it

closer to a huge teacup already waiting on a tray. It was decorated with robins and sprigs of holly. Pouring the velvety liquid
into the cup, she glanced at Adam. 'Could you pass me the jug
of cream, please? It's in the fridge behind you, the one nearest.
Top shelf.'

Adam got up to investigate, glad she'd only asked him for
cream and not some exotic ingredient he wouldn't even recognise. There was only one jug in there, thankfully, above a plate
of cooked chicken and a dish of butter. There were also several
bars of chocolate, posh ones too, not your run-of-the-mill ordinary stuff. He handed over the jug, watching as Judy stuck a
tiny electric whisk into it. She swirled the cream into the cup
over the back of a spoon, letting the froth she'd just created slide
in last.

'Holly sprigs?' she asked Midge, who nodded in reply. Judy
picked up a small canister with a series of holes in its top and,
pulling a sheet of card towards her, held it over the cup while
she dusted the cream with its contents. Once she had finished, a
perfect cocoa-dust holly leaf was revealed.

Midge checked her phone for the time. 'Perfect, Judy,
thanks a million.' She tucked her clipboard under her arm and
picked up the tray just as Judy added a plate of biscuits beside
the cup. 'Catch you later.' And with that, Midge was gone. The
whole process had only taken just over a minute.

'Sorry about that,' said Judy. 'But when Miranda first comes
on set she always does a piece to camera around the tree. And
the hot chocolate and biscuits are obligatory props.'

Fran smiled. 'I remember. It's so weird seeing such familiar
things from the show, only watching them from the other side of
the camera. One of the things I love about the show is the way
the format is always the same. It's comforting in a way. I hate it
when shows get messed with, just when you've got used to
them.'

'I guess...' said Judy slowly. 'Miranda does love everything just so, but sometimes you have to change it up a bit, or it gets stale.' She smiled. 'But what do I know?'

Adam frowned and glanced at Fran, who raised an eyebrow imperceptibly. Judy was a caterer on a cookery show. Did her comment smack a little of sour grapes?

With a sudden intake of breath, Judy turned abruptly to pick up a notepad and pen from the counter behind her. 'So, what are you going to cook, Fran?' she asked. 'Sorry, but we haven't got much time.'

A deep crease appeared in Fran's forehead. 'That's the problem, I haven't a clue.' She held up her hands in a helpless gesture. 'I'm normally fine with improvising if it's something for my family, but maybe it's the TV thing – my mind has gone a total blank.'

'I obviously have details of what Emily was going to cook, maybe you could do that? She *had* picked a baked Camembert, although her attempt at making it original is a little bland, in my opinion. And a honey and fig trifle. Nice flavours but apt to go very mushy.' Judy cocked her head to one side. 'It's up to you though.'

Fran, normally so decisive, was being unusually reticent and Adam couldn't really work out why. This was the kind of thing she did every day. She'd told him enough horror stories about past jobs where some calamity or other had occurred and she'd had to do a complete rethink on the fly. Maybe it *was* just the stress of being on the show.

Judy was being careful not to make it obvious, but Adam could see she was becoming a little impatient. 'I tell you what,' she said after several more moments of Fran staring at her vacantly. 'I've got to check a couple of things over in the stable, but I can give you ten minutes. Have a look through this.' She reached up to a cupboard above her head and took down a large and rather battered ring-binder, handing it to Fran. 'Don't breathe a word of this to anyone, because obviously the ideas are supposed to be yours, but have a look through some of my recipes, they might give you a little inspiration. I can't help you with the challenge this afternoon, I'm afraid, then you really will be on your own, but when I get back we can decide what you want to do. We've just about got time.'

'I might wander through to the stable as well,' said Adam. 'If that's okay with you?' He was rather conscious that Fran needed some time alone to think.

Fran nodded, and quickly bent her head to the recipe book. She had rather a tall order on her hands and Adam didn't envy her her task one little bit.

Midge was coming through the stable door as he and Judy reached it and he stood back to let her pass. She frowned at her clipboard as she hurried by with Tony in tow, muttering thank you. She looked increasingly more stressed each time he saw her.

'I hope Fran's okay,' he said to Judy, more for something to say than any other reason. 'It doesn't seem fair that she's had to step in when she's not even been able to practise. I know it can't be helped, but still...'

Judy gave him an odd look. 'Fran will get the help she needs, don't worry. Sorry, excuse me a minute.'

He watched as she walked away to speak to Harrison. He was standing at the rear of the room, chatting with Sam the cameraman and Woody, who was holding what Adam now knew was a sound boom and not a fluffy cleaning mop. By contrast, Miranda was settled in the armchair beside the Christmas tree, the tray of hot chocolate and biscuits on a table next to her. She looked around calmly, almost serene, the folds of her voluminous skirt carefully arranged around her legs. He noticed Hope hovering nearby, a small case in her hands. No doubt she was poised ready to give Miranda a dab of something, should it be required.

A minute later, the three men approached the tree and,

with very little preamble, began to film. Miranda picked up the cup, at first seeming to hold it unnaturally high until Adam realised it was so that it would also appear in the shot. Miranda gave a wide smile, tipped her head to one side and began to speak.

Adam had to hand it to her, she knew what she was doing. The words rolled out of her mouth without so much as a pause. No ums, no ahs and absolutely no searching around for what to say. He knew there would be a script, but Miranda delivered it so naturally you'd never know it. She ended the piece by bringing the cup to her lips and tipping her head slightly to meet it. As her mouth met the liquid she looked up through her lashes with an expression that said she'd just tasted heaven. She paused, held the pose, and then a few seconds later straightened up and plonked the cup back on the table. She licked her lips.

'At least it wasn't scalding bloody hot this time,' she said, rolling her eyes. 'Did you get that?' She smiled up at Harrison, her eyes darting sideways over his shoulder just for a second. From the far end of the room, Judy stood watching, an inscrutable expression on her face.

'Has anyone ever told you you have the most beautiful skin?' asked Hope.

Fran, who had hardly slept a wink and had looked in the mirror that morning with weary resignation gave a wan smile. 'Not recently.'

'I mean, you're how old? I'm thirty-six and you can't be much older than me. Thirty-eight, maybe?'

Fran blinked in surprise at the petite woman in front of her. She looked far younger than she claimed to be and was extraordinarily pretty, with elfin features, cropped black hair and, not surprisingly, expertly made-up. She certainly sounded sincere, her big hazel-brown eyes warm on Fran's.

'I'm forty-two,' Fran replied. 'It must be the freckles,' she added. 'They cover a multitude of sins.' Like when you couldn't sleep because you were a bag of nerves and consequently look like death warmed up.

Hope smiled. 'I've always wanted freckles,' she said. 'It's funny, isn't it? People spend so much time trying to cover them up when really, they're a part of who they are. I take it you'd like yours left au naturel?'

Fran nodded. 'I don't really ever wear much make-up,' she replied.

Hope picked up a large, round brush from a vast array of others. 'I'll just give you a little whisk over with something light then. You don't need anything else, but it will make sure you're not too washed out by the lights... or lack of sleep.' She paused. 'You don't need to be nervous, you know. Everyone here is lovely.'

Fran was beginning to realise just how lovely everything was. So far that morning she had attended the eight-thirty briefing with an exhausted-looking Midge, who had told them how lovely it was to see them all. Then she had met with Harrison, who discussed how lovely it would be to film a small segment with her later in the evening to get her reaction to the first day. After that, it was the turn of Woody the sound man, who asked her to stand at her workstation and say something so he could check the 'levels' – all lovely, followed by a similar conversation with the cameraman, who wanted to check her angles – just lovely... Finally, Midge had appeared to ferry her to see Judy and now she was in Hope's small trailer being subjected to intense scrutiny. She smiled to herself.

'Have you worked on the show long?' Fran asked.

Hope dipped a small brush into a pot of something and began to dab at Fran's under-eye area. She wrinkled her brow. 'It must be coming up to three years now,' she said. 'I was so lucky to get the chance to work with Miranda. A friend of mine put in a good word for me, and I was so nervous on my first day, I was nearly sick. I mean, someone like Miranda, you don't want to make her look rubbish, do you? She's so attractive... But I needn't have worried, Miranda was lovely, kindness itself, and we just sort of clicked.'

'Everyone certainly seems very friendly,' remarked Fran. 'That must really help, given that you're working such long hours together. It would be awful if you didn't all get on.'

'Wouldn't it?' Hope grimaced. 'I can't imagine what that would be like. I love how we're all so close. You really get to know people when it's like this – like a family, I guess.'

'Even families have their ups and downs though.'

'True. But I'm an only child, so I guess this makes up for it. The travelling can be a bit difficult sometimes. It's hard to have relationships when you're away from home so much, but I miss the show like crazy when we're on a break, Midge especially. Just close your eyes a second for me...'

Fran felt the brush whisk over her eyelids, prickling slightly as it did so.

'And... open?' Hope stared at her, eyes darting left to right as she took in all the details of Fran's face, assessing what she saw. 'Great... I'll just give you a little more colour to make sure the lights don't bleach you.'

'Midge does an incredible job, doesn't she?' said Fran. 'She's been so helpful, especially as she always seems to have so much to do. I don't know how she keeps up with everything.'

'I know, without her the show would fall apart.' Hope paused, eyes downcast. 'Harrison's pretty good, but he's more concerned with the production side of things – how the show looks – but if it wasn't for Midge he wouldn't have a show to produce. She keeps everything running to schedule, and everyone where they need to be. It's a massive juggling act, as you can imagine.' She blew a little powder from her brush. 'I wouldn't want her job, that's for sure.'

Fran pulled a face. 'Me neither. I'm not sure I'd be anything like as patient as she is. I heard Miranda teasing her yesterday – about her clipboard. I'm sure it was nothing more than that, and Midge seemed to take it in good spirits, but I thought it was a little mean, actually. Midge has so many things to remember, without that clipboard she'd be sunk. I'm just the same, I have to make lists of everything.' It was pushing the truth a little but Fran was interested to hear what Hope had to say.

'Miranda's not the only person who teases her about it. It makes me cross, actually. Like you said, where would everyone be if Midge wasn't so organised? And Miranda doesn't have to do anything other than film her segments. That's how it should be, obviously, Miranda is the star of the show; we wouldn't all be here if it wasn't for her, but she hasn't got nearly as many things to think about. Plus, no one shouts at her if things go wrong.' Hope turned around to rummage in a bag on the table behind her and when she turned back, her bright smile had returned.

'Now, how about a touch of lipstick? Or, if you prefer, this lip stain is fabulous, gives you just a hint of rosy colour without the full-on, made-up look.' She took in Fran's expression. 'We'll go for the stain,' she said.

They were cutting it fine. Fran had gone straight from make-up to the stable where Judy had been busy setting up her worksta- tion, but they were rapidly running out of time. Judy had promised to have everything ready for her and, as Fran approached, she could see she'd been true to her word. Jars of dry ingredients stood ready in serried ranks with fresh produce neatly laid out beside them. Judy was on her knees, adding items to the fridge. She stood up and closed the door.

'Right, that's everything,' she said. 'I think we're good to go. I've left the recipes for you as well, but remember that you might need to adjust the timings slightly to accommodate the changes you wanted to make.' She pulled a piece of paper towards her. 'I've jotted a couple of notes in the margin which might help.'

Fran smiled gratefully. 'Am I allowed to have them?' she whispered. She'd assumed they had to make everything from memory. She rarely used recipes when she was working – there simply wasn't time and she'd been a caterer for so long, she could do most of the basics with her eyes closed. She made notes, but that was entirely different.

'It's perfectly fine,' replied Judy. 'All the other contestants have them, and no one minds if you refer to them. Even the best memory suffers under competition conditions, and *you* haven't had any time to prepare.'

Inspiration had come relatively easily. Judy's file had been filled with a huge variety of recipes, some of which were very similar to those Fran used at home, but she still felt uneasy about the situation.

'I feel rather awkward using these recipes,' she said. 'Are you sure it isn't cheating?'

Judy gave her a wayward look. 'God, no. We'll just call them something else when we describe them for the voice over. I doubt Miranda will even realise.'

Fran looked down at the sheet, frowning slightly. 'Sorry, what won't she realise?'

'That they're her recipes.'

'Hers?' Fran stared at Judy in horror. 'But I thought you said they were yours.'

Judy tidied the sheets of paper and pushed them to one side. 'No, they're Miranda's recipes. I only called them mine because they're kept in my folder. I use it as a master copy for when Miranda does her speciality spot. She usually plucks something out of the air and it's much easier if I have the recipe to hand so I can ensure we have everything she might need.

That way I don't end up looking like an idiot. My memory's shocking.'

'Oh, me too,' replied Fran. 'I have to write everything down.'

Judy smiled, looking more relaxed. 'But I promise Miranda won't recognise them, just describe them differently when she gets to you.' She glanced at her watch. 'Okay, we've only got ten minutes to go. I've double-checked you've got everything, so try not to panic and you'll be fine. Good luck.' She nodded towards Harrison and Miranda. 'I'll just go and make sure no one else has had any last-minute hiccups.'

'Thanks, Judy.' Fran grimaced as she looked down at her workstation, her stomach somersaulting at the thought of what was about to happen. How on earth had she managed to get herself into this? It was crazy. She looked up as Midge appeared in front of her.

'Everything okay, Fran?' She didn't wait for an answer. 'Now, lucky you being right at the front because it means Miranda will be coming to you first. I suggest you pick up a jar of flour or something and look as if you're about to weigh it out. You'll hear them say when the camera is rolling, so just pause what you're doing when you see Miranda approach. She'll ask you a couple of questions about what you're making, you know the drill, so just be guided by her. I'm sure you'll be fine.'

Fran nodded. 'You look almost as nervous as I feel,' she whispered. 'Are you all right?'

'I will be once filming starts,' Midge replied. 'That's when I know that everyone is in the right place at the right time. I get a bit of a breather then too, thank God. I didn't get to sleep until four and I was up at six.'

'But that's awful.' Fran studied Midge, noticing the dark shadows around her eyes. 'Couldn't you sleep?'

Midge pulled a face. 'Partly... It took a while to clear up after the party last night, and then, when I'd actually got to bed,

Miranda called me over twice, said she'd heard someone outside her trailer.'

'And had she?' Fran frowned. That didn't sound good.

'Not that I could see,' replied Midge, shaking her head. 'I think she was a bit jumpy, after... you know...' She trailed off, her eyes following Miranda and Harrison down the room.

'Understandable, I suppose, but why didn't she call Harrison? He's closer, for one thing, and if there was someone poking around... I'm all for girl power, but, Midge, you shouldn't be dealing with things like that.'

'Yeah, but Miranda wouldn't call Harrison, would she? She doesn't want him to know what's been going on.'

'But she didn't have to explain,' argued Fran. 'She could simply have said she thought she heard someone.' She studied Midge's weary face once more. 'Listen, promise you'll give me or Adam a shout if she does that again, and one of us can come with you.'

Midge nodded, but Fran wasn't at all convinced she would do as she'd been asked. She looked peculiarly reticent for some reason. Fran was about to probe further when Midge dipped her head, directing her attention towards Miranda.

'Looks like you're up,' she said, giving Fran's arm a squeeze. 'I know you'll do brilliantly, but good luck. I'll catch up with you later.'

Fran smiled, watching as the young woman walked quickly back up the room. Her thoughts were full of questions but she had no time for them now, she really did need to focus on the task ahead. What had Midge said? Just pick up a jar of flour or something. She glanced at the recipe Judy had written out for her, trying to breathe as evenly as she could. Maybe that might stop her hands from shaking.

'Okay, Fran,' said Harrison, appearing at her elbow. 'We're going to film a quick piece with you now – your chance to tell us a little about what you'll be making today. Just follow Miranda's lead and answer her questions. You'll be fine.' He stepped aside to stand beside Sam and Woody.

Miranda stood a little distance away, waiting for her cue. She pulled a lock of hair over one shoulder as she readied herself.

'So, Fran, what are you cooking for us today? You've got a fabulous array of ingredients here.' Miranda smiled, flashing her teeth.

'I've gone for something which is a firm favourite with my family at Christmas. It's incredibly moreish, and always heralds the beginning of festivities for us. It's a blue cheese, pear and walnut twist, which I'll shape like a Christmas tree.'

'Oh, lovely, one of my absolute favourites, and something which works so well when you've a crowd of people. And what about your trifle? Is that something you make for your family as well?'

Fran nodded and smiled, remembering to look at Miranda and not the camera. 'Everyone loves a trifle, don't they? My mum used to make one every year, which we'd eat on Boxing Day. I guess I just inherited the tradition from her.'

'That's such a lovely story. But I suspect your trifle is a little different from the one your mum used to make, would I be right?' Another winning smile to camera.

'You would. I do love the traditional flavours of a classic trifle, but my daughter loves anything with caramel in it, so this one mixes a mascarpone cream with dulce de leche and squidgy brownies for the base.'

'And how are you going to decorate it?'

'I'm going to spin some sugar and lay it on the top.'

Miranda nodded. 'And you'll be able to get everything done on time?'

Fran paused. Did Miranda think it wasn't possible? *Was* it possible? Had she bitten off more than she could chew, no pun intended. 'I think so, yes.'

'Well, good luck. It all sounds lovely, and that trifle sounds right up my street, although I'm not sure my waistline would agree.' She flashed a demure smile.

Fran smiled back. 'I've often wondered how you keep your figure,' she replied. 'With so much tempting food around, I'd be the size of a house.'

'Cut!'

Fran whirled around. What had she done wrong?

Harrison was gesturing at the cameraman. 'Sorry, Fran, can we have that again? Only don't mention the weight thing. The other stuff you said was great, but we get complaints if we bang on about it too much.' He smiled. 'Let's just have that line again, Miranda, from where you wish Fran luck, and maybe this time, Fran, just smile, like you're agreeing. After all, Miranda does have an exceptionally fine waistline.'

Miranda scowled, eyes narrowing at Harrison before she looked away. There was an odd pause and then she turned back, the smile she'd worn before perfectly back in place. She paused again before delivering her line as if the previous exchange had never happened. It was fortunate that Fran only had to smile because she'd completely forgotten what she was supposed to do.

'Super, thanks, Fran. Okay, let's move on to Vinny.' Harrison indicated the next workstation just behind Fran, and the four of them moved off.

Fran stared at the ranks of ingredients in front of her, quite unable to process what lay ahead. She couldn't even think where to start. She took a deep breath, willing herself to keep calm. She was a caterer – she cooked every day of her life – it was like breathing, something she did almost without thinking. Pastry... that was it. Make the pastry. She reached for the flour and butter.

. . .

Adam had seen Fran cook on loads of occasions, he'd even had a hand in helping her on a few of them, but he'd never seen her quite so focused before. He hadn't intended to stay and watch, but the process of filming was fascinating and he'd never been on a TV set before; it was an experience he didn't want to miss. He was always on the lookout for unusual settings and locations for the computer games he designed. This could well come in handy.

It wasn't until Judy called out to the competitors that they only had ten minutes left to finish that he realised how much time he had wasted. He was supposed to be investigating the appearance of Miranda's latest present and there was one person in particular he wanted to talk to.

Betty was in the kitchen peeling vegetables when he caught up with her. She was singing softly to an old-fashioned portable radio playing in the background and had surprisingly dulcet tones.

'Can I help?' he asked, joining her at the sink. 'Fran says I'm a dab hand with a potato peeler.'

Betty's hand shot to her chest, still clutching a carrot. 'Blimey, you nearly frightened me to death. Don't sneak up on an old woman like that.'

Adam grinned. 'You're not old... are you? Apparently, it's rude to ask a lady how old they are, but isn't it better to know? Otherwise I could say you're in your eighties when you're nothing of the sort.'

Betty raised her eyebrows and wordlessly handed him a potato peeler, but not before he'd seen an amused twinkle in her eye. 'How's your friend getting on?' she asked a few moments later. 'I heard she got roped into the competition.'

Adam nodded. Betty had directed him to a pile of potatoes on the draining board and he was already halfway through the first. 'Hard to say,' he replied. 'I couldn't get close enough to see, but Fran's an amazing cook, I'm sure she'll be okay. That's if her nerves don't get the better of her.'

'This filming lark seems a bit of a shambles if you ask me,' she replied. 'I can't say I blame the young girl who left. Anyone could see how scared she was, it wasn't right to force her in front of a camera. I've watched these shows before and it might look all happy-as-Larry on the surface, but common sense tells you it can't be. You only had to hear what that producer chappie was saying to her to know it's all a pack of lies.'

'Is it?' asked Adam, blinking. 'Why? What did he say?'

'All but promised her she could win. I suspect he was just saying that to make her stay, but that's not right either. A nervous girl like that needs to win because she's good, not because someone insinuates he would bend the rules for her. How is she ever going to feel better about herself with that kind of carry on?'

It was a good point, and also confirmed Adam's suspicions that Betty was exactly the right person to be talking to. He'd bet she'd seen a lot of things since everyone had arrived at the house. 'It's shocking,' he agreed. 'Although maybe I won't mention that to my friend, I don't think she'd be very pleased.' He paused, looking at the potato in his hands. 'Are these for dinner?' he asked.

Betty nodded. 'I'm making a hotpot. Not as fashionable as what they'll be cooking over in the stable today, I don't suppose, but you can't beat a hotpot. Comforting and fills you up a treat.'

'I'm famished,' said Adam hopefully. 'I think it sounds delicious.'

Betty put down her knife. 'It'll be a while before you'll be eating it, but I've some cake in a tin if you'd like a piece to tide you over?'

Adam grinned. 'Could I?' he said. 'I don't know why I'm so hungry. Must be all this talk of food every minute of the day. I tell you what, Betty, why don't I make us both a nice pot of tea?'

He wasn't sure how long they'd been talking when the kitchen door suddenly flew open and Midge all but fell into the room. Her face was drained of colour, her eyes staring, round and frightened.

'Adam, you've got to help me, I don't know what to do...' She stared at Betty. 'Oh God, this is terrible,' she whispered urgently. 'Please, will you come with me?'

Adam got to his feet. 'Sure, but what's the matter, Midge? Is everything okay?'

Midge flicked the housekeeper an anxious glance, twisting her hands. Whatever was troubling her she evidently didn't want to say it in front of Betty. He steered her towards the door, mouthing an apology at Betty.

'Is it Miranda?' he asked as soon as they were outside.

Midge nodded, swallowing hard. 'What on earth are we going to do? This is all my fault.'

He frowned. 'What is, Midge?'

She pulled at his arm. 'Please... just come with me.'

He followed her from the guest wing, breaking into a run as she crossed the front of the house, heading for the trailers.

'Midge, slow down. What's the matter? Has Miranda had something else delivered?'

Midge whirled around. 'No, but...' She stared at him, her eyes filling with tears. 'I think she's dead.'

9

Adam had never seen a dead body before. Well, not one like this at least. The first murder he and Fran had investigated was of a young woman who'd been poisoned, but she had died in a hospital. Bodies number two and three he also hadn't seen, while body number four was an elderly man who had supposedly died in his sleep long before he and Fran had come on the scene. Body number five had been discovered by Fran when she'd literally fallen over it, but they had been in a wood at the time, in total darkness, and there wasn't really that much to see. Miranda was different.

She was sitting in a chair at her dressing table, the ring of brighter-than-bright lights which surrounded the mirror still illuminating every feature. The chair had slightly swivelled away from the table so it partially faced the trailer door, and Miranda looked for all the world as if she was about to start speaking. But her slack face and oddly sightless eyes revealed that she would never say another word. That, and the several inches of silver-coloured handle that protruded from the end of whatever had been sunk deep into her chest.

There wasn't even much blood, just a dark stain on the front of her dress which seemed to grow bigger as Adam stood there, rooted to the spot. It was a big thing to comprehend, that someone who he'd seen only recently could now have simply ceased to be.

'Is she...?' asked Midge, hardly needing to finish her sentence. 'Shouldn't we check? Call an ambulance or something?'

But Adam could see there was no need. 'Did you touch her?' he asked, eyes scanning the dressing table, moving to a mug which lay on the carpet, almost at his feet. Whatever it contained had spread into an even bigger stain than the one on Miranda's chest. Splashes of it had run down the cupboard beneath the small sink and, as he watched, another drip joined those already on the floor.

'No, I didn't get any further than where you are now. God, Adam, what do we do?' Midge darted a look behind her. 'Miranda's due back on set in less than an hour. What am I going to tell Harrison?' Midge's hands gripped the edges of her clipboard, her knuckles white. Whatever she had written there wasn't going to help her now.

'Come on,' he said gently, 'let's go back outside.' He touched Midge's arm, breaking her reverie. 'There's nothing we can do for her, and we have to preserve things for when the police get here.'

'The police?'

He nodded, seeing her vacant expression. 'Midge...?' He waited until her eyes met his, wide and frightened. 'Miranda's been murdered, Midge, we need to call the police.'

He saw it then, the realisation of what had happened sinking in. 'Yes, of course, I'll...' She fumbled for her phone. 'Damn, I don't know where it is.'

'It's okay, I'll call Nell. She'll know what to do.' That's what he wanted more than anything, someone who would know what to do, who could tell *him* what to do. He suddenly felt the full weight of responsibility finding Miranda's body had placed on him. And he really didn't think he was up to it. He tried to slow down his breathing and start thinking. 'We need to make sure no one comes anywhere near these trailers,' he said, feeling immediately better for having said something. Is that what Nell would do? Is that what she would say? He tried another question. 'Did you see anyone when you found her?'

Midge shook her head, several times. 'No, no one.'

'And when you left her to fetch me, did you see anyone then? In the courtyard, or the stable?'

Another shake of the head. 'No, but everyone is inside. They will have started filming the mini-challenge by now.'

Adam frowned. He pulled out his phone and located Nell's number with difficulty, his fingers didn't seem to be obeying instructions. The call made, he turned back to Midge, trying to push Nell's harsh response from his head. He always had to remind himself that she wasn't cross with him, it was just her manner. Tools of the trade, she had once told him. He thought he understood that better now. The things she must have seen. It was no wonder she used her words to conjure a protective force field. He swallowed and looked at Midge. She was staring at her clipboard again, eyes frantically scanning the lines of information as if she'd completely forgotten what she was doing, how to read even.

'So, what is everyone doing now?' he asked. 'On the schedule, I mean.'

Midge looked up and then back down again, the connection between his question and the information she held taking an age to form. With a deep breath, she visibly drew herself together. 'They'll be on the last segment now, where everyone has to make something from a set of ingredients which are revealed live,' she added, seeing his blank look. 'None of the contestants know what they are beforehand so it's a complete surprise. They only have an hour and Miranda's due back before they finish to film a few segments. Then there's the results and—' Her eyes filled with tears again. 'I have to tell them. We have to stop the filming.'

Adam was thinking hard because something wasn't quite right here. He could feel his brain scrabbling to make sense of things. 'So, everyone should be over in the stable?'

'Yes.'

'Then why wasn't Miranda there?'

Midge looked puzzled for a second, but then her face cleared. 'Oh, I see... no, she isn't needed during that challenge, so it's when she takes her break. She films all the linking sections in advance while the contestants are having *their* break and then she comes back here. I bring her a bar of chocolate and a drink at four, and then just before five she goes back to give her verdict.' She bit her lip. 'I thought I was going to be a bit late today, actually... I thought I was going to be in trouble. I dozed off and slept later than I thought I had. I couldn't find my phone, you see. Miranda can be quite particular about that kind of thing, but when I got here...' She swallowed.

Adam nodded. His brain had caught up with events and he tried to keep his face from showing what he was thinking. 'So, when Miranda came back here, that would have been about what time?'

'It varies, it depends when they finished filming her segments.'

'And would she have come back with anyone else?'

Midge shook her head. 'I doubt it, everyone else is needed on set.'

'Yes, of course. I just wondered who Miranda might have been talking to. See, she was sitting down when she was killed, so she either didn't get up to greet whoever came in, or she was relaxed enough to stay seated during their conversation. Either way, it strikes me that it must have been someone she knew.' He was feeling his way gently because there was really only one more question he needed to ask.

'I see what you mean,' Midge replied. 'I guess it could have been anyone but...' She frowned. 'It must have been before four because that's when the competition restarts and everyone would definitely have been over in the stable by then.'

Her eyes widened, and Adam winced as he saw Midge work out what was already very plain to him.

'They're going to think it was me...' She stared up into his eyes. 'Oh God, what am I going to do, Adam? They're going to think I killed her.'

He tried to reassure her as best he could, but what she'd said was true. Apart from him and Betty, everyone else should have been on set, and he obviously knew he hadn't killed Miranda, and it couldn't have been Betty because she was with him, so that only left Midge, the person who had found her, the person whose life Miranda seemingly made a misery...

Midge was visibly shaking now, but he really couldn't take her anywhere else. What he needed was Fran's very capable wing to tuck her under, but he couldn't go and fetch Fran either, she was in the middle of a competition for goodness' sake. Let alone the fact that to do so would mean leaving the trailer unguarded or, rather, guarded by Midge who, as she had just clearly deduced, could be the prime suspect. It would give her all the time she needed to get rid of any incriminating evidence. Not that he thought there would be any, just... His thoughts were firing in rapid succession. Even inside his own head he was gabbling.

He also couldn't risk everyone finding out what had happened yet either – not until the police arrived; the fewer people who knew, the better. People had a habit of behaving a certain way in situations like this – someone always wanted to take charge, or 'help' and, in reality, what that meant was a crime scene contaminated and a great deal of emotion to cope with. Adam wasn't keen on either of those things becoming an issue. He gave Midge as reassuring a smile as he could manage and thought about the possibility of hugging her. That's what Fran would have done. She would have known what to say as well, but Adam wasn't like Fran. He wasn't good with hugs, not with random people he didn't really know. He grimaced again, telling himself to shut up.

Fortunately, Nell arrived shortly after, which was just as well because Midge looked as if she might collapse. He was pretty shaken himself but at least he wasn't terrified of being arrested for murder. Nell's car swung to a halt in front of the main house and he raised an arm to attract her attention.

'This wasn't quite the update I'd been expecting from you,' she said on reaching them. 'Bloody hell, Adam, do you know what the chief super is going to say?'

'It wasn't my fault,' he said. Nell always managed to bring out his defensive side.

'Are you sure?' she asked. 'Because if it was, it would make my job a whole lot easier. A nice, neat arrest and conviction...' She blew out her cheeks. 'Not that any of it makes up for Miranda dying in the first place.' Her face softened. 'Miranda Appleby... Why do people do these things?' She directed her attention at Midge. 'Detective Chief Inspector Nell Bradley, we've spoken on the phone. You were a big help in getting Adam and Fran here in the first place, so thank you for that. Although I gather it was you who found Miranda?'

Midge managed a nod. 'Yes, just now.'

'And did you kill her?'

Midge's mouth dropped open. It was a tactic Adam had seen Nell deploy on more than one occasion, her lightning-fast question catching people unaware. And when they were unaware, and unprepared, you generally got a genuine response.

'No, I didn't.' Midge's eyes filled with tears. 'But I'm probably the only one who could have,' she added. 'That's what I can't understand... It doesn't make any sense.' She stared at Miranda's trailer and then turned her attention back to Nell, the confusion on her face clear to see.

Nell shot Adam a glance.

'Everyone else is filming,' he said. 'Over in the stable block behind the house.'

'Okay, we'll get to that in a moment. For now, who else knows about Miranda?'

'No one, just us two,' said Adam.

Nell's eyebrows arched in surprise. 'Well, that's something at least.'

'And neither of us have touched anything... obviously.'

'Okay, wait here a sec while I have a look myself.'

Nell wasn't gone long. No sooner had she mounted the steps to the trailer than it seemed she backed out again. Adam had never seen anyone assess a situation as fast as Nell could. And notice an extraordinary amount of things while she did so.

'So,' Nell said, walking back towards them. 'I would say Miranda knew her killer, given that she doesn't appear to have moved either immediately before, or after, death. Either that, or she was taken so unawares she didn't have time to react, which is possible. Midge... is that your real name?' She shook her head. 'Never mind, you can tell me later. We've already established that everyone is elsewhere, but exactly who does that encompass? And who's in charge?'

'That would be Harrison, Harrison Shaw. He's the show's director, but he also owns the production company. Then there are the regular staff: me, Judy Mulligan the caterer, Hope Fielding on make-up, Sam Ellis the cameraman, and the sound man Stuart Woodham, who's known as Woody. Apart from them, the only other people here are the contestants, six in total, including Fran, of course. Oh, and there's a housekeeper by the name of Betty. I'm afraid I don't know her last name. She works for the owners of Beresford Hall, but there's no one in residence at the house just now, only us.'

Nell paused a moment to digest what she'd been told. 'And every one of those people you mentioned is over in this stable block, are they?'

Midge faltered. 'Well, yes, they should be, filming will have started again.'

'All except for Betty,' put in Adam. 'But I was with her when Midge found me and told me about Miranda, and had been for a little while, so it obviously couldn't have been her either.'

Nell frowned. 'Why obviously?'

Adam glanced at Midge, doubting himself under the weight of Nell's gaze. 'Because Miranda would have been on set until quite recently, and then left to return to her trailer. Midge found her at four, so whoever killed her didn't have long in which to do it.'

Nell's eyes narrowed as she looked at Midge. 'And you're certain you found her at four?'

Midge nodded. 'Miranda has a break from four o'clock, which is when I bring her a drink... and a bar of chocolate. She's quite particular about things, doesn't like them to be late, so... I never am.' She dropped her head.

'And this was a regular thing?'

'When she was filming, yes.'

'So, apart from yourself, who else would have known Miranda's routine?'

'Everyone would, she always had...' Midge trailed off. 'Oh...'

'Exactly,' replied Nell. 'It's highly unlikely this was an opportunist crime. The chances of it failing are simply too high. It's possible someone got extremely lucky, but what's more likely is that it's been very carefully planned. Interesting... But at least we have a time frame to work with.'

Nell scrutinised Adam's face. 'Right, Midge and I had

better go and speak with Harrison and break the news.' She paused. 'You know, in all my years as a police officer this never gets any easier. I'm not a big fan of cooking myself, but I know Miranda was well-loved. It's going to come as a very harsh shock for a lot of people.' She stared into space a moment before shaking her head and refocusing on Adam. 'Can you stay here and direct traffic as best you can until I get back? It's going to be a circus here pretty soon. A couple of DCs should be arriving pretty sharpish, so if you could flag them down, I'd be grateful. But if the pathologist gets here first, send her in anyway.' She took a step forward. 'Oh, just one more thing before we go – the murder weapon – it looks like some kind of dagger, with a very ornate handle. Have either of you seen it anywhere before?'

'It's a cake slice,' replied Midge.

Nell did a visible double take. 'A cake slice?'

'Yes. Miranda won it a few years ago at an awards party. It usually sits on a shelf in her trailer. It rests on a plinth, you know, so it's fixed.'

'Quite,' replied Nell, raising her eyebrows. 'Now I've heard everything. Dear God, the press are going to have a field day with this one – charismatic celebrity cook murdered with a cake slice.' She inhaled a deep breath. 'Right, come on.'

10

———

Fran was halfway to Miranda's trailer before she realised she had left her pudding in the oven. Not that it really mattered now, none of it did. She hadn't seen Nell arrive straight away, only spotting her when she'd straightened up from replacing some cream in the fridge. The fact that she was talking to Harrison was ominous enough, given that he supposedly knew nothing about the real reason why Fran and Adam were there, but it was the look on Midge's face which told her something was very wrong. And when she realised that Miranda was also missing from the room, she dropped everything and ran.

She saw Adam almost immediately. He was standing beside Miranda's trailer, looking hunched and awkward.

'What's happened?' she panted. 'Is it Miranda?'

Adam nodded. 'She's dead, Fran. Someone's killed her.'

Even though it was what she had expected to hear, it made little difference to the way her stomach dropped away in shock. How could she have been so stupid?

'This is all my fault,' she said, staring at Adam in horror. 'Oh God, poor Miranda.' She hadn't exactly taken to the woman but no one deserved this.

'Your fault?' asked Adam, eyes wide. 'How can it be your fault?'

'Because I should have realised what was happening here, taken more notice of it and what it meant. Think about it, Adam. It started off with a card, then the dead roses, the tube of Polyfilla... a joke to start with maybe, or something that might be passed off as a silly prank, but this last present, the rotten meat, was an escalation and I should have seen where it was going, where it might end up.'

Adam touched her arm. 'Fran, you're not a mind-reader, or a police officer. There's no reason to suspect anything like this would happen. It's a very big leap from sending unpleasant gifts to actually killing someone. And you spoke to Nell about it. If she felt Miranda was at risk then...'

'And you're going to say that to Nell, are you?' she said, giving him a pointed look. What he said made sense and she knew he was trying to make her feel better, but she wasn't remotely consoled. She checked herself on seeing his expression. None of this was Adam's fault either. 'Sorry, I shouldn't have said that. But I can't help it, I feel responsible for this.'

'Not half as much as Midge does,' Adam replied. 'She's the one who found Miranda and although she obviously said she didn't kill her, she's by far the most likely suspect – the others were all in the stable when it happened, filming. And Betty was with me, so...' He let his sentence hang in the air.

'Poor Midge, she looked utterly distraught just now, no wonder.'

'I'm really worried,' said Adam. 'Because from what Midge said, she will be firmly at the top of the suspect list.'

Fran sighed. 'And I know how that feels. But it's a busy set, anyone could have slipped out... probably... couldn't they?'

Adam wrinkled his nose. 'Did *you* notice anyone missing?' he asked. 'Because from the way Midge told it, the window of opportunity was quite small, from the time Miranda finished filming to when Midge found her, so maybe only twenty minutes or so. The time you and the other contestants were on their break.'

'None of them were missing,' replied Fran. 'There are only six of us, it's not hard to spot if someone isn't there.'

'And before that time, Miranda would have been filming, so that would have involved Harrison and Sam, Woody... I'm guessing Hope would have been on standby too. What about Judy?'

'She was setting up the workstations for the next challenge. We only finished the last one at three, and she had everything to clear away before putting out all the new ingredients. I'm pretty sure she would have been in the stable the whole time, but I've no idea if that's true – you can't see into the main room from where we were sitting. And once the competition started again, people were milling about in all directions. I haven't a clue what everyone was doing.'

'So, again, it seems more likely the culprit is someone on the staff,' said Adam. 'Unless it was an intruder who killed Miranda, a stalker maybe, but it seems rather too convenient that she was killed during one of the few times she was alone. Nell seems to think this has been very carefully planned.'

Fran eyed the trailer. 'How did Miranda die?' she asked. 'Do they know yet?'

'The pathologist hasn't arrived so it's not confirmed, but the cake slice sticking out of her chest is a bit of a giveaway.'

'Cake slice?'

Adam nodded, lips pursed. 'Honest truth,' he said. 'According to Midge, it's some kind of award she won. It's normally displayed on a shelf.'

'Is that significant?'

Adam shrugged. 'I got the feeling Nell thought it might be.'

Fran didn't know what to say. She had spent so long in awe

of Miranda, of the way in which she had made ordinary food popular again and inspired so many people to cook for their families, *with* their families. Fran pretty much owed her career to her and, while meeting her hadn't been the thrill she thought it would be, Miranda was still a much-admired figure. Fran had promised they would get to the bottom of whatever had been going on but, instead, Miranda had been killed because Fran hadn't taken it seriously enough.

'It's so awful,' she said. 'And to have happened during the filming of the Christmas special as well. They were always Miranda's favourite shows. Whatever is Harrison going to do?' She looked at Adam in horror as another thought occurred to her. 'We've done it again, haven't we? Landed ourselves in the middle of a murder investigation where no one will be able to leave and we'll be stuck here, just like we were back in the summer at Claremont House.'

'Only difference is that maybe this time Nell will let us investigate.'

'Don't bank on it,' muttered Fran. 'Speaking of which...' She turned at the sound of several cars approaching. 'Here come the rest of the team.'

'Nell said if she wasn't here to point them in Miranda's direction and let them get on with it.'

Fran nodded. 'I'll go and speak to them.'

The first car to arrive had already drawn to a halt. It belonged to a detective constable by the name of Clare Palmer, who had been involved in the investigation of a previous case. Fran raised an arm and waited until Clare climbed from the car, as several other vehicles pulled in next to her.

'Hello, Fran,' said Clare, nodding at her, although not, Fran noticed, seemingly overjoyed at seeing her. 'I didn't think I'd be meeting you again quite so soon.'

'No, me neither,' she replied wryly. 'But I'm so glad you're here.' No matter how hard she tried to convince the young policewoman she posed no threat to her, it made no difference. 'Nell is over speaking with the producer of the show so she asked if you could "do the usual" when you arrived.'

'Will do. Is it really Miranda Appleby, the TV cook?'

Fran nodded. 'She was found by her PA around four o'clock.'

Clare shook her head. 'Awful... poor woman.'

Fran wasn't sure whether she meant Miranda or Midge. She followed Clare's line of sight, seeing her eyes narrow as she spotted Adam standing by Miranda's trailer.

'And that's where she is, is she?'

'Yes, no one has touched her.'

'That's something at least. We're going to have the press crawling all over this if we're not careful. Right – thanks, Fran. I'll get everyone sorted.' She leaned back inside the car, pulling out a folder. She was about to say something else when the sound of raised voices came from around the corner of the building.

It was Harrison, and he was clearly distraught. 'I can't believe you kept this from me. I've known Miranda for years. She wasn't just a colleague, but a good friend as well.'

Midge and Nell were walking with him and it wasn't altogether clear who he was shouting at.

'Did it never occur to you that had I known about these so-called gifts Miranda had been receiving, I might have been able to do something about it? Something which would mean she wouldn't now be dead—' He broke off suddenly, stopping in his tracks as he stared at her trailer. 'Oh God... How can she be dead? It doesn't seem possible.' His face crumpled, eyes glazing as he stood there. Then, with a shake of his head, he strode off again.

'I'm sorry, Harrison, but Miranda didn't want anyone to

know. She forbade me from telling anyone, even you.' Midge was struggling to keep up with him.

'Then you should have used your common sense, or have you not got any of that either? For God's sake, we all know Miranda could be touchy about appearances, but something like this... It should have occurred to you it wasn't a matter you should keep to yourself.' He halted again, whipping around so fast that Nell nearly cannoned into him. 'And someone *did* know, the bloody police knew! And *you* didn't tell me either.'

Fran wasn't close enough to see Nell's expression, but she could guess how it would look. She turned back to Clare. 'I might just go and...'

'He's all yours,' Clare replied, eyebrows raised.

The group were close to Harrison's trailer by the time Fran reached them.

'How long has this been going on?' he demanded. 'What else have you been keeping from me?'

Midge looked as if she was about to fall over. Her face was pale with livid red blotches and although she was desperately trying to keep her composure, Fran could see how much Harrison's tirade was affecting her.

'I haven't been keeping anything from you, but I don't work for you, Harrison. Miranda is – was – my boss and any PA will tell you that the ability to maintain confidentiality is very important. Miranda had to trust me with all sorts of very personal information, and she did. If she'd wanted you to know, she would have told you.'

He glared at her. 'Not good enough,' he said. 'And you didn't answer my question.'

Hi,' said Fran, deliberately interrupting. 'DC Palmer has just arrived, Nell, so I've asked her to carry on, like you said.'

Nell took a step forward to stand between Harrison and Midge. 'Thanks, Fran. Now, while my officers are getting to work, I suggest we take this conversation elsewhere so that they may do so undisturbed. Perhaps your trailer, Mr Shaw?'

Harrison was about to comply with her suggestion when he suddenly fixed Fran with a fierce stare. 'And what the hell has any of this got to do with you?'

She was about to answer when he very rapidly joined up all the dots.

'Oh, I get it, the writer and her "assistant" who are on set to get the low down on the show for a new book of Miranda's... A writer who just happens to be a really good cook as well... A writer who is also on first-name terms with the detective in charge of the case. I don't think so.' He looked at Nell. 'Start at the beginning, please. I want to know exactly what's been going on.'

Nell held out her arm, indicating the trailer's steps. 'After you,' she said.

Harrison's trailer was nowhere near as opulent as Miranda's, but it had a certain business-like importance about it, dark colours and dark wood in contrast to Miranda's much softer and more sumptuous furnishings. It was exactly how Fran imagined a typical bachelor pad might look.

Harrison clearly wasn't about to offer them a seat, so Fran touched Midge's arm lightly and steered her to the end of the trailer where a semicircle of soft seating was fixed against the rear wall. She could feel Midge trembling through the relatively light fabric of her suit jacket. Her face looked pinched despite the warmth of the afternoon, whether from cold or emotion, Fran couldn't tell.

'Perhaps I could ask you to make Midge a drink, if it's not too much trouble?' said Nell. 'Something hot? Finding Miranda like that is an awful thing for anyone to have to deal with.' She smiled at Harrison and Fran could see he would have liked to refuse. He wouldn't though. However much he wanted to find out what had been going on, he wouldn't risk appearing so heartless.

'Yes, of course... I'm sorry. This is all such a shock.'

'I can make them if you like?' offered Fran, getting to her feet.

'Thank you,' replied Harrison, 'but I can't let you do that. Is coffee okay for everyone? I have a rather natty machine which is surprisingly good.'

Nell nodded, throwing Fran a quick glance. 'Black for me please, no sugar.'

'Just milk, please,' added Fran.

Midge remained silent but presumably Harrison already knew how she took her coffee.

Nell waited until he was engaged in his task before drawing in a deep breath. 'This is a horrible shock for everyone concerned,' she began, 'and I realise a huge loss for you personally, Mr Shaw, but I can assure you that nothing untoward has been going on. I was asked by the district commissioner to have a look into a personal matter relating to Miranda and, in fact, it was Miranda's suggestion that someone join the set under the pretence of writing a book. She hoped that would allow the matter to be cleared up without involving anyone else. She also expressly wished that recent events be kept under wraps and confirmed that, thus far, only Midge was aware of what had been happening. As a result, Midge made the arrangements for Fran and Adam to join you and there was no need for anyone else to be involved. Consequently, as you know, one of your contestants pulled out of the show and Fran stepped up, again at Miranda's request, to fill the gap. Not an ideal situation, but one which at least still allowed both her and Adam to continue what they had originally set out to do.'

'But these so-called gifts you referred to... How long had Miranda been receiving them?'

'Over a period of a few months. Since April,' replied Nell.

'There was quite a gap between the first and second gifts arriving, less so with the last two, but although Miranda found them distressing, there was never any suggestion that anything sinister was going on. I appreciate you might have wanted to know about them, but the decision not to inform anyone was Miranda's and she was entitled to it.'

'But why was she being sent these things?'

'We don't know, and it's something we intend to find out. There is, however, at this stage, no evidence to suggest there's even a connection between the receipt of the gifts and Miranda's death. The two could be entirely unrelated.'

'Of course there's a connection. There must be,' replied Harrison, swearing under his breath as he fiddled with the coffee machine.

'Obviously, this is something we'll look into, and which will no doubt become clearer as we continue our investigation.'

Harrison regarded her silently for a few seconds, but seemed to accept what she was saying. 'So, what happens now?' he asked.

'A cordon will be put around Miranda's trailer while our initial observations are being made and forensic evidence is collected. Once the pathologist has been, Miranda's body will be removed. Do you know who her next of kin is?'

Harrison shook his head. 'Sounds crazy, but there was no one. She and her husband divorced a few years ago, but in any case he's dead now, and there were no children. I'm not sure about siblings, parents or other relatives, but if there are any then Miranda never spoke of them. We were her family. I guess that's why the show was everything to her.'

Midge cleared her throat. 'There are a couple of close friends,' she said. 'From years ago, before she was famous. But she was an only child and both her parents are dead. Judy told me that Miranda and her husband couldn't have children, so with him gone too there really isn't anyone. I guess her agent would know for certain though. Perhaps I shouldn't say this, but sometimes when she was feeling a little melancholy she used to say how truly alone she was. That when she was gone there would be no one. I often wondered if that was why she...' She shook her head. 'It doesn't matter.'

Nell nodded. 'We'll need to take statements from all the contestants, and they'll also be asked to comply with a few other requests, simply to eliminate them from our inquiries. Then I suggest they be sent home. We'll contact them if we need anything further. As for the crew, I'm afraid we may need to keep them a little longer but, under the circumstances, I'm sure they'll understand. Although this is all dependent on what our preliminary findings tell us, of course.'

Harrison remained silent, virtually motionless aside from pushing his glasses further up his nose. Nell raised her eyebrows in enquiring fashion but there was still no response.

'Mr Shaw?' she said. 'Is that all clear? Is everything okay?'

'No, everything is not okay. *Country Cooks* was Miranda's life and she always said that whatever happened the show must go on. She couldn't bear to let her public down. Apart from anything, I'm the bloody producer, and you deliberately kept information from me which, had I known about it, might have kept Miranda alive. I have a show to put on. Miranda's show, and I'm damn well going to do what she would have wished. You're not keeping me from that as well.'

'Mr Shaw, I strenuously recommend that you don't. It's going to make our investigation very difficult.'

'Be that as it may, I've explained how I feel. Have you any idea how many hoops have to be jumped through to put on a show like this? How many arrangements have to be put into place? How many people it involves? And that's discounting the cost. And a Christmas show... you can quadruple the number you first thought of. We don't even get a look in on the schedules unless we're a serious heavy hitter on the ratings front. And that's all down to our loyal viewers for whom, I might add, Miranda is the highlight of their week. The show is everything to me because it was everything to Miranda, and so we *will* be going ahead.'

Nell regarded him for a moment. 'First and foremost, what's important here is that Miranda's killer is apprehended. Surely that's more important than the show. Or have I got that wrong? Perhaps the show *is* more important.'

'How dare you!'

'It's a simple enough question.'

'And I'll give you a simple enough answer. Don't you dare accuse me of not caring, not when I've just lost a dear friend; not a colleague, you understand, Miranda could never be just a colleague. We've worked together for years, and that woman means more to me than...' He broke off, swallowing. 'See, this is just how it starts with you lot, twisting everything, putting words in our mouths.'

Nell's expression didn't flicker, but whether he realised it or not, Harrison had just made a grave error. Nell was as straight as they came and she didn't take kindly to people who made assumptions otherwise.

'Mr Shaw, may I remind you that a murder investigation is about to get underway and everyone here will be helping us with our inquiries, you included. Whether you like it or not, that investigation takes precedence over your show, however popular it may be. I am only too aware of Miranda's celebrity status and what you and the nation have lost, but what's vital here is that no time is wasted in apprehending the guilty party. And I shall take a very dim view of anyone who makes that difficult. A woman has lost her life, she deserves the very best we can give her.'

'We'll be doing the show in her honour, and if you think I'm going to be cowed by your threats that it will make your job difficult, I won't be. You do your job and I'll do mine. I'm quite sure there's room for both.'

'I hardly think that's appropriate under the circumstances.'

'I don't really care what you think, Detective, just watch me.'

11

_____

'What is it with these people?' asked Nell, twenty minutes later.

They were on their way back to the stable, following in Harrison's wake. He had pulled himself together and rushed over to ensure that the last segment's filming continued undisturbed. Nell had rather cannily dispatched Adam to follow him. As yet, no one else would be aware of Miranda's death, but if one of the crew members had been responsible, or even one of the contestants, then their behaviour might just give the game away.

'I get the whole show-must-go-on thing,' added Nell. 'But, really, when the star of the show has just died? The only good thing about it is that it means everyone will be staying here, but I will not have my investigation stalling because the director hasn't yet yelled "cut". Has he any idea how difficult it's going to make things?'

'Somehow, I don't imagine Harrison will let his grief at Miranda's death stand in the way of his show for too long,' said Fran. 'Not now that it is his show, of course.'

As expected, Nell gave her a long look. 'Explain,' she said.

'I don't know the whole set-up here, but although Harrison

owns the company which produces the show, I don't think he calls all the shots. Adam overheard him and Miranda arguing yesterday, something to the effect that he would never get control of the show. "Not while I live and breathe" was the phrase she used.'

'Did she now?' remarked Nell. 'That is interesting. Midge, do you know anything about this?'

Up until that point Midge had hardly spoken, her face still ashen. It was several seconds before she realised Nell's question had been directed at her, and another couple before she could formulate a reply. She nodded. 'Fran's right. Miranda isn't under contract to Harrison, it's more the other way around.'

'You mentioned earlier that Miranda had an agent. Would they know?'

'I'm sure she would, she managed most of Miranda's business affairs.'

'Excellent,' replied Nell. 'Can you make sure I get her contact details?'

Midge nodded. 'Her name's Louise Devereux. Miranda and Harrison *have* worked together a long time, but I've always had the impression it was at Miranda's behest.'

'Indeed,' replied Nell. 'And I can only imagine there would have been a queue of people lined up to take Harrison's place if Miranda had sought to ever change that arrangement. Were you aware of any animosity between them?'

'Not really. They had disagreements, and some of them were a bit heated, usually if something went wrong on set, but I'm not aware of anything else.'

Nell nodded. 'Okay. Will they have finished filming now?'

'I'm not sure. What's the time?'

Fran checked her watch. 'Just after five.'

'Then, yes, just,' replied Midge, looking even more worried. 'But Harrison will have to say something soon, the competitors will be expecting Miranda. She would normally be there by now to do the tastings and give her verdict.'

Nell stopped, frowning. 'Let me get this straight in my head,' she said. 'Between four and five o'clock the competitors will have been busy cooking for a challenge which lasted an hour.'

'Yes, that's right,' replied Midge.

'And Miranda would have been in her trailer the whole of that time, having a break?'

She nodded.

'So, who does all the announcements then? You know, "Cooks, you have fifteen minutes left", or whatever it is they say.'

Midge smiled. 'Not Miranda, at least not live anyway... That's the magic of television for you. She does say those things, but they're recorded separately, out of sequence, which is where the editing comes in. Scenes are spliced together so that viewers see Miranda giving the time call, followed by the competitors' supposed live reaction, but it doesn't happen in the order they see it. In actual fact, either Harrison or Judy give the live time checks, I do too sometimes – what viewers see is the competitors' reactions to those, not to Miranda. If we didn't do it that way, Miranda would be hanging around on set for hours.'

'Oh, I see...' Nell threw Fran a glance. 'I forget this is TV. It's all manipulated, isn't it? Nothing is as it seems.' She studied Midge. 'But Miranda would normally be over there now?'

'Yes.'

'Excellent, then let's get this over and done with, there are a few things I need to say.'

Fran felt her heart sink. It was happening all over again. The news of a death, the instruction for everyone to remain where they were, the taking of statements, fingerprints, the endless speculation. At least on this occasion she and Adam weren't in the frame for murder. At least she didn't think they were.

From the moment they walked into the stable it was clear people had guessed something was up. There was a quietly expectant atmosphere and a palpable tension which felt like air does in the moments before a storm hits. The contestants would already be nervous. They'd been cooking their hearts out over the last hour, praying that what they'd done would be enough. Praying that what they'd done would be edible. Each of them waiting for Miranda to pass judgement. And now someone had passed judgement on her.

Adam was sitting at the far side, not actually in Miranda's chair by the Christmas tree, but just beside it, chatting to Hope. She looked expectantly towards the door, her make-up case clutched in one hand. Harrison was at the rear of the room, talking quietly to Sam and Woody, and only Judy stood alone, close to the competitors, smiling what she presumably hoped was a reassuring smile. She came forward the moment she saw them, making a beeline for Midge.

'You dropped this again,' Judy whispered, shooting a nervous look at Nell. She slipped her hand into the pocket of her Puffa jacket and pulled out a phone, handing it across. 'What's going on? Where's Miranda?'

Midge silently shook her head, rubbing at a scuff mark on the phone's tough outer casing. Judy was about to ask again when Nell walked forward into the centre of the room, the exact spot where Miranda had greeted them all only that morning. She cleared her throat as the room fell silent.

'Hello, everyone... If I could have you all together, please?' She looked around, motioning that Judy, Hope and Midge should move down the room to join the others. 'I'm sorry to interrupt you all today, but I'm afraid I have some rather horrible news. I'm Detective Chief Inspector Helen Bradley of West Mercia police, and I'm here because, very sadly, Miranda

Appleby has been found dead this afternoon.' She paused as a ripple of shocked emotion passed around the room. 'I know there will be a lot of things you'll all want to know, most of which I won't be able to tell you. What I can say, however, is that we're treating Ms Appleby's death as suspicious.'

Fran scanned the faces in front of her, most of them registering surprise, some looking confused. Pea was close to tears, as was Hope. Others looked wide-eyed and fearful.

'I'm sorry, I know this has come as a huge shock.'

Nell had been a police officer for many years, but Fran knew she still found this aspect of her job hard. Nell's position dictated she get results, which meant asking questions, often harsh ones, and it was only those who knew her well, who could see behind her seemingly abrupt manner to the compassionate core beneath.

'And if I might suggest, some hot tea might be a good idea. I will try to explain as best as I can what will happen now, but the most important thing to say is that no one must leave this room for the duration, unless I say otherwise. There will be various things required of you, and the quicker we can get through them, the quicker I can let you go. Although that does mean staying on site for the time being, I'm afraid.

'The first thing we will need to do is to take a set of fingerprints from you all. These are solely for forensic purposes so that we may eliminate you from our inquiries. We will also need to take an initial statement from each of you. That may, in fact, be *all* we need, but obviously this will depend on what our initial findings tell us. The one thing I must stress, however, is that, as you are all aware, Ms Appleby was a very well-known person. As such, there will inevitably be a great deal of interest in her death from the media and this kind of interest can make our task here very much harder. I would ask you all, therefore, to refrain from talking about anything you see, or hear, to anyone outside of this room. That includes your family and friends. Tempting though it is to discuss such things, rumour and gossip may delay our work and I'm sure you'll agree the most important thing is that we find out what's happened here as quickly as possible.' Nell nodded her head. 'Yes?'

Christine had raised a tentative hand. 'Will we be allowed to go home? Only things haven't been going that well and I told my husband I didn't think I'd be here long...' She looked on the verge of tears and Pea went to stand silently beside her, giving her a gentle smile.

Nell looked pained. 'Erm...' She cast about for Harrison. 'I'm not really sure what the arrangements are for the show. Obviously, Miranda's death changes things, but perhaps when I've finished, Harrison, you could say a few words?' She smiled warmly at Christine. 'As for going home, that will depend on how the inquiry goes. Sorry, I can't say any more than that at the moment.'

Christine's anguish was very real and Fran felt for her. Watching the competitors' trials and tribulations on the screen at home was very different from being in the same room as them.

'I think that's all I have for the moment,' continued Nell. 'Unless there are any other questions?' She paused, but none were forthcoming. 'In that case then, thank you all for your cooperation.'

Nell turned and beckoned Fran over. 'Could I leave you and Adam to direct traffic here for a while? I need to get back across the way. Perhaps sort out some drinks, biscuits, that kind of thing – you know how long these things take, folks could be here for a while. Eyes and ears open, obviously.'

Fran nodded.

'And keep tabs on Midge, please.' She raised a single eyebrow, something which Fran often wished she could do. Nell's meaning was clear. In part it was a request to make sure

that Midge was okay, but mostly it was because Nell had her
eye on Midge and wouldn't take it off for quite some time.

Fran didn't know what to think. She'd been cooking, quite
possibly at the exact moment Miranda had been murdered, but
she'd also been very busy, focused on her work, and although
she didn't think anyone had been missing from the stable, they
must have been. She knew Adam, Miranda and Midge had
been absent, but who else? Fran looked across to where Midge
was standing, intercepting her glance and smiling. It was clear
the young woman knew exactly how things stood. She looked
around for Adam.

'Nell wants us to stay here and make sure no one leaves,' she
told him, her voice low. 'Did you notice anything when you
came across with Harrison earlier?'

Adam shook his head. 'No. When I got here it looked like
business as usual. Harrison went straight to talk with Sam and
Woody, while Judy had obviously just given the competitors
their "time's up" and was walking between all the workstations.
Hope was also moving between competitors, giving everyone a
flick of something or other – Pea especially, she looked a bit hot
and bothered.'

Fran nodded. 'She has cheeks like mine. They go red at
every opportunity.'

'Harrison didn't say anything, but everyone obviously
realised Miranda should have been on set. You could see the
conversations dwindling, people checking their watches. I heard
Judy ask Hope where Midge was. By the time you arrived, well,
you saw how it was.'

'Awful. It's so horrible for everyone. Even though I know
one of them must have killed Miranda, it doesn't seem possible,
does it? I mean, look at them.' She stared around the room,
watching as Harrison directed everyone back to the green room.
'Mind you, what's a killer supposed to look like?'

Adam nodded towards Midge. 'Let's hope Nell hasn't already made up her mind.'

Fran frowned. Maybe it was that simple – that the only person seemingly without an alibi was the guilty party. But something about it didn't seem right to her. 'I think I might ask Judy if she needs a hand with refreshments,' she said. 'Do you want to come with me?'

'I might just loiter a little,' he said. 'See what I can overhear. But I'll join you when the biscuits appear, obviously.'

He gave Fran a sheepish smile, which she returned. Honestly, Adam and his hollow legs. Midge was now speaking with Harrison, and seeing Judy on her own, Fran seized her opportunity.

'Can I give you a hand with anything?' she asked.

Judy flashed her a grateful smile. 'This is so awful, isn't it? I can't seem to take it in. I saw Miranda just before she left for her break. We even spoke about what she wanted to eat later this evening. And now she's... It doesn't seem possible.'

'It's a huge shock for everyone,' said Fran.

Judy nodded. 'Midge especially, the poor girl. How do you cope with a thing like that?'

'Like what?' asked Fran innocently.

'Midge found Miranda's body,' said Judy, leaning closer. 'Can you imagine? She said it was awful... I don't know the details, but...' She shivered. 'And now Midge thinks everyone's going to say she's the one who did it – killed Miranda, I mean.'

Fran did a double take. 'Is that what's happened? I thought the police just said they were treating her death as suspicious.'

'Yes, but that's what it means, doesn't it?' replied Judy, moving closer still. 'She was murdered...'

'I can't believe people would think Midge capable,' said Fran. 'Just because she found Miranda, it doesn't necessarily follow.'

'No, but from what she said, everyone else was in here, and

Midge was the only one who wasn't. She was over in the gardener's cottage where she's staying.'

'Maybe... but someone else could have been missing.' Fran shook her head. 'No, I can't believe it was Midge. Why would she kill Miranda?'

Judy raised her eyebrows. 'What, apart from the fact that Miranda made her life a misery, you mean?' She pulled a face. 'Sorry, I don't mean that. But we all know that Miranda took things out on Midge when she was cross. I don't know how she put up with it, actually. Hope knows more than I do, but I've seen how upset Midge was by Miranda's remarks on occasion. Not that I'm saying Midge had anything to do with her death, though. I'm not saying that at all.'

Fran smiled. She could recognise someone trying to deflect attention away from themselves when she saw it. 'She'd dropped her phone, hadn't she? I saw you give it to her when we came in just now.'

'Oh, she's always doing that,' said Judy. 'Why do you think she has it in one of those ultra-tough cases? It slips off her clipboard. I nearly walked on it, actually – it was just out in the courtyard, by my trailer. I expect she dropped it when she left to take her break.'

Fran nodded, looking around her. 'Shall we get those drinks sorted? And maybe put out some biscuits? I think everyone would appreciate it.'

'Please... although I'm not sure folks will be up to eating much.' She was about to add something else when she stopped and closed her mouth, an odd expression on her face.

'What?' asked Fran.

'I was just wondering where you got to earlier? I saw you dash out just before Harrison did, right before Midge arrived with that detective woman. Where did you go?'

Fran stared at her in horror. 'Oh my God, my pudding is still in the oven!'

She rushed over to her workstation, still littered with kitchen utensils, bowls and sundry ingredients. Everyone else had neatly presented the fruits of their recent labours on the end of their work surface, Fran's was... She pulled open the oven door, wincing at the plume of hot smoke which rose from it. She wafted at it furiously, but her nose had already told her what her eyes could now see – her dish was completely ruined, burned beyond repair. Not that it mattered now, but she'd been rather proud of her creation and had been looking forward to seeing if it had turned out the way she'd wanted. She pulled a face at Judy, who grimaced.

'What even was it?'

'A mincemeat spiced bread and butter pudding,' Fran replied. 'Damn.'

'That is a shame... Miranda would have liked that.' Judy stared up at Fran, eyes filling with tears. 'What on earth are we going to do without Miranda? This show is everything to me...' She cast about her. 'It's the same for everyone here. We're like family.'

'Well, if Harrison has his way, the show's going to carry on.'

Judy looked stricken. 'We can't do that, not without Miranda. That would be terrible. I know Miranda always said the show must come first, no matter what, but that isn't what she meant.'

'I think Harrison thought it was what Miranda would have wanted, that you'd all be doing it in her honour.'

Judy's gaze dropped to the floor. 'I suppose...' She looked back up, staring across the room to where Harrison was talking with Hope, a soft smile on her face. 'I can see where he's coming from, but...' She shook her head. 'It would be too difficult. Miranda was the mainstay of the show and we're on a tight enough schedule as it is. The logistics of getting someone to take her place, plus get them up to speed, don't even bear thinking about.'

'Maybe you should do it,' offered Fran, not entirely seriously. 'Or Harrison. You know how everything works and Midge would still be around to make sure things ran smoothly.'

Judy's mouth dropped open. 'Seriously?' she said, eyebrows coming together. 'That's a crazy idea.' But then she paused. 'But if that's what Harrison wants to do, we're going to have to think of something.'

Once the teas and coffees were ready, Fran popped back out to the main room to catch up with Adam. He was sitting at one of the workstations, an open notepad in front of him. There was no one else in sight.

'Is that part of your disguise?' she asked, tapping a finger on the notebook. 'The writer's assistant? Because if it is, I think I've just blown our cover.' She gave a wry smile. 'Listen to me, I sound like *I'm* in a TV show.'

Adam looked pointedly at her workstation. 'You are in a TV show.'

She tutted. 'You know what I mean. I dropped everything when I saw Nell and Midge come in earlier and went racing over to Miranda's trailer to see what had happened. I didn't even think what it would look like to everyone else, and Judy's just asked me where I went. I think I got away with it – I suddenly remembered I'd left my pudding in the oven and tried to distract her with my exceedingly burnt offering. We're going to have to be careful or we'll be of no use to Nell. People will clam up no end if they think we're working for the police.'

Adam nodded. 'I was over there too, though, don't forget. And what writer wouldn't be interested in a sudden death? You could always say I contacted you when I saw the police arriving.'

'Oh, good idea. We probably ought to check with Nell,

though, and make sure we're still supposed to be undercover. Have you heard anything interesting?'

Adam shook his head. 'Nothing untoward, although Harrison needs to work a little harder on his grief-stricken colleague routine. His mouth is saying all the right things, but his face isn't following through.'

Fran narrowed her eyes. 'What's his face saying, then?'

'Teensy bit excited,' replied Adam. 'Just a smidge.'

'Interesting...'

'Isn't it? So why would Harrison want Miranda dead? Not when she was earning him so much lovely money, surely?'

Fran nudged Adam's arm. Her attention had just been caught by the sight of Harrison coming in through the stable door with Midge. She was frantically scribbling on her clipboard as they walked, head bobbing as she nodded repeatedly.

'Looks as if Midge has already got herself a new boss,' she commented. 'I wonder whose idea that was?'

Adam was about to answer when he suddenly smiled instead. 'That has to be rhetorical question?'

'Well spotted,' replied Fran, smiling back. She waited until the pair were almost level before raising an arm. 'Sorry, Midge? Have you got a minute?'

Miranda's PA flashed Harrison an anxious look, who nodded and smiled graciously. 'Just come through when you're free,' he said.

Midge waited until Harrison had disappeared into the green room before pulling a face. 'Thank you,' she said. 'You should see the list of things he's given me to do,' she said. 'And I don't even work for him, not strictly speaking anyway.' She frowned. 'Sorry, is everything okay?'

Fran softened her look. 'Yes, I just wondered how *you* were holding up?'

At her words, Midge's face almost crumpled, and she only just managed to hang on to her composure. 'I'm okay, just... you know. But Harrison's adamant he wants the show to go on, Fran. I can't believe it. I thought all that back in the trailer with Nell was just bluster. Some people are like that when they're trying to hide their real emotions, aren't they? But he really wants to carry on. Says we should do it for Miranda, make it the biggest tribute to her we can. And he wants to change all sorts of things – I'm really not sure if it will work. Plus, none of it takes into account the fact that the contestants may not *want* to carry on. It's an awfully big ask, particularly with the police here. That's where he's gone now, to turn on the charm and convince everyone to stay.'

'Well, whether people stay or go is partly Nell's decision, not his. He'll find that out soon enough when she starts calling people for interviews and then wants to interview them again, and maybe even one more time. He's going to find that puts rather a dent in his schedules.' Fran pursed her lips. 'And you mustn't let him boss you around. You have enough to worry about.'

Midge dropped her head. 'I know, that's what's freaking me out. I can't think straight, and I know I'm going to make a huge mess of things. What am I going to do, Fran? I know the police think it was me who killed Miranda.'

'Nell's a good detective, Midge, she really is. She'll find who did this, and we'll obviously do all we can to help. If you're innocent, you don't have anything to worry about, but I know how hard it is. I've been top of Nell's suspect list myself once before, and it's not a nice place to be.' She gave Midge's arm a rub.

'Were you?'

Fran smiled. 'It's a long story.'

Midge drew in a deep breath. 'You've been very kind, Fran, and you, Adam, and I swear I didn't have anything to do with this. I'm not afraid to say there've been times when I could have cheerfully strangled Miranda with my bare hands, but however you feel about someone, murdering your boss is a big no-no as far as I'm concerned. Murdering anyone, come to think of it. I really didn't do this – please, you have to believe me.' Her breath juddered back out again. 'This job has turned into a nightmare and it was supposed to be a dream come true.'

'How long had you worked for Miranda?' asked Fran.

'Five years,' Midge replied. 'Four years and ten months too long.' She gave a tight smile. 'Actually, that's not true. Despite what I have to put up with, I love my job. I don't get much credit for what I do, but I still know that I'm part of one of the most successful cookery shows on TV. I love it when a new series starts. We take a bunch of people, from all walks of life, and throw them together into what is a, frankly, terrifying situation. At the beginning they're nervous, unsure about their abilities, shy and awkward, but gradually they begin to loosen up and realise what they're capable of. They begin to bond with one another too, and that's when you see what the real stuff of life is – because it's people who make the world go around. I always feel so humbled to be a part of it. Despite all the show-bizzy unreality of it all, when the contestants leave, they're different people – they've made friends for life and they're ready to take on the world.'

Fran studied Midge's face, the honest truth of what she was saying written there. 'And that's why you stay,' she said.

Midge nodded. 'That's why I stay.'

'And Miranda?'

'What can I say? You've seen what she's like – was like.'

'But when we first arrived you said Miranda had been particularly stressed of late, so has her behaviour changed recently? I'm asking because when we were in Harrison's trailer you said you often wondered if Miranda's lack of family had anything to do with... and then you stopped. What were you going to say?'

Midge fidgeted with her clipboard. 'Don't take this the

wrong way, but Miranda could be very selfish at times. That's what I meant about her lack of family – I just think she never learned how to share. Not as a child, and not as an adult either. She's never had to think about anyone apart from herself. It's quite sad, actually, because I don't think she was that way on purpose, or not all the time anyway, more that she never realised that's how she came across.'

'So, her behaviour hasn't particularly changed recently then, she's always been like that?'

Midge considered the question for a moment. 'Fundamentally, I'd have to say yes. What you've seen is pretty much standard fare. There were a couple of months, right at the beginning, what I now look upon as my honeymoon period, when she was kindness itself. Generous, full of praise, polite and considerate... but it was like, as soon as I knew what I was doing and my probationary period was up, she stopped bothering to be nice and reverted to type.' She looked between Fran and Adam, a soft smile on her face. 'I'm not doing myself any favours here, am I?'

Fran gave her a warm smile. 'On the contrary, I'd say you were extremely eloquent.'

Adam leaned forward. 'People are weird,' he said. 'I find them baffling most of the time – saying one thing when their face says another – pretending to be a certain way and then acting the opposite. It's often the people who profess undying love for the victim who are guilty. There's nothing wrong with good honest loathing in my book. You can't like everyone, can you? And let's face it, some people are really not very likeable.'

12

It had turned into a very long evening. And now, the next morning, Fran was feeling its effects. In fact, she was pretty sure they were written all over her face. She rubbed a hand across her forehead and blew out her cheeks.

Nell raised an eyebrow. 'That bad?' she asked.

They were sitting in Fran's room having breakfast, Fran having excused herself from joining the rest of the competitors over in the stable on the pretext of talking to her publisher.

She nodded at Nell's comment. 'Apart from anything, I'm having kittens about what I'm going to cook today.'

It would have been so much easier if everyone had said they didn't want to carry on with the show, but every single contestant had responded to Harrison's rallying cry and was now adamant that country cooks, cook, and nothing would stop them. Fran, who was very aware how much publicity the show would now receive on account of Miranda's death, couldn't help feeling a little cynical about people's motives. Even if they didn't win the competition, they were all taking part to some extent for the fame and glory a win would ensure, and the old adage was almost certainly true: all publicity was good publicity.

'I'll obviously do all I can to make that as difficult as possible,' said Nell darkly. 'I'm kidding, obviously. There's nothing I can do about the show. As long as everyone stays away from the crime scene, I'm happy, and Harrison assures me that people will be released as I need them. Apparently, anyone missing part of a challenge can do it at a later time, they'll just edit scenes together somehow and no one will be any the wiser.'

'I wondered how that was going to work,' replied Fran. 'And Judy is going to host, is that right?'

'So I've been told.' Nell raised an eyebrow. 'Apparently that was your idea.'

Fran rolled her eyes. 'I wasn't being serious,' she replied. 'Or not entirely anyway.'

'It seems one of the contestants also mooted the suggestion so, after a little discussion, Judy decided to do it. She could hardly let everyone down, could she?'

'Judging by your tone you obviously think there's something in that,' said Fran.

'I don't give a fig who does it, but call me cynical… Isn't it a little too convenient that Harrison's girlfriend just happens to end up presenting a show he's director of?'

'You're being cynical,' Fran agreed, smiling. 'Judy *is* the obvious person for the role. And, actually, we don't know for definite they *are* in a relationship.'

'No, but thanks to Adam's little titbit of gossip about a certain giggle that's something I shall be checking out very soon.'

Adam looked up from where he was sitting cross-legged on the floor, eating a very large bowl of sugar puffs. He grinned.

'And as I'm going to be starting with Harrison this morning,' added Nell, 'I'll be sure to ask him about his relationship with Miranda too. He doesn't seem half as distraught as he ought, given that the star of his show is dead. Plus, I still want to know who's behind the gifts Miranda had been receiving. They may not be connected to her death, but it seems likely that they are. I can't see any reason to keep their existence secret now, in fact, quite the opposite.'

'So, you think if we find out who sent the gifts, we'll find who killed Miranda?'

'Quite possibly. Miranda might have denied receiving any messages or threats with these gifts but that doesn't mean it's true. There had to be some point to them, or why bother sending them in the first place? And I want to know what that was.'

Fran nodded. 'So, who do you think are the main suspects? Apart from Midge, that is.'

Nell regarded her over the top of her coffee mug.

'She didn't do it, Nell, I'd swear to it. She has more reason to kill Miranda than everyone else put together, but I'm certain it's not her.'

'Granted, until I start questioning everyone I won't know for certain, but Midge is the only one who seems to have no alibi at all, or at least none which can be corroborated by anyone else. So, how do you explain that?'

'I can't. But that's my point, it's too easy. Someone's trying to set Midge up, I'm sure of it.'

'Yes, and they're doing a damn good job. Fran, there's no such thing as too easy in police work. The woman looks guilty. She has no verifiable alibi. She found the body. And Miranda treated her like something she found on the bottom of her shoe. If it looks like a duck, swims like a duck and quacks like a duck, then it's probably a duck.'

Fran hung her head.

'Just because you like her, Fran, doesn't mean she isn't guilty.'

'I know, but what if there's something else going on here?'

Nell smiled. 'Then we'll find out what it is,' she replied with just enough of a raised eyebrow to let Fran know it wasn't wise to push it any further. 'Meanwhile, I have the district commissioner breathing down my neck, whose wife is breathing down his. The sooner we can turn this around, the better.'

'So, what do we do about our cover story?' asked Adam. 'Fran nearly got caught out yesterday.'

'I think we keep it,' replied Nell. 'And if you could look slightly less excited about the word "cover", that would be good. I'm going to be busy conducting interviews for most of the day, and while I'm doing that I can't be picking up on what's being said elsewhere. Fran, try to engage the contestants as much as you can. You never know, there may be opinions voiced or comments made which can shed some light on all this. I think you're right, people will talk around you far more freely if they don't suspect you're connected to me in any way. Adam, you can obviously do the same, but with the staff. Continue to loiter, notebook in hand, and pick up what you can. It will be easier for you because you won't be tied to one spot. But, Fran, if you do need to see me, then you can simply say you're a potential witness as well and I'm questioning you. Or do what you did this morning and say you're speaking with your publisher or something. That way if anyone, such as Judy, questions where you've been, you can say you're simply following the story.'

Fran nodded with a look at Adam. 'So, what did the pathologist conclude?'

'Nothing we didn't already know. Miranda died from a single stab wound to the heart, and the time of death seems right too, around 4 p.m. or "nice and fresh" as the pathologist put it – she does a wonderful line in gallows humour. We're still waiting for forensics to come back, but obviously we have our murder weapon and I'd lay money on that being free of prints. It's the timing of this murder which intrigues me. It's so tight and that smacks of careful planning, unless the killer was incredibly lucky, of course, but somehow I don't think that's the case.'

Fran winced. 'So where does that leave us?' she asked.

'With another long day ahead of us,' replied Nell, staring into her mug, 'so we'd best go and make a start.'

It was quiet over in the stable when Fran arrived. Everyone was gathered in the green room, where Judy had set up breakfast, but in spite of last night's insistence that they do Miranda proud, the mood was sombre. Midge sat quietly with her clipboard on her lap, picking at a croissant, but Fran didn't need to look at her face to know she'd hardly slept.

Fran apologised for her absence and took a seat. 'Sorry, have I missed anything?'

Only Pea smiled. 'We were just talking about yesterday,' she said. 'The competition part.'

Harrison cleared his throat. 'Yes, and under the circumstances we've decided that any adjudications made yesterday will be null and void. Obviously, Miranda wasn't able to judge the final element and, Fran, you didn't actually manage to produce a dish, or one that was edible at least. I'm aware of Miranda's thoughts about the first segment of the day, but it seems unfair to send anyone home when you've all been so good about staying on. We'll therefore start again today as we would have, but instead of five contestants, all six of you will take part. However, today's challenges *will* be judged as normal, so one of you will be leaving us at the end of the day.' He threw a dark look at the green-room door. 'From the competition, at least. What our detective friend requests is a different matter. This will mean that at the end of the week we'll have one extra person still in the competition. We'll either leave it that way for the final, or, if things are clear-cut on the day before, we may choose to eliminate two of you at that point.'

He smiled. 'I know this is going to be very hard, but all I can say is that Miranda truly would have wanted us to carry on, I know she would. And once the show's viewers find out the devastating news, they'll want this last one to be an absolute knockout, so let's do all we can to make it so.' He reached forward to take another pastry from a plate on the table in front of them. 'Midge, would you like to explain about the other practicalities?' He sat back in his chair and bit a large chunk from his croissant.

Midge looked up, a little startled. 'Yes, of course... So, everything will happen much as it would have before. The only difference is that we will have to film far more scenes out of sequence than we normally would. This is so that if you are called to give a statement to the police and so on, you may do so. This might mean that some of you are cooking at different stages to the others, but in the spirit of the show we need to ensure that everything is fair and equitable for everyone.' She paused. 'As far as we can, anyway. I'm sure you'll agree this won't be a problem and will do all you can to afford your fellow competitors an equal chance to succeed.' She looked down at her clipboard, frowning as if she'd lost her place. 'Erm... Judy, maybe you'd like to run through what everyone will be cooking? Oh, no, sorry, I need to tell you that the eighty-thirty morning meetings will still be happening, but that we might also need a quick one after our evening meal in case anything else has cropped up during the day.' Midge looked up. 'I think that's it, sorry, I... If there's anything else, I'll come round and tell you all.'

Judy leaned forward and lifted a mug from the table, cradling it in her hands. 'Thank you, Midge. As Harrison explained, we will be starting today with all six of you. And, in fact, we're going to be changing the order of the challenges as well. There are several reasons for this, but mainly it's because we feel the difficulties we might run into while accommodating the wishes of the police will better suit certain challenges over others. We might also amend the programme a little, but I'll update you on the details once I have them. A few things are still in discussion.' She took a swig of coffee. 'We will start our first challenge at ten this morning, rather than eleven, which will be our hors d'oeuvres round – logical, if you think about it, to have the starters first.' She smiled. 'Maybe it's just me, but I could never understand why we did starters mid-week. Never mind... Anyone got any questions?'

Fran looked from face to face, but no one said a word. The reality of what was about to happen loomed large.

Judy looked at her watch. 'In that case, I'd better get a move on. I'll see you all in a little while.' She got to her feet and, with a smile at Harrison, they left the green room.

There were a few seconds of rather uncomfortable silence and then Vinny cleared his throat. 'Anyone regretting their decision to stay on?' he said. He tried to soften his words with a smile but didn't altogether succeed. It was clear he hadn't meant it as the jocular comment it could have been.

'It's going to be difficult,' said Tony. 'But what else could we do? Without us, there is no show and it's clear that the powers that be still want one, Miranda or no Miranda. This might not be a popular thing to say, but I'm just going to come out and say it – I kind of need to be here. I entered this competition to win, partly for my ego, but partly because I'm hoping to start my own business and winning could be the lift I need. Particularly on what might turn out to be the last series of the show...' He trailed off, swallowing. 'So, whatever the rights and wrongs of the situation, I'm going with it. I don't see I have much choice.'

'I agree,' said Pea. 'It's going to be a very different competition from the one we thought we were entering, but it can still be good, as long as we make the best of it.'

'Yeah, well, there have already been far too many changes to the "rules" for my liking,' said Vinny. 'And exceptions made. I'm not entirely sure there's a competition going on here at all. I'm not sure what is, mind, but...' He shrugged and leaned forward to take another croissant. 'I'm certainly going to use it to my advantage, be stupid not to. May the best man win and all that.' He got up and left the room.

Christine gave a nervous laugh. 'I thought I was going home yesterday, but it will probably just be today instead. I don't think anyone needs to worry about me.'

'Don't say that, Christine,' said Pea. 'Just look on yesterday as a dry run. You have just as much chance as anyone here.'

Christine smiled in response, but it was clear she didn't believe it. Fran didn't know what to think, except that the most pressing thing from her point of view was that she didn't even know what she would be cooking. As if reading her mind, Midge caught her eye.

'Could I have a quick word, Fran?' she asked. 'As you won't have seen them before, Judy has left you some details about today's first challenge. Do you want to come out to your workstation and I'll go through them with you?'

Fran got up, gratefully, and followed her out. But the smiling and helpful Midge of previous days was nowhere in sight. Instead, she could hardly meet her eye.

'I'm sorry, Fran, but Judy couldn't meet with you this morning. She's obviously got a lot more to do now she's stepping into the limelight and...' She frowned. 'Anyway, she's left a few suggestions for you in here.' She pulled open the top drawer of the workstation and removed a couple of sheets of paper covered in handwriting Fran already recognised. 'Like Judy said, you're all making hors d'oeuvres this morning and her recommendation was for this top one. I think she's already left the ingredients for you.'

Fran glanced at the recipes. 'But...' She studied Midge's face. 'Sorry, are you saying that's what I have to cook? If everything is already laid out, it seems rather like a fait accompli.'

'That's all Judy told me. I think she thought it might make things easier for you.' She looked nervously to one side. 'Don't forget, she doesn't know you're a caterer.'

It was a good point, but to Fran it felt more like Judy was trying to get her on side for some reason. 'True, but following other people's recipes is never quite the same as making something you already know. Couldn't I just pick a recipe myself? The fridges and cupboards here are stuffed with things – as long as I don't cook anything with particularly obscure ingredients, surely it will be fine? I'm quite happy to sort it out myself, there's still time.'

Midge wriggled her shoulders. Not quite a shrug, more an uneasy squirm, and as Fran took in her stance, and the downward slant of her head, it wasn't difficult to work out what was going on. Midge had clearly been told what to do and the last thing she needed was someone arguing with her.

'Midge, everything is going to be all right, you know,' said Fran. 'I understand you're worried about the position you're in, who wouldn't be? But Nell will thoroughly investigate what happened to Miranda, she won't just charge the first person who looks as if they could be guilty. She has to categorically prove there's no other solution and that means eliminating everyone else. There's a way to go yet.'

For the first time that morning, Midge smiled and looked up. 'It's like everyone is watching me,' she said. 'I'm sure they all think it was me. But Miranda was my boss, so I probably don't even have a job any more. She always said I'd never work anywhere else and now it's true. Harrison might order me about, but that's only because I'm useful to him at the moment. As soon as this show is over, I'll be on the scrap heap.'

'You don't know that,' said Fran, giving her a warm smile. 'You're good at your job, Midge – Harrison's an idiot if he can't see that. And if Judy carries on presenting the show, she's going to need help too. I'm sure one of them will snap you up.

Anyway, what do you mean, you'll never be able to work anywhere else? You've been on this show five years, you've got great experience.'

Midge looked startled, and instantly contrite. 'I know, and you're right... it doesn't matter.'

Fran frowned, convinced there was more to what Midge had said. She was about to follow it up when Midge shook her head.

'I'm sorry, Fran, I have to go find Hope. I'll come back and see you later.'

Fran could only smile as Midge scurried away, head bent.

Pursing her lips, she turned her attention to the recipes in front of her. One in particular she recognised from a Christmas book Miranda had published quite a few years ago – one of the first Fran had owned. She'd made the dish several times, but on each occasion had tweaked it slightly, finding the overpowering saltiness of the anchovies too much. She smiled, remembering how she and Adam had first met – at a party hosted by his mum, which Fran had catered for. She'd made some canapés at that event too, and Adam had discovered just how much he hated anchovies when he'd swiped a couple. Perhaps she would give the anchovies a miss, after all. But if not that, then what else should she make? She racked her brains, drumming her fingers against the countertop... What else? What else...?

'Someone's deep in thought,' said a voice. 'Is everything okay?'

She looked up to see Pea's smiling face approaching her. 'Just trying to decide what to cook,' Fran replied. 'I have a dreadful memory at the best of times and now my mind's gone a complete blank.'

'I forgot you don't have anything prepared. What a nightmare. I know what I'm doing, supposedly, and I think my mind's as blank as yours. It's not ideal all this, is it?' she said, lowering her voice.

Upfront, Judy and Harrison had just arrived with Sam and Woody in tow. Gone were Judy's jeans and Puffa jacket, as was the messy bun. In their place was a casual up do, designed not to look contrived but which was, and a ditsy-print long-sleeved dress, worn with coloured leggings and boots. Butter-wouldn't-melt sweetness à la Miranda it was not, but it suited Judy's Irish colouring, and was perfect for the show's country vibe.

Pea watched Judy for a moment before leaning in, her voice no more than a whisper. 'What do you think?' she asked. 'Is it just me, or does this seem a bit odd to you?'

Judy was now sitting in the chair by the Christmas tree where Miranda always gave her customary opening welcome. 'I get the whole show-must-go-on thing, and doing this as a tribute to Miranda, but if that were me, taking over her role, I'd be shaking in my boots.'

'Judy does seem quite relaxed about the whole thing,' commented Fran. 'Maybe she's been on TV before.'

'Hmm,' replied Pea, eyes narrowing. 'Maybe.'

'And it makes sense for Judy to host. In fact, I was one of the people who originally suggested it.'

'Tony did too.' Pea frowned. 'Perhaps it's simply that it doesn't look right, having someone else in Miranda's chair.'

Fran nodded. 'I'm sure that's all it is. It must be a hard act to follow.'

'Undoubtedly, but then again, what about them changing things up a bit? Those new ideas sprung up awfully quickly if you ask me.'

Fran stared at her. She was right. Less than twenty-four hours after Miranda's death and the show was swinging into motion almost as if nothing had happened. So, who was that down to? Harrison? Or Judy? Maybe it was both... She must make sure she mentioned it to Nell. And there was something else which had occurred to her.

'Was it me?' she asked Pea, 'or was there a bit of an atmosphere in the green room just now?'

Pea pulled a face. 'No, it's not you. Poor Christine got a bit of a bashing. She really didn't have a good day yesterday, plus, if you remember, she was the one who burned the caramel for the pecan tarts at the icebreaker. I didn't see what she made yesterday afternoon, but I don't think it was as good as some of the others, let's just leave it there.'

Fran raised her eyebrows. 'It would have been better than mine, I know that for a fact. Charcoal isn't top of most people's list of taste sensations.'

'Even so, I think most people, Christine herself, realised she should have been the one going home. But you heard what Harrison said, we're resetting the bar – Vinny didn't feel that was necessarily the best thing to do.'

'Ah...' Fran wrinkled her nose. That kind of thing was never pleasant. 'Poor Christine. Maybe the only thing she's lacking is confidence. It's one thing cooking at home in a familiar environment and quite another having to cook under pressure, with cameras and all the other stresses the show brings. Some people obviously adapt more quickly than others, that's all.' She didn't want to say outright that Vinny seemed very sure of himself, but some people took competitiveness a little too far.

Pea bit her lip. 'I'm afraid you got a mention too, Fran, so it was just as well you weren't there.'

'Me? What have I done?'

'Well, nothing, but I think Vinny thought you stepping in was a little odd. Contrived, was the word he used. Too many allowances being made.' She raised her eyebrows, darting a look to the rear of the stable where Vinny's workstation was set up.

'Contrived? No one was more surprised than me, I can assure you – it certainly wasn't my idea. Miranda sprang it on me. But, in hindsight, I'm not sure what else they could have done after Emily left.' Fran wasn't sure what she was being accused of, but she couldn't blame Vinny. If she *had* come on the show of her own volition she might well feel the same. 'I rather wish I hadn't needed to step in,' she added, 'but I'm here doing research, as you know. Apparently, this is the best kind there is, or so my publisher tells me.'

Pea smiled in sympathy as Judy got to her feet, walking closer. 'No offence or anything,' she whispered, 'but Judy Mulligan doesn't have the same kind of ring as Miranda Appleby, does it? That was a clever move, changing her name.'

Fran nodded before she registered what Pea had just said. 'Hang on, did you say Miranda had changed her name?'

'Mmm, years ago, before she got famous. I thought you would have known that, seeing as you're writing a book about her.'

Fran had to think quickly. 'Well, I'm writing a book about the show, really, and Miranda's part in it,' she replied, mentally kicking herself. 'I guess her life before she became famous isn't what the publishers want to focus on. But, blimey, what did Miranda change her name from? Was it really hideous?' She hoped her return to a more gossipy tone would hide her little slip.

Pea smiled. 'Do you know, I can't remember. Most likely read it in a magazine article or something.'

Fran watched as Miranda's replacement smiled for the camera. Well, that *was* interesting...

13

Adam was pretty sure Betty had taken what his mum would call a shine to him. He'd no sooner sat down in the kitchen of the guest wing when she appeared, ostensibly to clean the spotless sink but then, in very short order, producing a plate of biscuits and a pot of tea. She placed both beside him with a comment that she could see he was very busy but that he shouldn't forget to eat. Bizarrely, she reminded him of a butler in one of his computer games, who admittedly was a hologram, but who appeared whenever he was triggered by someone walking through a beam of light. He would then trot out one of his programmed stock phrases to the effect that your every wish was his desire. It seemed a little uncharitable to compare Betty in this way, when he was incredibly grateful for the treats she obviously enjoyed providing, but he couldn't help it. He had wondered idly whether she was actually flesh and blood or, in fact, a ghost, doomed to walk the hallways of the guest wing, forever dishing out refreshments. Then he'd realised he'd probably drunk too much coffee. He smiled, took another biscuit, and settled down to read.

Miranda's biography had been written about four years earlier, one of several that a quick search on Amazon had thrown up. Biographies, rather than autobiographies he was pleased to note, and unofficial ones at that, because Adam wasn't particularly interested in what Miranda had to say about her life, but rather what others thought of her. Gossip, to put it bluntly, was what he was after. Fran had sent him a hasty message earlier detailing Pea's revelation about Miranda's change of name and, in the absence of anything else to do, he was on the trawl for more information. Plus, the kindle version of the book was on special offer. Adam didn't even blink as he downloaded it straight to his phone.

Nell's direction that he should loiter, notebook in hand, was all very well, but everyone was so busy and, short of following them around, it was hard to know where he should be. He'd started the morning sitting to one side of the stable, but quickly realised that as soon as everyone started cooking, concentration levels ramped up to such a point that no one spoke much in between their short pieces to camera. Harrison had been called in to see Nell and, for a short while, Adam had entertained the idea of eavesdropping on their interview. Then he'd remembered the last time he'd tried to do that and the look on Nell's face when she'd caught him. Fran's request, therefore, was very welcome and it made sense too. People didn't leave the kind of gifts they had for Miranda without a very powerful motivation to do so, and that can only have arisen from something that had happened in the past.

An hour later, he was becoming increasingly bored. The tale of Miranda's life started early – her school years, her teens, her family willing her on to greatness as all good families do. It went into great detail about her desire to cook from a very early age, her triumphs and disasters, and how her indomitable spirit kept her going. Through college, through marriage and subsequent divorce, through the pain of not being able to have children, but always with that desire still burning away inside her. It was all very commendable stuff but none of it even alluded to a whiff of scandal. Either Miranda *was* a paragon of virtue and loveliness or she had very good lawyers who were adept at keeping anything negative out of the public domain.

He stared at the scant notes he had made. He wasn't sure he had the willpower to even finish the book. There wasn't anything he felt warranted delving a little deeper – the divorced husband was dead and there wasn't anyone mentioned who he felt could have turned into a present-giving psychopath. He began to flip through the pages, stopping occasionally to see how far he'd got in Miranda's life. He paused on the first page of a chapter entitled 'Leap of Faith' to read about her appearance in a cookery competition, one which had proved to be the turning point in Miranda's life. And suddenly the hand which held a biscuit halfway to his mouth stilled. He put down the Bourbon and pulled his laptop towards him.

He'd had no idea that Miranda had shot to fame after winning a competition, much like the one Fran now found herself taking part in. Fran had certainly never mentioned it, that's if she even knew. Shot to fame wasn't quite the right phrase, either, because it had taken Miranda three more years before *Country Cooks Cook* had been born and her star truly began its ascendance. Following that early competition, however, interview had followed interview, then there was a small guest slot on a regional radio cookery show and a feature in a glossy magazine. People had begun to notice Miranda and it had all started because of that win. He opened an internet tab and flipped forward a few more pages in Miranda's life.

The competition hadn't been televised, it was a one-off event that had taken place at an agricultural show of the type that were very popular in the rural area where they lived. The sponsors of the show were all big food producers and the event had been well-publicised in various farming magazines and the local press. It was obviously where the idea for *Country Cooks Cook* had been derived from, heralding a return to the type of food traditionally made in farmhouse kitchens all over the country. And Miranda, with her golden-blonde hair and peaches-and-cream complexion, was the perfect figurehead. The style of cooking had altered slightly over the years to accommodate changing tastes, but here was a very clear route to Miranda's past and what it had led to in the future.

Typing the details of the agricultural show into a search engine returned a large number of results, most of them providing details of recent shows or information for exhibitors; not really what Adam was looking for. He tried again, adding cookery competition into the search terms. The results were a better mix this time but after checking through several pages, there was still no mention of the cookery competition Miranda had entered. If it had continued to be a feature of the show it couldn't have been for long, and it certainly wasn't listed as one of the modern-day attractions.

Adam sat back and after a little more thought and another biscuit added Miranda's name to the string of search terms. Most of what came back ignored the terms 'agricultural show' or 'cookery competition' altogether, instead showing only mentions of Miranda, but after nine pages of results, he finally spied something which looked interesting. It was a Facebook page for a group taking a very nostalgic look at the show and its history, encouraging its followers to post old photos and memories. Adam needed to follow the group to see the individual posts, something which had him groaning in frustration, but forty minutes and endless scrolling later, he was rewarded with a grainy photograph. He peered closer and smiled. Gotcha!

Taking a quick screenshot of the photo, he checked the time, got to his feet and rushed out to see Fran. He was halfway across the front of the house when he spied Judy coming down the steps of Harrison's trailer. Given this was where Nell had temporarily set up her incident room, he could guess who she'd just been speaking to, and it didn't look as if it had gone well. Judy stopped after a few paces, putting one hand on the end of the trailer to steady herself. The other she held over her mouth as if trying to stifle her emotion. He waited a moment until she had set off again, and then quickened his pace to intercept her.

As he neared, he raised a friendly arm to signal hello. He wasn't optimistic of receiving much more than a smile, so he was surprised when Judy paused to wait for him. The confident air she had worn that morning had completely gone.

'Is everything okay?' he asked.

Judy gave a swift glance behind her. 'Adam, can I ask you something? This book Fran is writing, what sort of thing is it?'

Adam gave her a puzzled look. He thought Judy knew that already. 'It's a behind-the-scenes look at the show,' he replied, trotting out their stock response.

'No, I rather meant what sort of tone will it have? Is it a gossipy thing?'

Adam paused. He wasn't quite sure what Judy was getting at, but she was clearly bothered by something. Perhaps something which involved her and Miranda. If he asked the right kind of questions, maybe he could find out.

'It wasn't meant to be... Miranda's publishers commissioned it.' He let his sentence hang, allowing Judy to work out what he meant. 'Thing is, some of that changes with her death. I'm not sure, but I think the focus might be a little different now.'

Judy nodded, licking her lips. 'So, it's an exposé then?'

'I'm not sure I'd use that exact word but... Maybe you should speak with Fran?' he suggested. This was too good to keep to himself, Fran needed to hear it too. 'I was on my way to see her, actually. They're on a break now, aren't they?'

Judy checked her watch. 'They should be. Actually, I'm

sure they are, I left Midge keeping time.' She gave a weak smile. 'Thanks, Adam.'

They found Fran trying to clear away some of the mess she'd made that morning, while simultaneously drinking a mug of tea. Her cheeks were scarlet. 'This is crazy,' she said, holding her palms to them. 'It's as if time has been condensed on this show. It feels like a lead weight around my neck.' She grimaced. 'Sorry, this morning was tough.'

Judy eyed the tray on the end of Fran's workbench where twelve perfect-looking starters sat. 'I'm sorry I had to duck out of proceedings,' she said. 'Not least of all because now I'm going to have to sample those cold.'

Fran grimaced. 'No, it's not ideal, is it? Have you been to see the police?' she asked, flicking a glance at Adam.

Judy swallowed, with a minute nod of her head. 'I wondered if I could talk to you about something,' she said. 'Only, it's a little... awkward.'

Fran looked around her. 'Sure, shall we go back to your trailer for a minute, where it's quieter?'

Judy led the way, starting to speak the moment they were out of the stable and into the empty courtyard. 'I'm pretty sure the police think Harrison and I are in cahoots. That detective inspector is vicious, she outright asked me if I'd killed Miranda.'

'I think that's kind of her job,' said Adam.

'Maybe, but she doesn't mess around, does she? And the thing is... this is a bit awkward...' She paused to open the trailer door, ushering them inside and closing it firmly behind her. 'Me and Harrison are... we're seeing each other and because I'm now hosting the show as well, the detective's taken it to mean we're in league with one another. I don't know what she asked *him*, or whether he was the one who told her about us, but she knew all the same. She even suggested that Harrison and I killed Miranda so he could put me in the limelight instead of her. Like he was doing me some kind of a favour. Or even that I was doing *him* favours, of a very different kind, I might add.' She scowled. 'And it's not like that, it absolutely isn't. I really like Harrison, but I'm not the kind of girl who sleeps her way to the top. Harrison *is* ambitious and, sure, he disagreed with Miranda on occasion, but it was only because he saw the show differently from the way she did. He's younger, he has a different point of view, it stands to reason he would. But that doesn't make either of us murderers. Why on earth would either of us want to kill Miranda?' She choked slightly on her words. 'Sorry... I'm finding all this very difficult.'

Fran nodded. 'I know,' she replied. 'But you have to look at it through the detective's eyes. Stepping up to host, with all the preparation that must have entailed, plus the alterations to the show's content... it's all happened pretty fast,' she said. 'It's not even twenty-four hours since Miranda died and I'm sure the show does have to go on and all that, but you could argue that it smacks of unseemly haste. I'm not saying it is,' she added quickly, 'I'm just trying to put it the way the police might see it.'

If only Adam could have sat in on those interviews with Nell, but he knew it was out of the question. Something must have been said for Judy to be so anxious, though, and he was determined to find out what. As was Fran.

She smiled. 'I can understand how you might not have wanted to discuss your relationship with Harrison, but it's better to be honest. That way you have nothing to worry about, not if you haven't done anything wrong. The police are simply doing their job, and they have to ask questions, searching ones at times. Otherwise how can they ever begin to piece together what happened? DCI Bradley is simply exploring all possible scenarios for why Miranda was killed and, on the face of it, you and Harrison working together could be one of them. As long as you were honest, I'm sure you've satisfied that particular line of inquiry. I'd try not to worry about it.'

'I know, and I haven't done anything wrong,' insisted Judy.

'But there *is* something which makes it look like I could have. I didn't want to tell the detective, but I had no choice, it would have looked really bad if I hadn't. But will what I said go any further?'

'Sorry, Judy, I'm not following you,' said Fran. 'Will what go any further?'

Judy fell silent, head bowed as she chewed at the side of her lip. 'When I tell you, you're going to think all your Christmases and birthdays have come together – you're writing a book, for God's sake. Only, please, don't include what I'm about to tell you. For all her faults, Miranda *did* make this show what it's become, she doesn't deserve to have her name trashed.'

Adam frowned. 'Why would that happen?'

'The recipes,' Judy blurted. 'They're not hers.' She held his look for a moment and then dropped her head. 'I'm sorry, Fran, I know how much you admired Miranda.'

So, Fran was right. Adam knew that's what she had suspected, but it was still a shock to hear Judy say it. It turned everything Fran thought about Miranda on its head. The whole thing was a lie, *she* was a lie.

Fran nodded, giving Judy a soft smile. 'They're yours, aren't they? Oh, Judy... How long has this been going on?'

'A while...' She let out a long slow breath.

Fran studied Judy's face. 'I did wonder about the recipes when you gave me the file of them to read through the other day,' she said. 'It was the way you said it, *my* recipes, not *the* recipes or Miranda's recipes. And they're all in your handwriting too. You don't have to be a genius to work it out.'

Judy sighed. 'I knew you'd twigged. Thing is, no one normally sees that folder. If Emily hadn't pulled out of the show and Miranda insisted you be put in to replace her, I'd never have had to show it to you either. But you mustn't tell anyone, please, I'm begging you.'

'But I would have thought you would want people to know,' replied Fran. 'To get some recognition for your work.'

Judy looked puzzled. 'The recipes might be mine, but I could never do what Miranda did. She's the one who made the show successful and because of that, I get to work on the best show on TV. I wouldn't want her life – all that stress, the publicity, always having to look so perfect, worrying about growing old. No, I have the best of both worlds – I get to have real input into the show but without all the pitfalls. And I'm well paid for what I do – Miranda saw to that, she always looked after me. I owe her so much, she...' Judy faltered, looking anxious. 'I can't imagine what's going to happen now, without her, that's the worst thing. Maybe we can get someone else in to present the show, maybe it can continue and everything will be okay.'

Now it was Fran's turn to look puzzled. 'Yes, but you're hosting the show now.'

Judy made a derogatory noise. 'I'm filling in because Harrison wants the show to go ahead, but it's terrifying. I don't want to change what I do. I don't want anything to change. I guess it's going to have to though.' She bit her lip.

'And no one else knows about this?' asked Fran.

Judy shook her head. 'Not even Harrison. Miranda and I often talked about the recipes for the show, we had to, that's part of my job, so it really hasn't been that hard to keep it a secret. And it wasn't always the way it is now. The recipes *were* Miranda's to start with, and then... We did a show where everything seemed to go wrong. Nothing major, just little niggles, but the kind of stuff that sets everyone on edge. And then midway through, Miranda's publisher changed the deadline for her latest book, brought it forward, saying they needed to publish it earlier than planned for some reason. I can't even remember why now, but Miranda was furious. And very stressed. She had no new ideas for the book at all, and she came to me in a panic, asking for a recipe suggestion. When she used it, it felt incredible – that Miranda Appleby thought my recipes were good enough! After that, I'd make the odd suggestion, which Miranda took, and it just kind of grew from there. But I don't see why everyone has to know. I'm only telling you because I was worried you'd worked it out for yourself, or might find out now that I've obviously told the police about it. I'm terrified someone might let slip and the press could get hold of it. It doesn't bear thinking about.'

'Maybe it's for the best, though,' replied Fran. 'Secrets have a habit of coming to light, often when you don't want them to. It might be better to be upfront about it, but make sure it's put across in the way you want.'

Judy thought a moment. 'Maybe it is,' she replied. 'But I still think it's better to say nothing at all. That way, there's no risk of it being misconstrued. I know I did the right thing telling the police what I have, but it would be awful if Miranda's name got dragged through the dirt as a result. Please, I'd be very grateful if you could keep it out of the book you're writing.'

Fran smiled. 'Yes, I understand. And my publisher's instructions haven't changed that much since her death. The book won't be an exposé of any kind, but they have suggested that I delve a little deeper into who Miranda was. I took that to mean it would be as much a tribute to *her*, as to the show. I'll make sure I keep this conversation strictly between the two of us, and Adam, naturally. Although, if it gets into the public domain as a result of the police inquiry, then my hands are tied, but I'll do my best. There is one other thing though, something you can help me with.'

'Yes, of course,' said Judy, looking much relieved. 'I'll help if I can.'

'One of the other contestants remarked that Miranda wasn't her real name, that she might have changed it quite early on in her career. Is that true?'

'Well, if it is, it's news to me,' Judy replied. 'Who told you that?'

Fran shook her head. 'It doesn't matter. And it's not really important. Loads of people change their names, especially celebrities. I just wanted to check for factual reasons more than anything.'

Adam had almost forgotten the reason he had been going to see Fran in the first place, but now he was desperate to tell her what he'd discovered.

Judy shrugged. 'Harrison might know, I suppose. Out of all of us, he's known her the longest.'

'Thanks, Judy, I'll ask him.'

Judy left to 'gather' herself shortly afterwards while Fran finished her mug of tea. The morning's challenge still had to be judged and Adam was very aware how Fran must be feeling. He'd watched her cook on countless occasions, and he'd never seen her quite so stressed before. His discovery couldn't wait though. If he wasn't much mistaken, it could quite possibly put someone else in the frame for Miranda's murder.

He pulled her to one side of the stable, making sure they were well out of earshot of anyone else. 'Sorry, Fran, I know you're desperate for a break, but I need to talk to you about something I stumbled upon when I was looking into Miranda's change of name. Something which could shed a lot more light on the situation.'

Fran fanned her face, which was still rosy. 'But that's brilliant, go on.'

Adam pulled out his phone. 'I started reading a biography about Miranda this morning, not because I thought finding out about her name would be that easy – if it was, we'd all know about it – but I wondered if it might give me a few leads to check. And one of those leads was the information that Miranda had taken part in, and won, a cookery competition, a little like this one. It was years ago, and there was very little detail about it, but it did seem as if that success was what sparked the beginning of her rise to fame. So, I started fishing...' He navigated to the photos on his phone. 'And I found this.'

Fran squinted at the screen. 'What am I looking at?' she asked.

'Two things,' he replied. 'It's a photo I found on Facebook of the competition Miranda entered, taken at the agricultural show where it was held. It looks like it was originally from a newspaper article, which is possibly why it's so grainy, but check out the names underneath.' He pointed to the bottom of the picture. 'There are eight people in this photo and eight names underneath, and not one of them is Miranda Appleby.'

Fran looked up, eyes lit by excitement. She studied the photo again and Adam could see she was trying to work out which one of the figures was Miranda. She pointed to the person third in from the left. 'There,' she said, 'that has to be her.'

Adam nodded. 'I agree. Which means, if the list of names underneath follows the usual left to right convention, that Miranda Appleby formerly went by the name of Sally Grainger.'

'Adam, that's brilliant! So, it *is* true then. I wonder when she changed her name... and why? There might not be anything in it, but that discovery also gives us another link to check – someone might not have any past dealings with Miranda Appleby, but they could have had with Sally Grainger...' She broke off, frowning. 'Hang on a minute, you said there were two things I was looking at. What's the second?'

Adam grinned and used two fingers to zoom in on the photo so that just the row of faces was visible. He turned his phone sideways so Fran could see it better. 'Have another look,' he said, 'and tell me I'm not seeing things.'

Fran peered closer, her brow wrinkled, then took the phone from him, angling it against the light. He could see the moment when she worked it out, when her brow cleared and a spark flew into her eyes again.

'Oh my God, she looks very young, but that's—' She looked up.

'Yep,' said Adam. 'That's what I thought.'

14

'Well, well, well,' said Fran, 'that changes a few things.'

'Doesn't it just. Of course, it could be entirely innocent.' Adam raised his eyebrows.

'It could be,' replied Fran, handing back his phone. 'But judging by the look on your face you don't think it is either.' She grinned at him. 'Well done, Adam, that's a cracking piece of detective work. I'm not sure whether this is the kind of thing Nell's background checks would throw up, but we have to let her know – we have one person at least who has a past connection with Miranda.' She smiled a little mischievously. 'Shame, though. Part of me would like to keep this titbit of information under our hats for the time being, so we can follow it up ourselves.'

'There's nothing which says we can't do that, even once we have told Nell,' replied Adam, arching his eyebrows. 'We were sent here to look into who had been sending nasty presents to Miranda, and this could well be linked to that. So, in effect, all we'd be doing is following our original instructions...'

Fran smirked and tapped his phone. 'I'll see what I can find out. Right, I'd better get back to the others, the judging's coming up soon.'

Adam nodded. 'I'll carry on checking too. You never know, I might turn up something else.' He quickly looked over his shoulder. 'What do you think about Judy's revelations? I know you had your suspicions the recipes weren't Miranda's.'

'Yes, but I didn't know for definite they were Judy's. Plus, we also know that *you* were right – she and Harrison are having a fling. And despite what she said about him, and the show, that still throws up possibilities *and* motives.'

'She did seem genuinely worried that news about the recipes would get out, but I wonder if she was just saying that. You thought you'd blown our cover yesterday when Judy asked you where you had rushed off to. Maybe she suspects you and Nell might have some sort of connection and, if so, perhaps she's trying to protect herself from further scrutiny. From what she said, she'd already guessed you'd worked out the recipes weren't Miranda's and she couldn't risk you telling the police first, that wouldn't look good for her at all. But by spinning her story the way she has, it makes her look like a decent person, one who's not out to profit from Miranda's death, and if she manages to convince *you* that's the case, maybe she's banking on that being the message you take back to Nell. It could all be a massive bluff.'

'That's a very good point,' replied Fran, thinking. 'It doesn't really change the facts, merely our perception of them. She and Harrison still have to be prime suspects. I've been thinking about Miranda's presents too. It might seem a little obvious, but who's the person most likely to be able to get their hands on a lump of steak? That has to be Judy, surely?'

'Agreed,' said Adam, nodding. 'Let me know if you find out anything.' He smiled. 'And good luck for this afternoon.'

Fran pulled a face. 'I'm going to need it.'

. . .

Inside the green room, the others had gathered for a cup of tea and it was clear Fran wasn't the only one with murder on her mind.

'I can't see how we can be judged properly when the food we've prepared is now stone cold,' said Vinny. 'I know we've seen it on countless shows before – the ones in the summer where contestants have their ice cream melt, or their icing, whatever. It always appears as if it's taken into consideration, but you still get the feeling it's the contestant's fault and they should have picked something less volatile to cook. If I'd have known the food would be judged cold, I'd have cooked something that flaming well ought to be served that way.'

Jenny gave a nervous smile. 'I don't suppose they can help it,' she said. 'I think Judy has been very busy.'

'And there is a small matter of a murder to be solved,' added Tony. 'The show rather pales into insignificance beside it.'

Vinny shrugged. 'I guess. So which one of you did it then?' He grinned, but no one else seemed to find it funny. 'Although why they think it could be one of us is beyond me. Miranda was the show's judge apart from anything else. Given that we all want to win, we'd be nuts to bump her off, wouldn't we?'

Fran winced at his flippant comment.

'Unless whoever did it thinks they might fare better under Judy's regime.'

He raised his eyebrows and Fran was certain it was a dig at her. She ignored him.

'Someone did it, though,' said Christine. 'And, actually, it could be one of us. Why is that more unlikely than it being one of the crew members?'

'Maybe it was that Emily,' said Vinny. 'The one who went home, supposedly because she was ill. Maybe that was just a ruse to make it look like she was out of the picture when really she's the one who snuck back onto the set and killed Miranda.'

Blimey, thought Fran. Vinny's imagination was almost as good as Adam's.

'But what possible reason could she have for doing that,' asked Pea, 'when she doesn't even know Miranda? None of us do. All applicants are vetted to make sure there's no connection to anyone who works on the show.'

'Yeah, well, I wouldn't bank on that being as thorough as it ought to be,' said Vinny. 'I know for a fact their procedures are lax.'

Fran looked up, wondering if he was taking another shot at her, but strangely he seemed to be looking at Tony. She frowned.

Pea looked as if she was about to comment further when she was cut off by the appearance of Midge's head around the door. 'Judy's ready for the judging now,' she said. 'If I could have you all back in the room.'

Fran waited until everyone else had filed out before getting to her feet. She didn't quite know what to make of Vinny, but his comments were clearly designed to push a point of some kind. And she'd be very interested to know what that was. The list of questions in her head was getting longer by the minute.

The judging went okay. It could have been better, but then Fran's cooking could have been better too. If anything, Judy's comments were rather too generous. That could have been because Fran was up first but, given what had just happened between them, Fran was more inclined to believe she was being given the benefit of the doubt.

Overall, everyone's comments were very good. Only Jenny had had a disaster, attempting too many things so that she had run out of time. Her food was undercooked and also massively over-seasoned, if Judy's polite comments were anything to go by. Christine seemed to have fared best and Fran couldn't help an inward surge of glee. Certain other people may well have written her out of the competition already, but Fran, always the champion of the underdog, desperately wanted her to stay.

With the judging over, they waited nervously to hear the details of the next challenge – the surprise round, which no one had been able to prepare for. At least that meant Fran would be on an equal footing with everyone else.

'We wanted to focus on the spirit of Christmas for this challenge,' said Judy. 'Something which is all too easy to forget as we tuck in to heaps of rich food. But, for many people, Christmas is a time of real hardship, more perhaps than at any other time of year. And, as with most things, what we eat and drink has also become subject to runaway consumerism. Just think of all the adverts around at this time of year, our screens filled with images of tables groaning with food, and all of it synonymous with making Christmas a success. As if without these things, Christmas will be deemed a failure. I'll be the first to admit I've been very guilty of that in the past, but it does sit a little uneasily that the pressure to produce food in such quantity has become part of our Christmas traditions.' She smiled at the camera, just as Fran had seen Miranda do the day before.

'Notice I said quantity, however, and not quality,' she continued. 'Because I firmly believe that good food needn't cost the earth and that's as true at this time of year as any other. So, our challenge for you this afternoon is to produce a two-course meal for four people, for as little money as possible. It's up to you whether that's a starter and a main, or a main and dessert. On the edge of your benches are a set of ingredients, many of which have a distinctive seasonal feel. Each of you has the same items and you may use as much or as little as you like. However...' – another smile – 'the ingredients have been costed out beforehand, and in order to make things a little trickier, we're not giving you that information. You must therefore use your judgement to assess which of them you will use in your dishes. The judging will take into account the cost of the meal and also, importantly, how each course tastes. Needless to say, they should taste sensational.'

Judy walked forwards so that the focus of the camera would change and turn on the contestants instead. 'So, if everyone is ready,' she said with a beaming smile, 'country cooks, cook!'

Fran didn't know what to think. And it was clear no one else did either. There had never been anything even remotely similar to this on the show before. Harrison was obviously determined to make his mark. Or Judy was.

Lifting the tablecloth on the end of her bench, Fran pondered the ingredients she'd been given. There were so many questions spinning through her head, so many people she wanted to speak to, but for the next few hours she'd be unable to do anything about either of those things. With an inward sigh she turned her focus to the task in hand and got to work.

It was almost teatime before Fran managed to speak to Harrison. A couple of times he had drifted tantalisingly close to her, but she'd either not been at a point where she could have stopped to speak to him, or she'd been unable to attract his attention without alerting everyone else to the fact. Now, though, he needed to speak to *her* and she was determined to seize the opportunity.

'Looks like you've had a good day?' he remarked.

Fran nodded. 'Well, I've managed to finish both challenges,' she replied, 'which is something. How good what I've produced is, I've yet to find out.'

He smiled. The day's judgement was due to be meted out in about half an hour. 'Perfect timing then,' he said. 'I'd like to do your piece to camera now, if that's okay? Just a few words about how you've found the day, what you found particularly hard, or what you enjoyed. What your thoughts are now in relation to where you stand in the competition, and what your hopes are. How does that sound?'

'Terrifying, but yes, okay, provided I can string a sentence together.' She paused. 'Do we do it here, or go somewhere a bit quieter?'

'There's a corner of the courtyard we've been using. We get the stable in the background as we film you, with all the Christmas lights and decorations. It gives exactly the right vibe.' He looked around. 'I think the lads are just finishing up a piece with Judy, they won't be long.'

Fran followed him out, desperately trying to work out how she could turn the conversation around to Miranda without it looking as if she were interrogating him. Given the number of times he'd disappeared during the day, Nell must have done that several times over.

'Right,' said Harrison, turning around to face the stable. 'If you can stand there facing me, we should be good to go. I'll ask a question to start you off. Viewers won't hear it but it will make your answer sound more spontaneous if we do it that way.'

Fran nodded. 'And people don't know I'm not one of the original contestants, is that right?'

'Absolutely. We're filming far enough in advance that our publicity shots haven't gone out yet, so Joe Public knows nothing about you.'

'Okay, I just wanted to check before I go putting my foot in it. It's a shame in a way. It would be really good publicity to mention the book about the show, particularly now.' She smiled up at him. The sweetest smile she could manage. 'Actually, there's something you can clear up for me. A fact I need to check. It's no big deal, but someone mentioned Miranda had changed her name, presumably when her career in the spotlight started to take off. Do you know what it was?'

Harrison's face became instantly wary. 'Why would that be any concern of mine?'

'I'm not saying it would, I just wondered if you knew. It would help flesh out Miranda's backstory, something fans will obviously be keen to know. And details like that are so important, I'd hate to get them wrong. I'd ask a family member, only... I think you might be the closest thing she had to one.'

'Well, I'm sorry, I don't know. Miranda and I didn't start working together until she was already a successful chef, and she was always Miranda Appleby to me. If she had another name perhaps there are legal avenues you can use to track it down. I should ask her agent if I were you.'

It was a very good point and Fran made a mental note to check. 'Yes, of course, I'll do that. I just thought you might know, save me the bother. But it's no problem.'

Harrison checked his watch impatiently and stared over her shoulder, clearly hoping for the arrival of his crew members. She had to wonder if his agitation was due to a tight schedule, or something about Fran's line in conversation he was keen to be done with.

Her cringe-worthy camera piece over with, Fran made her way back across the courtyard just as Adam came into view. The judging was imminent, but she had enough time to have a quick chat first. She pulled him to one side as they went through the stable door.

'I've just been talking to Harrison,' she said, 'who seemed a little jumpy. I wonder if Nell's been giving him a hard time. In which case, maybe he does have something to hide. He also claimed he didn't know anything about Miranda's change of name, but I got the feeling it wasn't something he was keen to discuss.'

'Then perhaps he does know about her background,' replied Adam, thinking for a moment. 'He could also be aware of the connection between Miranda and one of the contestants, but did nothing about it. Don't forget he already made a bad judgement call over Emily, and if our new lead turns out to be the killer, Miranda's death might be all his fault. That's something the police could be very interested in.'

Fran nodded. 'Vinny was spouting about lax vetting procedures this morning,' she said. 'I wonder if it was bluster or whether he actually knows something.'

'Be worth finding out, wouldn't it?'

Fran grimaced. 'It would. There's only one problem with all this though... If we were able to recognise the face in the photograph you found, surely once Miranda had met all the contestants she'd have been able to do the same?'

'Maybe she did,' countered Adam. 'Maybe that was the problem.' He sighed. 'I have no idea why it would be a problem, but it's something to think about.'

'Hmm... Anyway, Harrison did say something useful, which was that we could probably check if Miranda changed her name through legal channels. Or via her agent. *We* might not be able to do that, only the police, but I wondered whether there are public records we could check.'

Adam grinned. 'I'm way ahead of you,' he said. 'That's one of the things I've been looking into this afternoon. And the good news is that there's a thing called The National Archives, which lists various ways of searching for name changes depending on when that change occurred. For records from 1945 to 2003, which I'm guessing would be applicable to Miranda's case, you simply have to search "The Gazette".'

'Why do I get the feeling there's bad news as well?'

Adam pulled a face. 'Only deed-poll records which were enrolled appear on the list. A permanent record is created in the supreme court of judi... judi-something-or-other. But they reckon only one per cent of records were ever recorded, give or take. And, you've guessed it, I've searched the list and Miranda's name doesn't appear. Drawn a blank, I'm afraid.'

'Damn...' Fran sighed. 'That would have been too easy,

wouldn't it? Never mind, it was worth a try. I don't suppose you managed to find out anything about our other friend, did you?'

Adam shook his head. 'I've drawn a blank on that too, so far. But I'll keep looking. You never know, I might turn up something.'

Fran nodded as Harrison reappeared. 'Looks like the judging's imminent,' she whispered. 'Can you send me that photo you took of the agricultural-show clipping? If all else fails, maybe I'll just have to start asking questions.' She paused. 'Look, here's Judy now, I had better get back to my station. Just pray it isn't me who gets sent home.'

Fran's heart began to pound uncomfortably fast as Judy took up position in the centre of the floor. She waited while Hope fussed around her, whisking a brush across her nose before adjusting a clip in her hair. Eventually, after another check of the light, Judy was ready.

'Goodness, what a day,' she said. 'But one you've got to the end of, so thank you all for your hard work, and under trying circumstances too.' She paused to give them a warm smile. 'Would you all like to gather round?' she said. 'I'm sure you know how this goes, although in a way it's my first competition too. I'm probably as nervous as you are. However, I've been incredibly impressed by the food you've all prepared, and if this first day is an indication of things to come, I can see we're in for a belter of a contest.' She took a deep breath. 'I'm just going to say a few words to camera and then I'll move on to whose dishes have been commended, and the horrible announcement of who will be leaving us tonight. It's so sad because I'm only just getting to know you all, but one of you does have to go.'

She turned to Harrison, who murmured to Sam and then gave Judy a thumbs up. 'In five, four, three...'

'Hello, everyone. Before we go on to the judgements can I just say that you've all made my job here today incredibly difficult – what a standard you've set! You all deserve the biggest pat on the back, so well done. Miranda would be immensely proud of you all.' Judy turned slightly, angling herself a little further to the camera. 'So, today, we gave our contestants two challenges. The first was to make an array of sumptuous starters, and the second, in quite a departure for *Country Cooks Cook*, was a new challenge, that of making a two-course festive meal fit for a king, and queen, that didn't tax the budget. And I think you'll all agree we've seen some fantastic cooking. From Vinny's superlative soufflés, an incredibly risky dish to make, but one which was a total triumph, to Christine's unbelievably inventive Christmas dinner and dessert, which was a total taste sensation. Fran, too, must get a mention for her sinfully wicked layered pudding, which looked and tasted far more complex than it actually was. Very few ingredients as well, which was a brilliant way of keeping the cost down.'

There was a pause as the camera panned back to them while Fran did her best to look modest. Did that mean she had got through to the next round? As had Christine, surely? Her heart began to beat even faster.

'Sadly, some of you didn't have such a good day, but, even so, you mustn't lose heart. You are already very successful cooks – you wouldn't be here if you weren't. And cooking here, under hot lights and competition conditions, is very different from cooking at home. It's always horrible when we lose someone from the competition, but unfortunately that's the only way we can find our winner. And today, the person who will be leaving us is...'

The camera panned back around, as the contestants stood, sweating nervously while the beats of silence ticked by.

'Jenny... I'm sorry, Jenny.'

As one, they all moved forward to give Jenny a hug, waiting in turn to give their commiserations. Jenny gamely received them all in good grace, acceding that the decision had been the right one, but she was obviously disappointed. And the truth of it was it could have been any one of them going home. The competition was hard, much harder than Fran had expected, which made Vinny's smug expression all the more surprising. Naturally, he tried to mask it, but he didn't quite succeed and Fran hoped to goodness Jenny hadn't seen it. She turned away from him. With any luck, tomorrow would be his turn to go. Fran usually tried to give everyone the benefit of the doubt, but she was finding that tough where Vinny was concerned. Perhaps it was just as Adam had said – some people really weren't very likeable.

Once the congratulations and commiserations had died down, the camera moved away to film one final comment with Jenny, leaving Fran staring at the others, not knowing quite what to say.

'I'm exhausted,' said Pea with a wan smile. 'And starving. I don't think I've eaten anything the whole day, too nervous.'

Fran fanned her face. 'Me too, but I need some fresh air, it's so stuffy in here.'

'Too many hot bodies,' said Pea. 'And hot ovens too, of course.'

'I was thinking of taking a walk before dinner,' Fran replied with a glance at Adam. 'Would you like to come?'

Pea hesitated, checking her watch. 'I promised I'd give my daughter a call, but, yes, that would be great. My head's in a spin.'

'Mine too. Blimey, what a day.' Fran fell into step beside Pea.

'I'm just glad it's over and I'll live to see another,' said Pea. 'Plus, I haven't had to speak to the police yet, so that's a bonus. I don't think you have either, have you?'

Fran shook her head. 'No, I expect they're questioning the staff first. Horrible as it seems, they're probably the most likely culprits.'

'Yes, it's all rather worrying, given that someone among us could have... well, you know.'

'It doesn't seem possible, does it?' replied Fran. 'Everyone here seems so lovely.'

'Maybe that old adage is true after all – that you can't judge a book by its cover.' Pea gave a guilty smile. 'Except possibly Vinny. I think he wears his cover on his sleeve.'

Fran laughed. 'You may well be right. He looks like he might have one or two secrets up his sleeve as well. Speaking of which, I wondered if I might ask you something? Only the other day when you mentioned Miranda had changed her name, you said you thought you might have read it somewhere... That's not actually true, is it?' she added gently. 'You knew Miranda years ago, when you both entered the same cookery competition...'

15

At first Fran thought she'd made a mistake and Pea was about to deny everything. Conflicting emotions crossed her face as she stared at Fran in shock, but then she gave a rueful smile and shrugged. 'I might have known you'd find that out. You're a writer, used to doing research, checking facts...' She shook her head in amusement. 'I nearly had heart failure when Vinny said he knew the vetting procedures were lax. I thought he was talking about me.'

Which is interesting, thought Fran, because *she* had thought Vinny was talking about *her*. Yet it wasn't her or Pea, Vinny had actually been looking at Tony.

'But when I filled in my application form,' continued Pea, 'and ticked the box to say I didn't know anyone connected with the show, that was the truth. The competition with Miranda was years ago and I wouldn't say I knew her then either. Sure, we talked to one another and so on but the competition was only over two days, so it was chit-chat, nothing more. We didn't keep in touch and I haven't seen her since that day.'

'But...?' Fran smiled. 'There's always a "but",' she added, raising her eyebrows.

Pea stopped, her eyes searching Fran's face. She was weighing up whether Fran could be trusted. 'You're right, but before I tell you what that "but" might be, can I ask you something? What was your impression of Miranda?'

That was a difficult question to answer but if Fran was to gain Pea's trust, she couldn't be anything less than truthful. 'A very conflicted one,' she said. 'Like a lot of people, I was in awe of Miranda. I'm a woman of a certain age and more than aware of the passage of time and the havoc it wreaks on our bodies. I'm not particularly vain, I think I'm actually pretty comfortable in my skin, but – heavens – who wouldn't want to look like she did? And I absolutely admired her ideals – that food shouldn't be some mystical art that only a select few initiates have access to. I liked that she brought back simple, honest cooking, of the kind I grew up with. Miranda inspired my passion for food. I was at a crossroads in my life – bored by a succession of uninspiring jobs and with a daughter who was rapidly growing up – it was time for me to find something I really wanted to do, and I did. Without Miranda, I doubt that would have happened.' Hopefully her reply was vague enough to avoid having to reveal the absolute truth.

'So, this is where the but comes into *your* sentence...?'

Fran laughed. 'You're absolutely right. Because I held those thoughts about Miranda right up to the point when I met her and discovered that not everything was as it seemed. What I've realised is that everything I felt about her was a fiction, probably created by publicists or someone who read the zeitgeist right and predicted what the next big thing was going to be – and Miranda simply became its face. She was just a character playing a role, one which didn't reflect her true personality at all. She performed that role beautifully, however, I can't knock that. She had me and thousands of others fooled, but the reality, the real Miranda, wasn't anywhere near as nice as we'd all been led to believe.' She pulled a face. 'That sounds awful, when the poor woman has lost her life, doesn't it? But I'm disappointed she didn't turn out to be the kind of person I'd built her up to be. Even so, I still think she was incredibly good at her job, and there's no denying the success of the show, that has to account for something.'

Pea nodded, eyes narrowing as she stared into the distance. 'Let's head away from the house,' she said. 'Then I can explain as we walk.'

If Pea had subjected Fran to some kind of test, Fran had evidently passed it. Moments later, the two of them walked through the orchard and on past the cottage where Midge was staying. Fran suddenly realised she hadn't given a thought to Miranda's dogs – who would look after them now? Although she had a feeling she knew the answer. If the dogs were inside the cottage, however, they were silent as she and Pea made their way into the gardens which lay behind the house.

'How much do you know?' asked Pea once they had settled into the rhythm of walking.

'Not much,' replied Fran. She pulled out her phone. 'Literally this...' She paused to show Pea the picture Adam had sent her. 'That's clearly Miranda, and this... is you?'

Pea squinted at the photo. 'Blimey, me when I was young and slim.' She gave a wry smile. 'And you only have to look at that photo to see what we were all up against. Eight contestants, all about the same age, all presentable enough, but then there was Miranda, who might have looked good before she died, but back then was truly stunning.'

Fran nodded. She could see exactly what Pea was getting at, but it was a cookery competition, not Miss World. 'So her looks were a problem, were they?'

'You could say that. Despite the fact we were all there to cook, Miranda clearly thought her looks entitled her to pretty much anything. And you have to remember this was the nineties, and times were not as enlightened as they are now.

Plus, it was an agricultural show full of burly farmers, who came from a long line of burly farmers with chauvinistic tendencies. Put it this way, the stalls advertising combine harvesters were all manned by very young girls in very skimpy clothes. It's just the way it was, I didn't think anything of it at the time.'

'So what happened?'

'As competitions go, it was just a bit of fun. Organised by the Egg Marketing Board, would you believe? The prize money was paltry, I can't even remember what it was. The actual cookery wasn't difficult either – Victoria sponges and quiches, that type of thing. I grew up on a farm, cooking for my brother and sister from an early age, so it was bread and butter to me, no pun intended. There were six rounds, three on the first day, three on the second, with overall judging taking place just before the close of the show on the final day. The competitors were pretty evenly matched, all apart from two, Miranda and one other girl.'

'You mean they were ahead of the rest of you?'

Pea shook her head. 'No, they were behind...'

Fran gave her a sharp look.

'Exactly... The other girl couldn't cook at all, I'm not sure why she entered, and Miranda was okay but, for example, she forgot to put sugar in one of the cakes, and she burned her scones, which looked like bricks anyway. In fact, at the end of the first day she was the one wailing she was going to lose. And that didn't improve on the second day. Her first two makes were okay, but the last was a pavlova and Sally's – that's who Miranda was then – was so overcooked, it nigh on shattered when the judges tried to cut into it.' Pea paused to frown. 'I should have realised something funny was going on because, despite the judges' reaction, Miranda just beamed, tossing her hair and pouting.'

Fran stared at her. 'So Miranda won the competition. She *cheated...*'

Pea nodded. 'I have no proof of this, you understand, but we think the judges were bribed in some way. There was certainly a distinct change in their attitude towards her. One of the other girls said she'd seen Miranda at the end of the first day, sobbing in very dramatic fashion, while her father and mother exchanged pointed looks. She reckoned Miranda's father had "had words" with the judges. She said he looked the sort – rich, entitled and very obviously wrapped around Miranda's little finger.'

'But did no one complain?'

'Yes, they did. Someone else's father waded in with cries of "it's a fix" but he was booed out of the tent. Miranda was a darling, she had everyone rooting for her, and in the end, we all decided it looked worse if we made a fuss, that it smacked of sour grapes, so she got away with it.'

And she may well have been getting away with it ever since, thought Fran. Adam had come across the clipping about the show when he'd been looking into Miranda's early years, and it was very clear that this first competition had provided the launch pad for her career.

Pea's information was interesting, but as they walked, another far more disturbing thought came to Fran. 'So, who should have won?' she asked. 'If not Miranda?'

But she could tell immediately from the expression on Pea's face who that was. 'I came second,' she replied.

'So, logically, it should have been you?'

Pea nodded. 'Yes, and I might be in my fifties now, and a grey-haired, rather large lady, but Miranda wasn't the only one who was photogenic back then. You've seen the photo, I like to think I held my own.'

It was true. And on Fran's phone was the proof. Without Miranda standing by her side, Pea would easily have been the most attractive girl in the photo. 'So, you think you could have had the success Miranda did?'

Pea paused, looking awkward. 'I'm not saying that exactly... And it shouldn't be about looks, should it? But I'm a good cook. I *was* a good cook. Haven't you ever done the "what if" thing? Got to a point in your life and wondered if things might have been different.'

Fran, who had, completely understood.

'I'm not saying they would have been, but...' Pea shrugged. 'I'll never know, will I?'

Fran didn't know quite what to say.

'I know... you think I'm deluding myself,' added Pea. 'Don't worry, I've reached that conclusion myself, but you did ask.'

'I wasn't thinking that at all,' replied Fran. In fact, what she had been wondering was far worse. 'But I do think you might need to be a little cautious how you recount that story in certain quarters.' She raised her eyebrows, hoping Pea would understand what she was getting at.

'Oh, don't worry, I shan't be letting Vinny know. He strikes me as the sort who'd make trouble.'

'It wasn't actually him I meant,' replied Fran.

Pea stopped dead, eyes wide. 'Shit, I didn't think. Bloody hell, Fran, the police are going to think I killed Miranda in some kind of revenge attack. I didn't, before you ask, I swear I didn't. I might not have liked her all that much, or her morals anyway, but do something like that? I couldn't.' She looked suddenly panic-stricken. 'What am I going to do?'

Fran would have liked to tell Pea that Nell would understand but she was supposedly a writer with no connection to the police, so that wasn't something she should even have an opinion on. Secondly, more importantly, Pea did actually have a motive for murder. Admittedly a little far-fetched, but Fran had seen in the past how easily simmering resentment could become something far worse. There was also the question of who had been sending Miranda those horrible gifts. Could that have been Pea as well?

'I think you have to tell the police what you've told me. Don't try to hide it, because they'll only find out and that will make things look ten times worse. Go to them before they come to you.'

Pea nodded. 'Maybe they don't know Miranda changed her name so I could offer what I know as information. That way, I look like I'm helping rather than trying to hide something.'

Fran made a non-committal noise. She wanted to believe Pea, but she couldn't overlook the possibility of her involvement in Miranda's murder. And neither would Nell.

'You won't tell anyone, will you?' asked Pea, grimacing. 'Only I meant what I said about Vinny, I don't want anyone else making trouble for me. Despite what happened, I really haven't borne Miranda a grudge all these years, and I don't want people making out I'm just a sour-faced cow who can't handle competition.'

Fran smiled. 'I won't say a word. Adam knows, obviously, but he won't say anything either.'

'Oh, the book! I'd forgotten. Please don't put this in, that would be awful. It would have been bad enough if it came to light when Miranda was alive, but now...' She swallowed. 'The gossipmongers would have a field day and I'd hate to be responsible for that.'

Fran studied Pea's face, anxiety written across it. It was strange how everyone wanted to protect Miranda's good name. In fact, they were so worried about being labelled a sourpuss they allowed Miranda to get away with all sorts rather than face the potential consequences for themselves. First Judy and now Pea. Fran hated to admit it, but they were probably right too. Miranda *was* the nation's darling, and anyone who tried to say otherwise would more than likely come off worse.

'Pea, I don't intend to put anything derogatory or gossipy in the book, it really isn't meant to be an exposé of any kind. And however I feel about Miranda personally, I don't want her to end up looking like a fraud either. Adam was simply fact-checking when he came across the photo of you and Miranda in the competition, so if you weren't here now, I wouldn't know a thing about it. There is one last thing you could help me with, though. I don't suppose you know when Miranda changed her name, do you? It would be interesting to find out when she chose to leave Sally Grainger behind.'

Pea shook her head. 'I've no idea, sorry. Like I said, I never kept in touch with Sally, why would I? And I had no idea what she'd been doing in the intervening years – she only came on my radar about the same time as everyone else's, and by then she was already Miranda Appleby.'

They walked in silence for a couple more minutes before Pea stopped. 'Actually, Fran, I might head back now, if you don't mind. I really do want to give my daughter a call and it's been a bit of a day, one way and another. I think I'll have a shower and get some rest before dinner.'

Fran smiled. 'Sure, I'll catch you later.' In truth, she was glad of the opportunity to be alone with her thoughts for a while. The competition had been far more arduous than she'd imagined, and the combination of raised adrenaline levels all day, coupled with the sheer number of thoughts in her head, was exhausting. She was also very aware that she ought to speak to Adam as soon as possible – what she'd just learned from Pea was too important to keep to herself. But the early evening air was calming, maybe another ten minutes wouldn't hurt.

She was approaching the orchard on her return journey when she caught sight of Midge up ahead. She was walking with Hope, Miranda's two dogs bouncing around them. As Fran watched, it became clear Midge was on her way somewhere. She bent down to kiss each of the dogs' heads in turn and then gave Hope a brief hug before turning away with a wave; her normal quick pace seeming even faster as she hurried down the path away from them. Fran had been aware of Midge calling out the odd timing check during the day's competition, but as she replayed the day in her head, she realised Midge hadn't otherwise been in evidence much at all. And now she was rushing off again.

Fran took her time, walking leisurely through the trees, smiling when the dogs bounded over, sensing a potential new playmate.

'They get a bit excited but they won't hurt,' called Hope, following anxiously.

'Oh, they're fine, don't worry,' Fran replied, bending down to pick up a ball one of the dogs had obligingly dropped at her feet. 'They're beautiful... They're Miranda's, aren't they?'

Hope nodded as Fran reached her. 'Yes. Poor Midge, she seems to have become well and truly lumbered with them.' Hope's brown eyes were dark with concern.

'Only in the short term, I hope?' replied Fran. She threw the ball and watched as the spaniels chased after it. 'I know Midge dotes on them, but helping to look after them is one thing, making that arrangement permanent is something else. How will she cope? She's far too busy. Surely there's a family member who could have them?'

'Miranda has no family.' Hope bent down to pick up a stick which was nestled in the grass, gazing after the dogs as she straightened. 'Or at least not any she kept in touch with.'

'That's sad,' replied Fran, studying Hope's face. 'For her to have been so alone in the world.'

Hope shrugged. 'Maybe Miranda preferred it that way. I certainly got that impression, but yes, it is sad. I'm not really sure what will happen to the dogs. Midge loves them to bits, but I know she worries about them being trawled from set to set – it's hardly an ideal life. But if she can't look after them, or no one else can, I guess they'll have to go up for rehoming.'

Fran couldn't bear the thought. The dogs seemed so settled and happy with Midge and even though she wasn't their legal owner, they were obviously thriving under her care. Clearly it wasn't just people who would be affected by Miranda's death.

'At least Midge has you to help her,' said Fran. 'The dogs are enough of a worry, but she must be frantic over the police investigation.'

'What do you mean?'

Fran was puzzled by her question. Hope was good friends with Midge, surely she must know the strain she was under?

'Being so obviously a suspect in Miranda's death,' she replied. 'I don't believe she's guilty for a minute, but if things don't go well for her, the dogs will have no one.'

Hope's eyes widened. 'Shit... Do you really think it will come to that?'

Fran gave her best reassuring smile. 'I'm sure it won't,' she said, bending down to fuss one of the dog's ears.

She left Hope playing with them and made her way back to the guest wing feeling rather guilty. Hope obviously hadn't realised how serious the situation could be for Midge. On one hand that was a good thing – Hope clearly thought her friend innocent and, right now, Midge needed to be surrounded by people who believed in her. But she would also need support if things deteriorated, someone who understood what could be facing her. Fran had been so busy she'd hardly given poor Midge a thought today. She pushed open the door of the guest wing, resolving to put that right.

'If you've got something to say, Vinny, maybe you should just come right out and say it?'

The voice was Tony's, quiet but deliberate, and Fran halted, not wishing to either eavesdrop or interrupt their conversation. However, it soon became apparent that it wasn't a particularly private discussion.

'Jenny has only just left, for goodness' sake, why don't you say something nice instead of belittling her? What does her background matter anyway?' It was Christine speaking this time, sounding huffy and belligerent.

Fran made her way down the hall and into the sitting room. The three of them were grouped around the coffee table, a plate of biscuits and a pot of tea between them, no doubt courtesy of Betty.

'Hi,' she said breezily. 'God, is there still tea in that pot? I'm desperate for one.'

Tony hastily got to his feet. 'I'll go and get another cup,' he said, leaving Christine still glaring at Vinny.

'Did I hear you say Jenny has already gone?' Fran asked, plonking herself down in a chair. 'That's a shame, I wanted to say goodbye.'

'She has,' replied Christine. 'And at least some of us were sorry to see her go.'

Vinny raised his hands in a 'who me?' gesture. 'All I said was that given her background, I was surprised she entered in the first place.'

Fran frowned. 'Sorry, what background?'

Vinny raised his eyebrows in a teasing gesture which Fran found instantly irritating. She certainly wasn't going to play his games and beg for information. Fortunately, she didn't have to.

'Vinny's just annoyed 'cause Jenny has more money than he does,' replied Tony, returning to the room. 'Apparently, coming from a wealthy background means you shouldn't bother having the same hopes and aspirations as everyone else.' He gave Vinny a very direct look.

Vinny rolled his eyes. 'Oh, come on, what difference to her would winning the competition make? I doubt she'd use it to lay ground plans for her future. I expect Daddy will just top up her allowance if she falls short.'

'You don't know a thing about her circumstances,' replied Christine, beginning to look very upset. 'You have no idea whether what you've said is true and, in any case, it's a horrible judgement to make about someone.'

Fran was so taken aback by Vinny's derogatory comment she openly stared at him. She was shocked that he could say such a thing about someone he scarcely knew, but something else also struck her as rather more important: 'Can I ask how you know these things, Vinny? Or think you know them?'

He gave her a cool look, and then slowly tapped the side of his nose. 'Because I made it my business to know,' he replied. 'I find, in most things, it pays to know who you're up against.'

'I think you've just made it very clear who *we're* up against,' said Tony. 'More's the pity.'

'Why, because I'm speaking the truth? At least with me what you see is what you get.'

'And what's that supposed to mean?' demanded Tony.

'I think you know very well what it means.'

For a moment the two men squared up to one another, and Fran wondered if they would come to blows. What on earth was going on? But then Tony shrugged and tried for nonchalance. 'You're such a wind-up merchant,' he said.

'Oh, am I?' Vinny gave a lazy smile. 'And what if I'm not? What if I do know the odd secret? Maybe I do know something about you...'

'Don't be so bloody ridiculous! What's there to know?'

Vinny chuckled. 'Shall I tell everyone? They'd probably like to hear it... No, maybe I won't, maybe I'll keep it to myself for just a little while longer. You never know when it might come in handy.' He got to his feet. 'I shan't be joining you for dinner, I'm afraid, I've got a prior arrangement. So I'll say goodnight and see you all in the morning for another fun-packed day of competition. May the best man win and all that.'

No one said a word until he had left the room.

'What the bloody hell was all that about?' asked Christine. 'What a horrible man.'

'He's probably trying to psych everyone out,' said Fran. 'Not a nice thing to do, not a nice way to be either, but, if it helps, it's probably because he's severely lacking in confidence and doesn't much fancy his chances.'

Tony eyed the door through which Vinny had just left. 'I think it's much simpler than that,' he said. 'I think it's because he's a total bastard.' He flicked a defiant glance at Fran and Christine, shifting uneasily in his seat.

Fran had no idea why, but underneath the bravado, she'd have said he looked scared.

16

Dinner was a surprisingly jolly affair, given what had happened around the coffee table. Although Fran wondered if perhaps it was *because* it happened – no one wanted to have the evening spoiled by Vinny's outburst and were determined to prove they could have a very nice time without him.

Pea, who had been in the shower and heard none of the argument, had been horrified to hear what Vinny had said, but the look she threw Fran reminded her of their earlier conversation. So Vinny *had* been looking at Tony when he'd spoken about lax vetting procedures. The question was, was he just being obnoxious and stirring trouble? Or did he know something about one of the contestants? Even perhaps know something about them all? That wouldn't bode at all well for Pea, nor Fran for that matter.

Adam had missed the whole drama as well, mainly because he had opened his bedroom door to see whether Fran had returned from her walk, heard the harsh voices and beaten a hasty retreat. Fran didn't blame him – the episode had left her rather shaken. She had quickly filled him in on what had happened and, now dinner was over, they were sitting in Adam's room nursing a mug of cocoa each, courtesy of Betty.

'I have far more questions than answers,' she said, sipping at the frothy sweetness. She had already recounted the details of her conversation with Pea, the implications of which had Adam hopping around in excitement until she'd reminded him that Pea would appear to have an alibi for the time Miranda was murdered. An alibi provided by Fran herself, and all five other contestants.

'Every time we discover something that seems to open up a whole load of possibilities,' she continued, 'it comes to nought when we remember that motive is nothing without opportunity.'

'So, let's run through everyone again,' said Adam. 'Because, very clearly, someone *did* kill Miranda, so there *was* an opportunity. We just need to spot it.'

Fran gathered her thoughts. 'Okay, let's start with staff,' she said. 'Midge is still the person at the top of the suspect list. She found Miranda, so was categorically with her very close to the time of death, a time when everyone else was seemingly busy, and also, she has no checkable alibi. She was asleep.'

Adam frowned. 'Don't you find that odd? If you were the murderer and trying to cover your tracks, why give yourself such a lame alibi? One which could never be corroborated by anyone else.'

'Unless you weren't sleeping alone...'

'Yes, but Midge hasn't claimed anything of the sort.'

'True. Go on.'

'So, in my mind, that seems to suggest she's telling the truth. It's unfortunate because it leaves her wide open to suspicion, but as she's made no attempt to at least make herself look innocent, then it's either a very clever bluff or she really didn't kill Miranda.'

'A clever bluff?' Fran asked. 'Sorry, I've got a very tired brain, why is it clever?'

'For exactly the reason we've just theorised. It makes her look innocent. Plus, if there's nothing else which can tie her to the murder – no forensics, no tangible motive, no other proof – then the fact they can't prove her alibi isn't sufficient reason to charge her with murder. They can't prove either way whether she was, or wasn't asleep, whereas if she had invented another perhaps more plausible alibi...' Adam cast about for a suitable example. 'Like she was out shopping or something, then it's possible she could be caught out. The best lies are always the simplest.'

Fran nodded. 'That make sense. So, which is it, bluff or innocence? I'm inclined to say innocence... Not just because I like her and don't believe she's guilty, but because I'm not convinced she has sufficient motivation.'

'Miranda did treat her appallingly.'

'Then why kill her? Why not just get another job and—' She stopped suddenly, looking at Adam. 'I've just remembered something Midge said to me this morning. Harrison seems to have adopted her as his PA, giving her an endless list of things to do. But Midge worked for Miranda personally, not Harrison's production company, so strictly speaking she no longer has a job. When I tried to reassure her that it would all turn out okay, she commented that Miranda had always said she'd never work anywhere else, and now it had come true. I didn't think about it at the time, but doesn't that strike you as odd? Midge seems more than capable, in fact, I'd say she goes above and beyond the call of duty. I would have thought prospective employers would snap her up.'

Adam licked a curl of cream from the top of his lip. 'Maybe Miranda had some hold over her? We need to find out because, despite what Midge said, with Miranda now dead, surely she's free to work wherever she likes? Not sure that's a plausible enough motive for murder though. It seems a bit extreme.'

Fran nodded. 'See, there we go again, another question.' She paused. 'Okay, let's leave Midge alone for a minute and look at Judy. She has to be pretty high up the suspect list, so what do we know about her?'

'The most important thing has to be the revelation that Miranda used Judy's recipes, both on the show and in her books, passing them off as hers. Despite that, Judy swears she had nothing to do with Miranda's demise and wants us to believe she doesn't want her good name to suffer either.'

'Hmm,' mused Fran. 'I'm not sure I completely buy that. She also mentioned that Miranda had always looked after her and paid her well too, which means Miranda's death might be a real blow to her. Despite what Judy says, I can't help feeling there must be some resentment there. The question is whether that resentment had simmered to the point where it made her take action. Miranda used Judy through and through, profiting hugely by it, yet now Judy's happy to keep the secret.' She wrinkled her nose. 'Really? I don't think I would be. Plus, now she's effectively taken Miranda's place on the show, doesn't that give her even more reason to spill the beans? To set the world straight and claim what's rightfully hers?'

Adam nodded. 'It might, although there's no guarantee the show will continue to be successful. From what you've said, Judy seemed to do a very good job today, but I would imagine viewers are very fickle. With Miranda gone, what happens if they start switching off? Could Judy even prove the recipes were hers in the first place?'

'That's a good point. But I still think she's profiting from Miranda's death in some way. Judy's made out that the limelight is not for her and that she's only filling Miranda's role on a temporary basis.' She pulled a face. 'I'm annoyed with myself for suggesting that Judy step up, because now she can argue it wasn't her idea and was never her intention. Even so, the changeover on the show has been far too slick for my liking. It should be in disarray with its star gone and a police investigation going on, but it isn't. It's almost as if Judy and Harrison rehearsed what would happen if Miranda wasn't around.'

'And we know that Harrison and Miranda had disagreements over the show's content. Disagreements that, as his girlfriend, Judy could have been privy to. In fact, she could have been part of his solution.' Adam paused a moment, thinking. 'Plus, I still think Judy is the best person to have got hold of a lump of steak, so she could be the one behind Miranda's presents.'

Fran sighed, staring into her mug. 'So, onto Harrison then, who, as we know, is in a relationship with Judy. There's obviously nothing wrong with that except that it could be seen to be a very fortuitous liaison for them both, particularly if Harrison has designs on making the show his own. We already know he and Miranda had fought over certain aspects of it, and with her gone he gets carte blanche to do as he likes *and* gets a bigger slice of the pie at the same time. It would be interesting to see whether contractually that's even possible.'

'And you said he was a bit jumpy when you asked him about Miranda's change of name?'

'Yes,' replied Fran. 'Categorically denied knowing anything about it and seemed almost annoyed I'd asked him – tried to point me in official directions.'

'He wouldn't necessarily know, would he? Just because Miranda and he had worked together for many years it doesn't have to follow. Remember how adamant Miranda was that no one, not even Harrison, find out about the presents? I think she was very good at keeping things to herself she didn't want other people to know.'

'Yes, but why be desperate to keep details of a name change private?'

'Unless she *did* cheat at the competition she entered with Pea, and her previous name is the only link to it. She'd want to keep that quiet.'

Fran frowned. 'So maybe Harrison *did* know about her name, and he *did* know about the competition with Pea, and was just as keen as Miranda to keep those facts hidden. He wouldn't want anyone else discovering she was a fraud... In which case I'm not sure how he's going to feel when he finds out that his girlfriend had been providing Miranda's recipes.' She groaned. 'Argh, this is all just going around in circles.'

Adam shook his head. 'But somewhere in all these questions is the one which will lead us to the answer.'

'We also have one of the other contestants insinuating things. Pea, we know about, but where does Tony come into this? I can't make up my mind whether Vinny is simply trying to stir things up, or whether he genuinely knows something about Tony. And if he does, what?'

'And where has he got his information from in the first place?'

Fran thought for a moment. 'Same place we do probably, the internet.'

Adam's eyes lit up and he flexed his fingers. 'I feel another search coming on,' he said.

'There's just one problem with all of this though,' added Fran, with a rueful smile. 'And that's the inescapable fact that everyone seems to have an alibi. The contestants certainly do, we were all together, and I'm pretty sure Judy and Harrison do. As far as I know they were both in the stable throughout the whole time the murder could have taken place. And if they were, then numerous other people would have seen them too.'

Adam rolled his eyes. 'Maybe they're all in it together,' he said.

·   ·   ·

'That has to be the most ridiculous thing you've ever said,' replied Nell the next morning. They were enjoying a cooked breakfast courtesy of Betty, the other competitors having long since gone over to the stable for theirs.

'I bet it isn't,' replied Adam. 'I'm sure if you think back you'll remember countless other occasions.' He gave Nell a cheeky grin, guaranteed to have her rolling her eyes.

Instead, she gave him a long look, knife and fork poised over her plate. 'Yes, thank you. I might also mention that I've seen at least six adaptations of *Murder on the Orient Express* and read the book as well. And while having multiple murderers worked very well for Agatha Christie, that's fiction, Adam. Here in the real world, Miranda was killed by a single person, of that I'm certain. Although quite how they did it is beyond me at this moment in time.' She viciously speared the end of a piece of sausage and stuffed it in her mouth. 'Although what you said about Pea is interesting, Fran. I thought these kind of TV programmes were supposed to have stringent vetting procedures.'

'They do,' answered Fran, pulling a face. 'Which, if you think back to the argument Adam overheard between Harrison and Miranda when Emily was threatening to leave, is supposedly Harrison's job.'

'Yet they missed Pea's prior connection with Miranda,' Nell commented. 'Can't be all that stringent then, can they?'

'I don't even know what the checks amount to,' added Fran. 'It might be no more than verifying the details on an application form, so what you leave out won't be checked…'

So far, she'd only picked at her breakfast, which could only bode well for Adam. He was concerned for her wellbeing, of course, but they were very fine sausages and it would be a shame if they went to waste.

'Plus, there could be applicants like Emily,' said Adam, 'who might not be the most worthy contestant, but might make for good television. It would be interesting to know exactly how they pick people to appear on the show.'

'Wouldn't it just.' Nell swallowed. 'I'll make a note to pick that up with Harrison, particularly given that Vinny seems intent on casting suspicion onto some of his fellow competitors.'

'I could ask Midge as well?' offered Fran. 'The answer we get from her might be considerably different from the one you get from Harrison, and I'm sure she knows.'

'Good idea,' said Nell. 'And better if you ask her. It's understandable under the circumstances, but I think I make her nervous.'

Adam smiled. Nell made everyone nervous. 'So, is there anything else we should know?' he asked. He had a few ideas he wanted to follow up, but it didn't hurt to ask.

Nell's response, however, was far too predictable. She raised an eyebrow. 'Nothing that you couldn't already have worked out,' she replied. 'We haven't spoken to all the competitors yet, but we've taken everyone else's initial statements and, so far, drawn a blank. Everyone's movements check out. Judy says she was in the stable during the time when Miranda must have been murdered. When I asked Hope who else was in the stable with her during that time, she says Judy, Harrison, Sam and Woody. I ask Sam what he was doing and he says he was chatting with Harrison. Who else was there? He says Woody, Hope and Judy. You get the picture... Multiple people in the same locations, at the same time, and all providing alibis for the others, quite naturally and with no hesitation.'

'Yet obviously someone did kill Miranda, which means someone must be lying,' said Fran. 'Or colluding with someone else for some reason.'

'That's one possibility,' replied Nell. 'The other is that Midge is guilty.'

Fran sighed with frustration. 'But what about background checks?'

'We're still in the process of pulling those together. It's slow and, in Miranda's case, made slower by the fact she had very few relatives, and none she kept in touch with. We're aware of her change of name but, as you know, she kept details about her personal life very private, so from the moment she became Miranda Appleby, there's very little to go on. Even her agent can't shed much light. There was a husband, whom she divorced and who later died, but that's about all we know. If there were other relationships she kept them very well hidden. Information about Sally Grainger is also being checked, but unfortunately these things take time. Your lead about Pea is probably the best we have so far.'

Nell lifted her mug of tea and swallowed its contents. 'As for everyone else on board the good ship Miranda, nothing stands out so far. The crew are well established – they've all worked on the show for a number of years. Hope is the newest member of the team, but even she's already clocked up three years, so, again, well known. They all speak highly of Miranda... that's to say they were honest about her less-than-agreeable character traits but still respect that she was very good at her job. The common feeling seems to be that what they gain from the show far outweighs any negative aspects.'

She shrugged and then got to her feet. 'Right, I must go and gather myself. I was due to interview Pea this afternoon but, thanks to your information, I think I might bump her up the list. Good luck with today's competition, Fran.'

Fran groaned. 'Don't remind me,' she replied. 'I'm tempted to cook extremely badly to ensure I get sent home, but that's the rub of this whole thing – I can't. At the end of this week I'll still be running my business and can't afford to have people thinking I'm a rubbish cook.' She checked her watch and pushed her plate away. 'I've got to go, or poor Midge will be after me and she has enough to worry about without—' She stopped dead as Midge's head appeared around the door.

'Ah... I would appear to have found you. Are you on your way?'

'Yes, yes, just coming—' But Midge had already turned on her tail. Fran grimaced. 'Do you think she heard? Me and my big mouth,' she muttered. She hastily drained the rest of her tea and hurried out the door. 'Midge, wait!'

Nell watched her leave, both eyebrows raised. 'And on that note, I too must be away. I'll try to catch up with you later, and needless to say,' – she leaned a little closer to Adam – 'if you do see or hear anything today that I should know about, don't keep it to yourself.'

Adam nodded. 'Absolutely. Not. I mean, yes, I'll tell you... straight away...'

The corners of Nell's mouth twitched. 'Excellent.'

Once she'd gone, Adam stared at the door, wondering what to do first. The most obvious thing would be to finish Fran's breakfast, but then again, maybe he should—

'There we are then,' said Betty, coming into the room. 'Everyone gone, have they?'

Adam nodded, swiping a sausage from Fran's plate before Betty could remove it.

She frowned at the sight of Fran's uneaten food. 'Poor thing, couldn't she face it?'

'She's a bag of nerves,' replied Adam, shaking his head. 'It was absolutely nothing to do with your amazing cooking, Betty, that I do know.'

The diminutive housekeeper blushed alarmingly. 'Oh, get on with you.' She turned away to clear the plates, but not before Adam had seen her bashful smile.

He got to his feet. 'Tell you what, you wash and I'll dry.'

Betty positively twinkled.

.   .   .

'So, what do you know then?' he asked, grinning as Betty began to fill the sink with water. 'What's the word on the street?'

Betty gave him a wayward glance. 'I don't know what you mean.'

But she did and Adam smirked. 'Don't try to fool me, I've seen you hobnobbing with Midge. So, who's your money on for the win? Has Fran got a chance?'

'More than a chance, I'd say,' replied Betty. 'Midge overheard Judy saying she's very good – was quite complimentary, apparently. That's all I know, so don't ask me any more.' She turned off the tap. 'One thing I do know, though – that detective of yours is a bit scary, isn't she?'

He nodded. 'She terrifies me.'

'And poor Midge seems to be on the receiving end at the moment. Honestly, as if anyone could possibly think her guilty of such a thing as murder. You only have to look at her to know she's innocent.'

Adam smiled. If only it were that easy. 'So come on then, Betty, who's your top suspect?'

Betty narrowed her eyes. 'One of the men, I expect. I don't much like men, present company excepted. Not when they're around good-looking women anyway,' she said. 'You only had to look at Miranda to know she'd broken a few hearts in her time. And, in my experience, men do very strange things when their hearts are broken, it's like they lose all sense of reason.' She paused. 'Or maybe they never had it in the first place. Anyway, my money's on Harrison. I don't like his hair, it's too...' – she waved her hands about her head – 'artificial-looking, like he spends far too long preening himself in the morning. I'm not a fan of that. I always liked a man who was neat and well-cared for, but not too aware of himself, if you know what I'm saying. And I don't like that Vinny chap either. Snooping about in other people's business and then pretending he's not.'

Adam stared at her. 'Hang on, Betty, do you know he's been

snooping about, or did you just hear something? Only there was a bit of an argument last night and...'

'Well, I don't know for definite, but coming out of someone's room when they're not there is wrong, surely? No matter what they say.'

'And what did they say? I mean, *he* say?'

'That Tony had forgotten his pen and asked Vinny to fetch it for him. Lame excuse, if you ask me. Don't they have pens over where they're filming? Unless it was given to him by his grandfather and is a good-luck charm, then it doesn't make any sense to send Vinny to fetch it. Why all the fuss over a pen? And Vinny looked shifty. Jumped out of his skin when he saw me.'

'So, Vinny was coming out of Tony's room?'

Betty nodded, swilling tomato ketchup off a plate. 'That's what I said, didn't I?'

'And when was this?'

She thought for a moment. 'Yesterday afternoon, not long after lunch.'

Adam nodded. 'You're right, Betty. I don't like the sound of that either. We'll definitely put him on our suspect list.'

The conversation ranged back and forth for a while until all the dishes were washed, dried and put away. Adam was desperate to get on but Betty liked the company and she was turning into a remarkably good informant.

'Will you be in here again today with that computer thing of yours?' she asked, hanging up the tea towel.

'I expect so, yes. Some of the day anyway.'

'Then you'll be wanting tea and biscuits, won't you?' she replied, with a tilt of her head. 'Half eleven suit you?'

Adam beamed. 'Perfect.'

He had no idea where Betty went when she wasn't in the kitchen. And he still wasn't altogether convinced she couldn't just appear at will. She had a habit of popping up at the exact moment she was needed, but Adam certainly wasn't about to complain. There *were* a few things he wanted to check on his laptop, but they could wait – first he had to do some snooping of his own, something which Betty would surely frown upon. As would Nell, but then as he wasn't planning on either of them finding out...

It took only a couple of minutes to equip himself with what he needed. A little bit of kit which had come in extremely handy on quite a few occasions since he'd met Fran. The first time was when she'd been locked in a shed by a would-be murderer and he'd had to go to her rescue. Not that she'd been all that happy about it to start with, but once she understood he might actually have saved her life, she agreed his ability to pick locks was quite fortuitous. He looked down at the little pouch in his hand and smiled.

Triple-checking that Betty had disappeared back to wherever it was she went, Adam let himself silently into Vinny's room and looked around. My, how the tables were turned.

The room was untidy and smelled slightly sour, as if too many unwashed socks had been left lying around. He grimaced and resolved to let his eyes skim over those kind of details – he had far more important things to look for. But where to start?

The furniture was similar to that in Adam's room, solid mahogany stuff: a wardrobe, chest of drawers, bed with table beside and a wing-backed armchair covered in brocade. Vinny's suitcase had only been partially unpacked and lay on the floor beside the chair, a good portion of its contents strewn across it. The bag had multiple side pockets, the exploration of which was tempting, but Adam decided to leave them until later. The potential for dirty sock discovery was simply too great.

The wardrobe was probably the least obvious place to find anything, so Adam checked it first in order to exclude it. Hanging trousers and shirts, a smart jacket and a pair of shoes, but nothing else. He closed the door and moved on. The chest of drawers was probably a much better bet.

The top drawer was empty, and he groaned inwardly in frustration when he saw the second one was too. He closed it and almost turned away, but then he stopped and looked back, eyes narrowing. He'd almost walked away, almost, but not quite... He dropped to his knees and pulled open the bottom drawer. At times Adam really didn't understand why people did the things they did – who chooses to use only the bottom drawer in a chest? Not many people, he would have thought. But then, *exactly* like a lot of people, Vinny had chosen to hide his notebook among his underwear. Adam memorised its exact position before lifting it out and, sitting back on his heels, began to read.

Vinny was evidently a consummate notebook user. He made notes about everything, some of it relating to the competition – ideas for recipes and lists of ingredients – but mostly the notebook seemed to contain random thoughts, none of which made any sense to Adam. In the back was a list of phone numbers, and the name Lucy with a date beside it. A birthday? Anniversary? Adam pulled a face and flipped back to where the last entry had been made. The following few pages were blank, but then at the top of the next page the letters 'CCC' had been underlined twice. And below them was a list of names. Adam read, eyes widening as he did so. Not only was Vinny judgemental in the extreme, he was also very observant. Most of what had been written there was obvious conjecture, but several words leaped off the page, stopping Adam in his tracks. Fact or supposition? He had no idea, but there was only one way to find out.

Pulling out his phone from a pocket, he took a snap of each of the pages, checking first that none of the images were blurry before carefully replacing the notebook, exactly where he had found it. He got to his feet, giving the room one last look, but he was pretty sure he'd found what he needed. He left as silently as he'd entered.

Back in the kitchen, after first collecting his laptop, Adam sat for a moment, staring at the wall ahead of him. He ought to tell Fran what he'd discovered, not least of all because the information affected her as well, but she would be just about to start the first challenge, there was no way he could interrupt her. Besides, if everyone was busy cooking for the next few hours, it meant nothing else would be happening, and that bought him some time. He probably ought to find Nell as well, but she had mentioned interviewing Pea first thing and that was just as important an avenue to explore. Plus, there was the fact that Adam only had a one-word clue right now. And he had no idea whether it had any substance beyond the wanderings of Vinny's mind. Surely it would be better if he found evidence first, got the backstory, if there was one. That would be of far more use to Nell.

He stared at the image on his phone, at Vinny's neat handwriting and the notes he had made beside each of the competitors' names. Beside Fran's was the word 'police' – no prizes for guessing what that was about. But it was the word next to Tony's name which had sent Adam's pulse racing and, mind made up, he opened his laptop and got to work.

17

'Midge, wait!' Fran called again as she hurried to catch up with the young woman. They were almost halfway across the front of the house by the time she drew level. She caught hold of her sleeve. 'Midge, hang on,' she panted.

Eventually Midge stopped but, when she turned, the bleakness of her expression took Fran by surprise.

'Midge, what's wrong? I know you're under a lot of pressure at the moment, but I'm worried about you. What's going on?'

'What, aside from killing Miranda, you mean?'

Fran had been prime suspect in a previous case and she knew exactly how that felt – as if the walls were closing in and time was running out. As if nothing you said would be believed, and anything you did say sounded incriminating, as if you were making excuses. She had even felt guilty, for goodness' sake. 'But you didn't kill Miranda,' she said gently. 'I know it feels as if everyone is against you, but honestly, they aren't.'

'But what if I did kill her?' Midge shook her head. 'I think I'm going mad,' she added. 'Actually mad. Properly lost the plot. I'm scared I've done something and for some reason I'm blanking it all out.'

'Oh, Midge...' Fran gave her a warm smile. 'I'm sure it feels that way, but it's just the stress of the situation. You have so many things to think about, and everything feels out of control. It's horrible, but it doesn't mean you've done anything wrong.'

'But the facts don't lie.'

'What facts?'

'There's no one else who could have killed Miranda,' replied Midge. 'Only me. Talk to anyone and they'll tell you.' Her eyes searched Fran's, wild and staring. 'What if it *was* me? What if I killed Miranda and I just can't remember?'

Fran didn't know what to say. 'I'm sure you'd remember something like that,' she replied. 'People forget little details when they're stressed, not big whopping ones like that. And you had no reason to kill Miranda.' That wasn't strictly true, but Fran didn't think it would be helpful to mention it under the circumstances.

Midge swung her head around, checking they were alone. 'Promise me you won't breathe a word of this, but when I was younger, and I swear it only happened a couple of times, I went sleepwalking. The second time was when I was seventeen. I had a part-time job on the weekend and I got up and got dressed in my uniform, utterly convinced it was morning when really it was the middle of the night. I was eating breakfast when Mum found me.'

Fran frowned. 'But if it only happened a couple of times, I'm sure you've nothing to worry about.'

'It was a few months after my dad died, so my mum put it down to stress. But what if it wasn't just that? What if it's something I always do when I'm stressed and it's happened all over again?'

'But surely you've only been stressed *since* Miranda died. Were you really that stressed beforehand?'

Midge stared at her. 'No... No, I don't think I was. No more than usual, anyway.'

'There you are then. I'm sure it's nothing.' She rubbed Midge's arm. 'It sounds a stupid thing to say, but try not to worry. Nell is working hard on this, so are Adam and I. We'll get to the bottom of it, I promise.'

Midge nodded, but her eyes were still full of despair.

'Speaking of which,' added Fran, hoping a change of subject might help Midge from dwelling on her predicament. 'There's something you can help me with, actually. I said I'd ask you how people get to be on the show. I'm guessing there's some kind of application form?'

Midge nodded. 'Yes, there's an initial form, which is pretty straightforward. Essentially what's important is that people aren't professional caterers, or don't cook for a living. Um, obviously you do, but you're different. We ask for some details about their level of competency and who they cook for – just family, or do they throw dinner parties, that kind of thing. Also examples of something they've done recently which particularly illustrates their skills and a recipe they've devised on their own, although it can be one they've modified.'

'Okay, and these things are checked, are they?'

'Oh yes, particularly the professional cook thing. You'd be surprised how many people enter thinking we won't find out they run a tea room, or work in a restaurant, however small their role. Oh, and people have to live in the county we're featuring, that's important too. So, we check addresses and so on.'

'And then what do you do once you've got all the forms? How do you whittle people down? And who does it?'

'Miranda and Harrison are supposed to do it together. They always used to but...' She pulled a face. 'The last couple of years or so, Harrison's done it by himself. I help, and I did try to flag things up for Miranda, but essentially it's Harrison's choice.'

'So how does *he* whittle them down?' It was all beginning to sound a little too vague for Fran's liking.

'We have to ensure a good mix, so older people, younger

people... men and women, you know what I mean.' Her eyebrows raised a little.

Fran studied Midge's expression, the years of being a PA showing there; being privy to all sorts of confidential information meaning she often had to be a little guarded. 'So what you're saying is that the ratings help decide who gets to be on the show?'

'Sometimes...' Midge chewed at the inside of her cheek. 'It's important our contestants are a balanced representation of society.'

'That's the official line, Midge. What actually happens in practice?'

'The way the forms are phrased allows for the applicants to give us a little insight into their characters, and...' She narrowed her eyes, weighing something up. 'Some people just make for better television,' she finished.

'People like Emily?' Fran suggested. 'Who Miranda called flaky and Harrison said would endear herself to the public?' Midge was still being far too reticent. 'Bottom line, Midge, does Harrison cherry-pick who he wants based on his whims, for want of a better description?'

Midge dropped her head and it was all Fran needed to know.

'They still have to come to the elimination rounds,' added Midge. 'We get hundreds of applications, so we reduce the number to about thirty or forty and then hold two preliminary heats. The best cooks from those rounds are the people who eventually get to come on the show. And even then, there are occasions when people pull out, or can't make the filming schedule, are ill, all sorts of things. So, on occasion, Harrison has to accommodate certain... changes.'

They were getting closer to the truth, but Midge was still holding back for some reason. The faithful PA was partly it, but there was something else, Fran was sure of it.

'Midge, why are you so afraid of losing your job? Did Miranda threaten you?' It was a sharp change of tack on Fran's part, but it did the trick.

Midge's face crumpled. 'I lied on my CV,' she confessed. 'I so desperately wanted this job, I pretty much made up everything and because Miranda never checked things, she took me on. She found out later, of course, and threatened to fire me, but by then she'd also realised she couldn't do her job without me, so she began saying she'd tell all if I ever left. And, believe me, she knew enough people in the business to make sure I never worked in TV again.'

'Oh, Midge... But you're so good at your job and all that was years ago now, you've more than made up for your lack of experience.'

'Yes, but you don't know Miranda, what she could be like. I was so scared that if I wasn't good enough at my job, or said things I shouldn't, that she'd fire me anyway, out of spite. I've seen what she can do to people, people she took a dislike to, and I honestly believed her when she said she'd make sure I didn't work again.'

'So, you kept your head down and didn't rock the boat?'

Midge nodded.

'And even now, you still don't like saying bad things about her, do you? Even when she's dead and has no hold over you any more. Even though you're in the frame for her murder.'

'But I never wanted to go anywhere else, really I didn't. The way Miranda treated me was horrible at times but, like I said before, I've loved working on the show. I don't know what I'd do if it wasn't this. I'm on my own, I have nothing else. This show... it's like my family.'

Fran tutted with frustration. 'Honestly, Midge, how anyone can think you were responsible for Miranda's death is beyond me.' Fran shook her head, staring out towards Miranda's trailer, still fluttering with police-cordon tape. She was beginning to see a much bigger picture about life on the show, about who Miranda really was and, importantly, who she wasn't. But there was something else which occurred to her.

'Just now, you mentioned that on occasion Harrison has to accommodate changes to the planned contestants. Is that what Emily was? An accommodation? Only Adam overheard an argument with Miranda where she clearly blamed Harrison for Emily pulling out and leaving the show in the lurch.'

'Emily was complicated,' replied Midge, sighing. 'And she should never have been on the show in the first place. Her application form made reference to some struggles she'd had in the past with her self-confidence and that cooking was the only thing which made her feel good about herself. A lot of people have similar issues and it can be good when you see how the show changes them, how they grow. But in Emily's case there was something about what she'd written which suggested a much deeper problem. We have a duty of care to people and it was thought that the stress of coping with the show might be too much for her. Harrison disagreed, however, and thought she should be given a chance.'

'So, what happened?'

'She came along to one of the preliminary rounds, and she was lovely, very nervous, but understandably so. When compared with the others, however, she wasn't the greatest of cooks, that much was evident. Judy helps out at these rounds and she recommended that Emily be dropped because she wouldn't cope with disappointment particularly well. And that would have been the end of it, if two other people hadn't pulled out. One suffered a bereavement, and the other was offered a job overseas and so wasn't available for the show. Harrison put Emily forward as a replacement. In fact, he became adamant that Emily be on the show. He said the shows were too "nice". That they didn't have enough bite and viewers didn't want saccharine-sweet all the time. He wanted to toughen things up, not show people suffering exactly, but having a hard time because then, when they won, the payoff for the viewer would be even greater. Perversely, the show would become even more popular.' Midge held her look and Fran suddenly realised what she was implying.

'Midge, are you telling me the show is rigged?'

'No... maybe. Look, I really don't know, not for certain. But please don't breathe a word of this to anyone. It only happened on two or three occasions that I know about, odd times when Harrison saw an opportunity to have things his way, but—' She broke off, looking nervously towards the stable. 'I really wasn't happy about it, particularly in Emily's case. Quite a lot of chatting goes on at the preliminaries. It's far more relaxed an environment and less pressured than the actual shows – it helps us to get to know people. But the more I chatted with Emily, the more concerned I became about her. Just little things she'd said, references to problems with her mental health in the past.'

Fran didn't like the way this was going one little bit. 'What did you do?'

'I told Harrison, but he didn't listen, so I told Miranda too. Trouble was, Miranda didn't listen to much of what I told her, and a lot of the time she... It was like she was bored with the show. Don't bother me with trivia, she used to say. But when I told her about Emily, she said she would take it up with Harrison. I believed her, but obviously she did nothing of the sort, because when I got the confirmed competitors' list through, Emily's name was still on it. I argued about it with Harrison, but he said I was being alarmist and everything would be fine. In fact, he had a feeling that Joe Public would love Emily and that this show would turn out to be one of our best yet.'

Things were beginning to make a lot more sense for Fran – how Miranda had become a starlet bored by the demands her success made on her, and only interested in the success itself. It was why Judy had started providing the recipes, why people like Midge were doing all the work, why standards on the show were slipping with entrants appearing who shouldn't, and results which were tantamount to being fixed. More worrying than any of this, though, was the fact that Miranda's attitude may well have been what led to her murder. It all came down to how much Harrison might have wanted his own way, and how much Miranda didn't...

'I have to tell Nell about this, Midge, it could be important.'

Midge stared at her, only then realising the ramifications of what she'd revealed. 'Oh God, I should have mentioned it sooner. Do you really think Harrison might have had something to do with Miranda's death?'

'I don't know what to think, Midge, but don't you dare go blaming yourself for this as well. I'll speak to Nell and it will be up to her to deal with it.'

Midge glanced at her phone, grimacing at the time. 'But we've already taken too long, Fran, I need you over in the stable. We're about to start filming.'

Fran shook her head. 'I'm sorry, Midge, but I have to speak to Nell. Tell Harrison I'll be over as soon as I can. The others will just have to start without me, and I'll catch up as best I can.' It wasn't ideal, but under the circumstances, she had no choice.

Midge nodded, anxiety clouding her face as Fran watched her walk away.

Predictably, Nell was not at all pleased to hear what Fran had to say. 'Oh for goodness' sake, our job would be an awful lot easier if only people would tell the truth.' She caught the look her DC gave her. 'Yes, I know. I'm aware that's a stupid statement. But, honestly, people think it doesn't matter – *it was only a little lie, I didn't think any harm would come of it*. I spend my days and nights picking up the mess because people didn't think it mattered or wasn't important enough to mention.' She scowled.

'Needless to say, I shall be asking Harrison Shaw some very difficult questions.'

'Do you really think he could be responsible?' asked Fran.

'I'm not thinking anything yet,' replied Nell. 'But we don't exactly have much else to go on at the moment, and we know he and Miranda had been arguing. Maybe their relationship wasn't as sweet as Harrison's been making out.' She paused. 'Even so, I'm sure differences of opinion occur all the time on shows like this and, generally, that doesn't lead to murder.'

'So maybe there's a reason why it's particularly important to him,' suggested Fran.

'Mmm, that's what I was thinking. Palmer, have we had the financial report back on Harrison yet?'

Clare shook her head. 'No, Boss. Should be any time though.'

Nell's eyes narrowed. 'Okay, make sure I know the minute it is, please.' She checked the time. 'Aren't you supposed to be cooking?' she asked Fran.

'Yes, but I didn't think this could wait.'

Nell nodded. 'I was going to interview Pea this morning, but that will keep. Thanks, Fran.' She turned to her DC. 'Right, let's have Harrison in again. He won't be expecting it and you know how I like to catch people unawares.'

Adam had disappeared down that many rabbit holes in his search for information, he was beginning to feel like Alice in Wonderland. And each time he had exhausted one rabbit hole, he had to backtrack and return to his original starting point, following up his next thought, his next lead. He was well past his half-eleven tea and biscuits by the time he had even a glimpse of his quarry, and from there it took another couple of hours before he finally found what he was looking for. Goodness knows how long it had taken Vinny, but that didn't matter now...

Adam shook his head. Of course it mattered. Vinny had deliberately set out to obtain information about Tony. Fran and the other contestants too, for that matter. But why? What was he hoping to gain from it? Knowing that could be just as important as the information he'd uncovered in the first place.

Adam slid his beanie from his head and ran a hand through his hair. Aware he was breathing a little fast, he sat back and tried to keep calm. Thinking logically, the information didn't mean anything, not on its own. There was no connection between Tony and Miranda, or none that he could find. He glanced at his phone. Damn, it was much later than he'd thought.

Fran was the only one still cooking when he arrived at the stable. Working at speed, she began to plate up her food while Midge stood to one side, hand spiralling in the classic wind-it-up gesture. He could already see the camera moving around, getting ready for the final shots.

'And... cut,' said Harrison, with a signal to Sam. 'Well done, Fran, thanks. We've got enough to cover the closing stages. No one will be able to tell you've been on your own once we're done with the edits.' He flashed a smile and withdrew, leaving Midge to give Fran a hug. She returned it, looking oddly sanguine.

Adam raised a hand to alert her to his presence.

Giving Midge a quick squeeze, she hurried over. 'Is everything okay?' she asked.

'I'm fine,' he replied. 'But what about you? How come you were finishing on your own?'

'I started late, I got held up chatting to Midge and then Nell.'

Adam gave her a heartfelt look. 'You don't look flustered though,' he remarked. 'Does that mean everything went okay?'

She shrugged. 'Not sure I can be that bothered any more,' she replied. 'Given that the competition may well be rigged.'

'What?'

She turned to look over her shoulder. 'In fact... let's step outside a minute. I've got quite a bit to tell you.'

Adam hesitated. Whatever Fran had uncovered didn't sound good, but it was probably nothing compared with the possible identity of the murderer. He nodded. 'Me too.'

Fran's expression was quizzical. 'You've got that look on your face again,' she said. 'Excited, but a little panic-stricken at the same time. What's going on?'

Adam steered her towards the stable door. 'I think I might have found our murderer. I don't know the whys and where-fores as yet, but—' He broke off at the sight of Fran's face.

'Yes, Harrison, I know,' she whispered. 'But how did *you* find out?'

He stared at her. 'Harrison...?'

'Yes, we think he's been rigging the show and Miranda found out—'

'But it isn't him, Fran, it's Tony...'

They were outside now, standing in the courtyard, the gentle autumnal sunshine warming their backs so at odds with the line of Christmas trees which decorated the space.

'I think I'm missing something here,' said Fran, pulling a face. 'I spoke to Midge earlier, and it turns out Emily coming on the show was at Harrison's behest, but she should never have been allowed on. She was actually knocked out of the prelimi-naries, but when someone else couldn't make the show after all, Harrison insisted Emily be pulled back in. He wanted her on the show because he thought her self-confidence issues would make for good television, and I'm pretty sure he was going to rig things so that Emily would win as well. He may even have promised her that. Of course, he didn't know she was going to pull out once she got here, but—'

The door to the stable opened sharply and Vinny strode into the yard. He visibly started when he saw them and turned his head away, intent on passing by unheeded. But Vinny going on a walkabout was too much of a coincidence for Adam to ignore.

'Hi, Vinny,' he called. 'How's it going?'

'Great!' he replied, a bright smile on his face. 'Sorry, I just need to rush back to my room for something.'

'Yeah, sure... Your room? Or rifling through someone else's?' Fran stared at him.

As did Vinny. 'I beg your pardon... What did you say?'

Adam quailed a little. In his head it had sounded like a good thing to say, but now that his challenge was out in the open, he wasn't so sure. Vinny was considerably bigger than he was. He cleared his throat. 'I wondered if you were going to your room, or Tony's,' he said.

'And what business is that of yours?' Vinny demanded.

'As much as anyone else's,' Adam replied. 'It struck me it wasn't the kind of thing you should be doing.'

'And who says I've been doing it?' But then Vinny sneered. 'Oh, I get it... Although it isn't just me who's supposedly been snooping, is it? That accusation's a bit rich coming from the pair of you, when you've been leading everyone a merry dance.'

'Okay,' said Fran in the voice Adam knew she usually reserved for her teenage daughter, 'that's enough. I suspect this isn't a conversation any of us want to have out here. Shall we go somewhere a little more private? Maybe back to your room, seeing as you were headed there anyway.'

Vinny glared at her, but Fran stood her ground.

'Or we can pick it up with the chief inspector if you'd prefer?'

Adam smiled to himself. Fran was so good at this – not knowing a single fact about a situation but still making out that she did. He often wondered if it was a mum thing. He wished it was a skill he could learn. Adam had a feeling that a lot of the time he looked like a small animal trapped in the glare of headlights.

'Fine,' muttered Vinny savagely, striding off across the courtyard.

Not a single word was uttered until they were safely in Vinny's room, Adam trying his best to appear as if it was the first time he'd been there. Vinny wasted no time in picking up the conversation right where they had left off.

'Would you like to tell me what it is I'm supposed to have done?' he said, closing the door. 'Although why you get to be all holier-than-thou when the pair of you are pretending to be something you're not is beyond me.'

'He knows we're working with Nell,' said Adam for Fran's benefit, in case it wasn't clear. 'But I'd like to know how you've come to that conclusion.'

'So would I,' muttered Fran.

'It's pretty simple,' said Vinny, 'given that I've already had an interview with the chief inspector. She asked me lots of questions about any past associations I've had with Miranda and what my movements have been over recent months. She *also* said the police had been investigating a series of incidents relating to Miranda which may have culminated in her death. Now, I don't know what those are exactly, but I saw you talking to her when you thought no one was watching. The old "I'm writing a book ploy" which conveniently changes when a contestant just happens to leave the show, allowing you to take her place. It doesn't take a genius to work out that something has been going on for a while and you two were obviously sent here to find out what. Except that someone killed Miranda first, I don't suppose that went down too well.'

'A woman is dead,' said Fran, her voice cold. 'Those aren't words I'd use to describe something so horrific. This isn't some game, Vinny. Miranda was murdered by someone standing close enough to look in her eyes as she died.' She lifted her head slightly. 'And just last night you were boasting about certain secrets you were aware of. Secrets you then threatened to reveal, saying that other people might be interested in them. Then you changed your mind, saying maybe you'd keep the information to yourself for a while longer because you never knew when it might come in handy. That doesn't strike me as a particularly friendly thing to say. In fact, it sounds horribly close to a blackmail threat and, given that someone *has* been killed, the chief inspector is going to be very interested in anyone making threats.'

Vinny swallowed, not surprisingly. Adam had seen Fran mean business on several occasions now, and she could be pretty scary when she wanted to be. Perhaps now Vinny had the measure of what he was actually up against, instead of idly boasting he might begin to take things seriously.

'So, what were you doing in Tony's room?' Adam asked, hoping to catch Vinny off guard.

'Nothing! I mean, I haven't been in there. Who says I have, anyway? It sounds to me as if you're the ones doing the snooping.'

'I think you're rather missing the point,' replied Adam. 'We're police consultants, *you* are not.' It was stretching the truth somewhat and Nell wouldn't approve one little bit, but then when had that ever stopped him before? 'And you didn't answer my question. Why *were* you in Tony's room? Because we have a witness who saw you go in.'

Vinny was about to argue again when his face suddenly relaxed. 'Oh, you mean when I went to get Tony's pen, when Betty saw me. Oh, yes, of course... Sorry, I thought you meant on some other occasion. No, it was just as I told the house-keeper, Tony forgot his pen and he asked me to fetch it for him.' He nodded as if to reinforce that he was telling the truth.

'And would Tony say the same thing if we checked with him?' asked Fran, smiling sweetly.

A blood vessel pulsed at the side of Vinny's head. 'Yes, of course he would.'

Fran nodded. 'Good, we'll be sure to ask.'

'Does he keep his room locked?' asked Adam. 'Only I'm just wondering if he gave you any keys?'

Vinny's brow furrowed as he made a show of remembering. 'I'm not sure...' His eyes narrowed even further. He had a fifty-fifty chance of getting it right, and Adam was quite intrigued to hear which he would pick. 'No, actually, I think it was unlocked.'

Adam nodded. 'Hmm... odd, only it's locked now.'

'Well, it wasn't then,' replied Vinny, defiantly. 'It's his room. I guess he can lock or unlock it as he sees fit. I'm not his keeper.'

'Okay, fair enough. And when you were in his room, fetching his pen, did you notice anything else which happened to be lying around?'

'Like what?'

Adam shrugged. 'Nothing in particular. I just wondered how you'd come by the little gem you have on Tony, the secret you were boasting about. Only it strikes me as the sort of thing Tony might be keen to keep private, so I'm intrigued to hear how you found out.'

Adam obviously couldn't give away what he'd learned without revealing how he'd done so, by methods which weren't exactly conventional. But he was also very aware that Fran didn't yet know what he'd discovered. He had no other choice but to bluff his way through this.

Vinny shrugged. 'I overheard Harrison talking about it with Miranda, if you must know, on the very day we arrived. So, I don't think it's quite the secret you thought it was.'

'And you're certain?' he asked, his pulse beginning to race. 'What did you actually hear them say?'

'Miranda said that Emily was one thing, but playing the same trick twice with Tony was quite a different matter. She was practically hissing at him, furious, but Harrison almost laughed at her, told her to calm down. Said for heaven's sake, Tony went to prison for manslaughter and had served his time, it wasn't like he'd murdered anyone.'

18

To give her her due, Fran hid her surprise very well, probably better than Adam had. He just had to hope Vinny was so busy trying to figure out what was going on that he hadn't taken much notice of either of them.

But Vinny's revelation had introduced another layer of mystery to the situation. If Harrison and Miranda both knew about Tony's background, then why was he still on the show? There was one last thing Adam needed to check.

'So, when you heard Miranda and Harrison talking, what did you think?' he asked. 'Only, the other day, you made what could be construed as a threat towards Tony. What exactly are you planning to do with this information now that it's fallen into your lap?'

Vinny looked first at Fran and then at Adam. 'Isn't it obvious?' he replied. 'I was going to make damn sure I won the competition. Anybody who comes on this show and doesn't think it's rigged is an idiot. Well, two can play at that game. Information is power... and if things weren't looking as if they were going my way, I was going to remind Miranda and

Harrison that Joe Public would be very keen to hear tales of underhand goings-on with their favourite show...'

'I must be so naïve,' said Fran, a few minutes later. They had watched Vinny make his way back to the stable and were now safely tucked away in Fran's room, out of sight, and hopefully earshot too. 'In all the years I've been watching this show, it never crossed my mind it could be rigged.'

'But we don't know for definite that it is,' replied Adam. 'Vinny obviously thinks it is, but then he doesn't exactly have a high moral code, does he?'

Fran pulled a face. 'Indeed. It would make sense though. Emily was supposed to be the underdog, the contestant everyone would be manipulated into rooting for. Then, lo and behold, when she won, people would have their choice validated and everyone would be happy and, importantly, keen to tune into the next series.'

Adam nodded. 'And when that little plan fell through, Harrison could have set his sights on Tony instead. The question is though, does Tony know his secret is out and that he's become Harrison's latest project? Because if he does, I wonder how he's feeling.'

Fran caught his look. 'You mean he might not be all that happy about it? And *unhappy* enough to want to do something?'

'Maybe he already has,' said Adam, raising his eyebrows. 'Both Miranda and Harrison knew about Tony's past, and now one of them is dead.'

Fran stared at him in horror. 'Are we really saying Tony could be our murderer? He seems such a gentleman. Honestly, he's so polite, I can't imagine him as a crazed killer.'

'Can you ever imagine anyone in that role, Fran?'

'Okay, point taken.'

'And what about the presents Miranda had been receiving?

Do we think Tony might have been responsible for those as well?'

Fran wrinkled her nose. 'It's possible, but that would mean Tony has some past association with her. The first present was left months ago and, as far as I'm aware, the uncovering of his past has only happened recently. We've been tying the two things together, the presents and Miranda's murder, but maybe they're not connected at all.'

'We shouldn't rule out Vinny though,' added Adam, 'because he's obviously not averse to snooping, so maybe he's not averse to sneaking into places and leaving little gifts behind either?'

Fran nodded. 'We need to speak to Nell, and soon. You and I have been in enough situations like this to know that someone who's killed once doesn't stop to think twice about their next victim, particularly when their secrets look like they're about to be revealed. Vinny hasn't exactly kept quiet about his intentions, he could be putting himself in real danger. And Harrison too, for that matter. If Tony knows that both he and Miranda were aware—' She broke off as a quiet knock sounded at the door. She sighed, getting up to answer it. 'That's probably Midge telling me I'm supposed to be elsewhere.'

But it wasn't Midge. It was the last person she'd expected to see.

'Sorry, Fran, I know you're probably trying to have a break, but I wondered if I might have a word with you?'

Fran stood back, heart hammering. 'Tony, hi... Adam and I were just having a bit of a chat, about the, er, book, you know.'

Adam got to his feet, moving to her side.

Tony still looked apologetic. 'I hope you don't mind, only I saw you leave the stable earlier. And when I spotted Vinny leaving not long after, I wondered if you'd arranged to meet. I went out to the courtyard but you'd both gone.'

Fran didn't know what to say. Should she admit it? Or

pretend she didn't know what Tony was talking about?

'I've kind of been keeping tabs on Vinny myself,' added Tony, pausing to give a small smile. 'Bit pathetic, really, but wondering when he's going to make good on his promise is driving me mad. Did he tell you about me? Actually, don't bother to answer that, I can see by the look on your faces he has.' Tony's shoulders slumped. 'In a way I'm quite relieved, you know. The tension has been almost unbearable. I found you because I wanted to tell you myself. I thought if I came clean, maybe you wouldn't think so badly of me.' He stood, hands clasped, awkwardly waiting for a reply.

'Do you want to come in?' Fran asked. 'Sorry, it's just a bit of a surprise.' It might end up being the biggest mistake she ever made, but Fran couldn't bear the expression on his face. He looked like a small animal that had been kicked repeatedly.

Tony nodded, running a hand over his hair. 'Thank you. I'm not sure why I'm here really, I...'

Fran pulled out a chair from under the dressing table, turning it around so he could sit down. 'I've been told I'm a good listener,' she said.

'What I don't understand is how Vinny found out,' said Tony, sinking onto the chair. 'It's not the kind of thing you bring up in polite conversation. Although Harrison knows, of course, and I assume Miranda did too. I declared it on my application form because I knew if I didn't, they'd only find out from the checks they do.' He paused. 'But it's not what you're thinking. Actually, maybe it is.'

Fran gave him an encouraging smile.

'We are talking about the same thing, I suppose? The prison thing? I ought to check in case I'm about to make a total prat of myself.'

Fran nodded gently. 'Do you want to tell us about it?' she asked.

'I'd like to know what Vinny told you.'

There was no point in lying now. Whatever the situation, Fran could see it had taken enormous courage for Tony to speak to them. 'Not much,' she said. 'He mostly tried to deny he'd been snooping around, and that there was nothing wrong with making what sounded suspiciously like blackmail threats. He said you'd been in prison, for manslaughter.'

Tony hung his head. 'It's true, I'm not going to deny it. I was convicted when I was eighteen, served eight years, released when I was twenty-six. I'm now thirty-two. And during these last six years I've done everything I can to rebuild my life. Coming on this show was supposed to be a celebration of how far I've come. I've a long way to go yet, I know that, but...' He closed his eyes. 'I guess that's it now. Dream over.'

Fran gave Adam a wayward glance. 'Why is it dream over?'

'Because I can't see Vinny keeping his mouth shut, can you? I mean, he's obviously spoken to you because you're writing a book about the show. No doubt he thought you'd be very interested in his juicy bit of gossip.'

'Actually, Tony, that wasn't it at all. We followed him because *we* wanted to talk, not the other way around.' She looked over at Adam, eyebrows raised, and received an answering nod. 'Maybe it's time we were honest with you as well.' She paused, seeing his confusion. 'I'm not writing a book, Tony, and Adam isn't my assistant,' she said. 'I'm a professional caterer, but I also happen to know the DCI investigating Miranda's murder. You could say Adam and I were asked to come here on a consultant basis.'

'Oh God,' groaned Tony.

'And we were rather concerned that Vinny claimed to have knowledge of certain secrets.'

'Is this to do with what the detective said about Miranda? That they had been investigating a series of incidents prior to her death?'

Fran nodded. 'Except that, tragically, she was killed before we could work out who had been responsible for those incidents.'

'Look, I swear, I had nothing to do with any of this, despite what Vinny has told you, he—'

Fran leaned forward. 'Tony, Vinny doesn't know any of the details, he simply overheard Miranda and Harrison talking about you. That's how he found out.'

Tony looked at Adam and then back at Fran. 'Harrison and Miranda? Why, what were they saying?' Either Tony was a very good actor, or he had absolutely no idea what Harrison's plans for him were. Plans for him and the show.

'There wasn't much detail, but they were arguing – about you. Vinny thinks the show is rigged,' Fran explained, 'and so when he overheard you being discussed it struck him that he might be able to use that information to his advantage, especially if he thought he was about to be sent home. He wants to win and, rather unfortunately, you seem to have become his insurance policy.'

'Me?' Tony clearly still wasn't seeing the bigger picture. 'But the show isn't rigged, that's daft...' He swallowed. 'Is that what you think, too?'

'We've uncovered some other information which suggests it's probably true, yes.'

'And you think I'm in on it as well?'

'I didn't say that,' said Fran quickly. 'If you're saying you didn't know anything about it, then I believe you.' She held his look, praying she was right to trust her instincts. 'I don't know what Harrison had planned, although it seems likely that, whatever it was, Miranda didn't know about it. When she found out, she certainly didn't approve, but now that she's dead we have no idea whether Harrison intends to make something of it or not.' She swallowed. 'But we think that might be his intention.'

Panic struck Tony's face. 'This can't happen,' he blustered. 'It would mean I'd be essentially profiting from someone's death and I won't do that under any circumstances. God, that's... sick. What kind of person could possibly think my past is some kind of sensationalist story? I *have* turned my life around, and I'm proud to have done so, but I don't want to capitalise on it. Can you imagine how Stephen's mum would feel, knowing that I'd used the death of her son as some kind of springboard for my career?' He shook his head, utterly distraught. 'Winning this competition would mean the world to me, but I want to win it fairly and squarely. I'll have to leave, it's the only way.'

Fran put out her hand to stop Tony rushing off there and then. 'No, Tony, wait! Listen... We need to bring this to Detective Bradley's attention. She's already had Harrison answering questions about the show so she's going be very interested to hear this as well. If it's any consolation, he'll be lucky to have a show left at all by the time she's finished with him. He certainly won't be rigging anything.'

'Yes, but word will still get out. The press will get wind and that'll be the end of it. I've learned a lot of things since I left prison, and one of the most important is that it doesn't matter how hard you try, people always see the bad in you first. That's exactly why I don't tell anyone unless I have to. Haven't you ever made a mistake in the past? Or maybe you have, but you got lucky and that mistake didn't blow up in your face and turn into the single most defining thing of your life. Maybe your mistake got overlooked by people. Maybe the universe was smiling on you the day when it could have all gone wrong and steered you back onto the right path. And when it did, maybe you listened instead of thinking you knew best.' He turned his head away in frustration. 'You both thought the same as everyone else will... You might not have meant to show it, but it was there all the same.'

Adam cleared his throat. 'You're right,' he said. 'And of all people I should know how it feels to have assumptions made about you, it's been happening to me my whole life. Assumptions that were wrong because nobody bothered to find out the truth. Instead they labelled me. It turned me into a near recluse and it's only since meeting Fran that I've begun to realise that people aren't all bad. When I heard you'd been to prison, my imagination conjured up some kind of pantomime villain, someone who is nothing like the man sitting in front of me. And that was wrong, I'm sorry.'

Fran smiled at Adam, nodding her head gently. When they'd met he'd been in a cupboard, so keen was he to hide away from the outside world. Admittedly, she'd been hiding in the cupboard too, but that was another story. Adam's somewhat different view of life had set him apart from his peers while at school, and his intelligence, which couldn't be measured in conventional ways, had been overlooked and ignored by an education system which didn't know how to bring out the best in him. He'd come a very long way since then.

Tony smiled too, colouring slightly, and Fran could see he'd accepted what Adam had said. And he'd been right. The man sitting in front of her may have done something awful at one time in his life, but he was no villain now. He was casually dressed, in neat, pressed clothes which were neither the height of fashion nor from yesteryear. His hair was cut conservatively, and he wore a simple watch with a plain strap. It was the kind of look which, in the nicest possible way, didn't draw attention to itself. He was softly spoken, and had been polite, courteous and quietly good-humoured. And he was humble. She had seen him at work, and although his passion for what he did was clear to see, it wasn't born of arrogance and overconfidence, but instead had arisen through hard graft and application to his craft.

'You probably thought I was the one who killed Miranda, didn't you? Anything to protect my secret from coming out and, let's face it, if I'd killed once, no doubt I could do it again.' Tony gave a wry smile. 'I don't blame you. If I wasn't me, I'd probably think the same and I guess you were only trying to help. But I swear, I had nothing to do with Miranda's death. This competition is part of my future, a future I've tried hard to cultivate. Why would I want to throw that away?'

Adam nodded. 'Yes, I can see that.'

'Why don't you tell us what happened?' suggested Fran.

Tony was quiet for a moment, looking for a place to start. 'My story's no different to a lot of people's,' he began. 'I was young, too young to know any better, and I fell in with the wrong group of people. Before I knew it, I was drinking heavily and dabbling in drugs. I was a nuisance, and not very pleasant, but nothing worse than that. Until one night, me and a group of so-called mates went out on the booze. Long story short, I wasn't really sure what I'd taken, there were plenty of things on offer and before the night was over, things between us turned sour. We took our fight outside and, in the heat of the moment, I shoved one of the lads, Stephen, I shoved him hard. He fell into the road, straight into the path of a car. He was killed instantly and—' He broke off, visibly trying to control his emotions. 'And that was that. I still remember the awful moment when I realised what was happening. How I tried to save him, tried to pull him back, but my hands just pawed at empty air... he had already gone.'

Fran was about to say something, when Tony put out his hand to stop her. 'No, don't tell me you're sorry, or that you understand. I deserved everything that came my way. I had the same choices everyone else did, but I made bad ones. No one forced me to do any of the things I did. I could have turned my life around at any point, but I didn't, until it was too late. People try to be kind and say I was a victim of circumstance, or something similar. Maybe there's a degree of truth in that, but it's no excuse. I caused another man's death and I went to prison for it.'

'You said you served eight years.'

'Yes, that's right, and prison is where I learned to cook. I got put on kitchen detail and, believe me, when you're in there, there isn't much you look forward to. It crept up on me slowly, realising how good it felt to make something which people enjoyed. And when the other inmates began to take notice of what I was doing, it made me feel better. Nothing had done that in a very long time. They teased me, made fun of me and my cakes, but I know it was only because they'd enjoyed them. And it was enough. Plus, I was lucky – the chef there was the real deal, once upon a time. Life had dealt him a few hard knocks along the way, but he had just enough spark left to recognise someone who wanted to learn. And he pretty much taught me all I know. When I got out, I worked in a series of cafes and greasy spoons, anywhere an ex-con could work and be left alone and I thought about what I wanted for my future. It's where I met Nat, my wife. She didn't care what I'd done before, she just cared about where I wanted to go and, more than anything, she wanted to go with me. So, we've worked and we've scrimped and saved and now, finally, we have enough money to start a business of our own.'

'So, winning a show like this would be a real boost?' said Fran.

'It would. I knew there was no guarantee I would win, but I hoped that even appearing on it would be enough to give me the start I needed. I've dreamed for so long about getting up every day and doing something I love, but also because the very best thing about having my own business will be that people stop asking questions. No more application forms, no more interviews. No one will want to know where I've come from, they'll only be interested in what I'm doing now, and where I'm going next. But I'm not taking part in the show if there's the slightest chance it isn't above board. So whatever Harrison has planned, he can think again.'

Adam nodded. 'This isn't going to be easy, but I think you need to speak to Nell. It would only have been a matter of time before they found out about your past anyway, they're running background checks on everyone.'

'Which will shoot me straight to the top of the suspect list, no doubt.'

'Perhaps, but getting there first and telling her what you've just told us has to count for something,' said Adam.

'And, don't forget, you also have an alibi,' added Fran. 'You were with me when Miranda was killed. We were all in the green room having a break between segments.'

Adam stared at her.

'It's true,' she said. 'Tony was there the whole time.'

'That's what I don't understand about any of this,' said Adam. 'According to Midge, everyone had an alibi.'

Fran nodded. 'Mmm, everyone except her. To the point where the poor girl's even been wondering if she might have killed Miranda while she was sleepwalking.'

'And yet, somehow, someone must have had an opportunity to kill Miranda and—'

'What? Have you thought of something?' interrupted Fran.

Adam frowned. 'I don't know. There's something, but...' He growled in frustration. 'It's like it's on the tip of my tongue but whatever it is just won't make itself known.'

'That's usually my line,' Fran replied. And it was. She had a photographic memory, and over the course of their last three cases it had come in very handy. She had seen small details during the investigations which had later become pivotal pieces of evidence, she just hadn't known it at the time.

Adam shook his head. 'Never mind, it'll come to me.'

'So, what do we do now?' asked Tony.

'Speak to Nell – DCI Bradley – as soon as we can,' said Adam. 'I'll go and see her.'

Fran nodded, checking her watch. 'And *we* had better get back over to the stable,' she said, smiling at Tony. 'Our break is nearly over and you've got a competition to win.'

19

Adam's knock on the trailer door landed just a fraction of a second before it opened. In fact, had he not stepped smartly backwards, he would either have been knocked flying or had Nell land virtually in his arms, neither of which was a pleasing prospect. Nell stared at him, bemused, almost as if she'd forgotten who he was.

'Is Fran in the stable?' she asked.

Adam nodded. 'But she's about to start cooking again.'

'Oh... I wanted to fill her in about my little chat with Harrison.' She frowned. 'I had him squirming like a worm on a line but, sadly, I think we drew a blank as far as the murder is concerned. He pretty much came clean about Emily, admitting he might have been a little over-zealous and "misguided" about her role in the show, but that was all. However, he categorically denied there was a rift between him and Miranda. He said they might have had a few words about the situation, but no more than that, and Miranda certainly never threatened to do anything about it. He also reiterated that it made no sense for him to kill Miranda, not when she was the star of his show.'

'It's not his show though, is it?' countered Adam. 'At least, it wasn't... Remember the argument I overheard between him and Miranda. She told him he'd never get control of the show. "Not while I live and breathe" is what she actually said. There's also something else you should know – Harrison might have come clean about Emily, but it seems his ambitions to control the competition didn't stop there.'

He quickly recounted the conversations he and Fran had had with both Vinny and then Tony, the details of which had Nell looking as if she might explode.

'I don't bloody believe this,' she muttered, looking across at her DC. 'Palmer, would you mind fetching Mr Shaw, please. Again. And I don't care what he's doing, I want to see him now.' She smiled sweetly. 'Thank you, Adam. That's very useful.'

Adam certainly wouldn't like to be in Harrison's shoes. He would, however, like to be a fly-on-the-wall when Nell questioned him, but as that obviously wasn't possible, there was nothing for it but to go back to his laptop and carry on a little digging of his own. First though, there was something else he wanted to check.

Midge looked just as harassed as she had the last time Adam had seen her. In fact, she almost collided with him as she came around the corner of the courtyard. She stopped suddenly, cursing as her phone slid off her clipboard and onto the hard flagstone floor. Adam rushed to pick it up.

'Sorry,' they both said at the same time.

'No, it was my fault,' said Midge. 'I wasn't looking where I was going.' She reached out to take back her phone. 'Now you know why I have such a heavy-duty case on this. It would be in smithereens otherwise.' She peered at it anyway, giving him a sheepish smile. 'No harm done.'

'It was you I was after, actually,' replied Adam. 'Do you have a minute?'

'I have about thirty-six,' she said, pulling a face. 'I was just going to let the dogs out for a wee. Can we walk and talk?'

Adam nodded. 'Fran and I were talking about everyone's alibis earlier and she mentioned how convinced you are that Miranda's death was your fault. Even to the point that you might have murdered her in your sleep. If you don't mind me saying, that's a rather curious thing to admit to when everyone else is busy strenuously denying their guilt.'

'Yes, well, as I said, the facts don't lie. And everyone else has an alibi. I don't. It's very simple.'

'Everyone else *seems* to have an alibi,' replied Adam. 'But clearly someone doesn't, because that someone murdered Miranda.'

Midge gave him a curious look. 'Thank you. I know you're trying to be kind, but I've plotted out the whole thing, virtually minute by minute, everyone's movements, and there's only me unaccounted for.'

Adam studied her face: pale, tired-looking, and entirely open and honest. 'When you say you've plotted everyone's movements, do you mean written down? Or just in your head?'

'No, I have it written down,' Midge replied. 'On a big graph thing, like a timeline. I can show it to you if you want, but it won't do you much good. All it will tell you is that I killed Miranda.' She straightened the paper under the clip of her board. 'I didn't, of course, but on paper, I definitely did.'

Adam had never been inside the cottage where Midge was staying but, although tiny, it was beautifully formed. The front door opened straight into a small sitting room, with a flagged floor. It was almost entirely covered by a rug which could have come straight from a middle-eastern souk, while a fireplace dominated the wall opposite. To his right, a spiral staircase rose to the room above.

'I'll just let the dogs into the garden,' said Midge as they entered, dropping her clipboard and phone onto the sofa. 'Come through.'

The kitchen was a long, thin strip, which ran along the back of the house. Another room had been tacked on at one end, and as Midge opened the door, there was a mad scramble of fur as both dogs came hurtling through the gap. They launched themselves at Midge, who dropped to her knees.

'Hello, boys...' She wrapped her arms around both dogs as they wiggled with delight, clearly overjoyed to see her. 'Have you been good?' she asked.

At her words, the spaniels sat, rooted to the spot, but trembling with excitement.

She laughed. 'They're not daft, as you can see. "Have you been good?" is code for "would you like a biscuit?"' Reaching into a cupboard, Midge withdrew a packet of bone-shaped treats and held one out for each dog. Her fingers almost disappeared into the mouth of the smallest, who was a little too exuberant in his haste to eat his snack. Midge just smiled.

With their biscuits finished, she opened the back door and the dogs shot outside into the garden. 'I love them to bits,' she said, rinsing her fingers under the tap. 'But they don't half make a mess. And the drool is revolting.'

'What will happen to them now?' asked Adam.

Midge shrugged. 'I'll keep them,' she replied without hesitation. 'No one else wants them, and I'm not having them passed from pillar to post. Poor things don't have much of a life as it is, but...' She tipped her head to one side. 'Maybe when all this is over, I'll be able to make a few changes. My job for one.'

'But I thought you loved working on the show?'

'I do. I *did*. Let's just say it's not the show I once thought it was and, despite the fact that Harrison doesn't seem to have realised it yet, I don't actually work for him. I worked for Miranda, and obviously...' She pulled a face.

'What will you do?'

'I have a little money saved,' she replied. 'We spend a lot of time on the road and when we do, my accommodation and food is paid for so that helps. Plus, we're so busy I don't get much time to spend money. I'm not really sure what I'll do, but I think what I need most is some time. Time away from the show, so I can relax a bit and think properly about my future. That's if I don't end up in prison, of course...' She blinked. 'Sorry, you want to see my timeline thing, don't you? I'll go fetch it.'

It was another of those moments when Adam wished Fran was here. She would know exactly what to say, whereas he felt horribly awkward in the face of Midge's emotion.

'Would you like a cup of tea?' he asked. 'I... I could make one for you, if you like?'

Midge glanced at the clock on the wall. 'I'm not sure I really have time,' she said. 'But, thank you.' She gave him a small smile. 'I don't get tea made for me very often.'

'Then I'll make one anyway. If you don't have time to drink it here, I'll take it to wherever you're going next. How's that?'

She dipped her head. 'I'll get the plan,' she said, blushing a little.

Spending so much time with Fran had taught him lots of things, and one of those was how to find his way around almost any kitchen. Working comfortably in unfamiliar places was something Fran took in her stride, but she had taught him a few pointers and, so far, they'd proved to be true. 'You just have to think about your kitchen at home,' she'd said. 'Think about where your mum keeps her mugs – I bet you any money they're in the cupboard over the kettle.' In this case, Adam didn't even need to look, the mugs were hanging on a small tree beside the cooker. He selected one and carried the kettle over to the sink, where he filled it with water.

He wasn't sure what he expected Midge to return with, but it certainly wasn't the huge scroll of paper she laid out on one of the work surfaces.

'It didn't start off this big,' she explained, 'it sort of grew.'

He stared at it in astonishment, peering closer. 'This is incredible. How long did it take to do this?'

Midge wrinkled her nose. 'Not that long. I have all my notes, you see, so all I had to do was copy everything down.'

He was looking at several sheets of A4 paper sellotaped together. They had been filled with a grid, along the top of which Midge had written everyone's name: Harrison, Judy, Hope, herself, Sam, Woody and all of the contestants. Even he and Fran were there. Along the side of the grid were five-minute interval markers, starting from a point fifteen minutes before the window of time when Miranda had been killed, right up until ten minutes past the point when Midge found her body at four o'clock. Within each time interval the movements of every single person had been added.

'And this is accurate, is it?' he asked, although there was really no need to check.

Midge nodded. 'As I said, most of it came from my notes, because even if I'm not around, I know where everyone is supposed to be. And I've checked the details. It's easy to do when there's a group of you because it's rare that anyone does anything on their own.'

Adam studied the information, picking a name and following it through the timeline. It was a complete picture of the exact situation at the time of Miranda's death, and seeing it like this, in visual form, made getting a feel for what had happened very easy. On the day in question, Miranda had been filming in the stable until a quarter to four. She had gone back to her trailer, where Midge found her dead fifteen minutes later and, during that time, everyone, apart from Midge, was accounted for. He frowned, peering closer at a detail on the chart.

'What are these?' he asked, pointing to a red asterisk beside one of the time stamps. The page was littered with them, green ones too.

'Those are where I've checked the alibi, that people were where they were supposed to be. The red asterisks are where one other person has provided the alibi... so there, for example, where you have Judy and Harrison in the stable, they have each alibied the other. And where there are green asterisks, multiple people can verify the alibi. That's mainly true of the contestants because they were all in a room together.'

Adam nodded. He didn't need to point out what was clearly evident – Midge had already long since worked it out for herself. The only gaping hole in the whole grid was the one left by her, when she had been catching forty winks, right here in this cottage. Unaccompanied, unaccounted for and un-alibied. What must it feel like to be staring an apparently incontrovertible truth square in the face?

The kettle came to the boil with an audible click as it switched itself off. Adam smiled. 'I'll make the tea,' he said.

'Pretty damning evidence, isn't it?' remarked Midge a few minutes later as she gratefully sipped her drink.

'It's an amazing piece of work,' he replied, sidestepping her question. 'Why haven't you shown it to Nell?'

Midge stared at him. 'Are you mad?' she asked. 'She'll have me in handcuffs quicker than you can say you're under arrest.'

Adam winced. 'I would hope not,' he said. There was still something niggling he couldn't put his finger on. 'The key must lie on this grid somewhere, the one which unlocks this whole thing. Because if you didn't kill Miranda, then the answer to whoever did is on those pieces of paper.'

'Where exactly?' asked Midge, eyebrows raised. 'I've been over it time and time again. There are no gaps in anyone's movements.'

There certainly didn't seem to be.

Midge blew across the top of her mug. 'I started this to prove I was innocent, and when I found it proved exactly the opposite, I decided it was better kept to myself. It's not really rocket science though, is it? Anyone could have done the same. The timings on the show are strict, they have to be, and the crew are old hands. They're used to the routine – on different shows, and in different locations, admittedly, but essentially it's the same.'

'Then those notes you keep on your clipboard – why are they so necessary?'

'Because, as you've seen, the show isn't filmed in a linear fashion. The viewer sees a chronological order of events, but that's only because the show is edited to look that way. We film introductions, end pieces, interviews with competitors, all out of sequence in the gaps the schedule provides. It's so we can utilise everyone's time more efficiently, otherwise people end up endlessly hanging around. Miranda hated it, she wouldn't do it, in fact. So I keep lists of what goes on each day. That can change depending on where we are in the competition, and what Harrison wants to shoot or reshoot. Then I fill in the gaps as best I can, depending on who else is free. I always think it's a bit like being an air-traffic controller. There are all these things going on simultaneously and someone has to keep them on track. The Christmas shows are way easier because there are less competitors. The regular shows have twice as many, so it's far more complex.'

Suddenly, Adam could see how if someone wanted an opportunity to slip away unnoticed then, with knowledge like Midge's, it would be very easy to do. And, as she'd just said, if she could do it, then theoretically so could anyone else. There had to be a gap somewhere, he just had to find it.

'Can I borrow this?' he asked. 'Just to look at. A "two heads are better than one" kind of thing.'

She paused. 'It's my only copy,' she replied. 'Do you really think you might be able to find something? Something I've missed?'

'I can't promise,' he said. 'But I'll do my very best.'

Midge looked down at the spread of paper, still unsure whether to agree to his request. Adam understood, it was the only thing making her feel she had any control over the situation.

'How about if I promise not to show it to Nell?' he added hopefully.

With one final look and a decisive nod, Midge folded up the paper and handed it over. 'It's weird,' she said. 'When Miranda was killed, I thought my world had come to an end. But only two days later, I've begun to think about how my life could be, the choices I might have, the freedoms.' She swallowed. 'Do your best, Adam, I'd quite like to have a future.'

It was fruitless, of course. Another two hours of staring at Midge's grid had given Adam a stiff neck and a vague headache, but that was about all. He was no further forward. The answer was there, he was sure of it. He just needed to look at things from a different point of view.

The afternoon's competition would soon be drawing to a close and Adam desperately wanted to catch up with Nell to see how her questioning of Harrison had gone. Midge might have had the opportunity to kill Miranda, but Harrison surely had the motive.

'Categorically denied knowing Tony had a prison record,' said Nell when Adam finally caught up with her. 'Acted very surprised when I told him... badly, I might add.' She rolled her eyes. 'I mentioned that the last time I looked, I didn't have the word gullible tattooed on my forehead and, seeing that we have a witness who overheard him and Miranda arguing about Tony, he might like to revise his statement.'

Adam put a hand over his mouth to hide his smile. 'And did he?'

'Oh yes. Couldn't wait to tell us how he only had Tony's best interests at heart, and truly wanted what he thought was best for him. He spoiled it slightly by then rolling out a sob story about how difficult the industry is, and how hard it is to keep momentum going on a show that's been popular for many years. He said there had been a few "differences of opinion" with Miranda, who wanted everything to stay exactly the same as it always had, whereas he could see certain elements needed a bit of "freshening up".' She pulled a face. 'So, you were right – Harrison definitely sees the show as ripe for a bit of a make-over. He was very quick to defend his thinking about the probable benefit to Tony's career following a show win, but when I pointed out that it was actually quite a serious breach of trust and a data-protection issue, he back-pedalled at speed, saying he quite understood that Tony might want to keep things quiet.'

She gave a tight smile. 'Harrison has finally and very sensibly concluded that he's a person of importance to us and has decided to cooperate fully. He can say all he likes, however: Miranda was the one obvious person standing in the way of his plans for the show and we've all seen how quickly those plans swung into place as soon as she was dead. Unseemly haste doesn't even begin to describe it. And that's in addition to putting his girlfriend at the helm. Harrison is beginning to look as guilty as they come, I'm afraid, which is somewhat of a shame.'

'A shame?' repeated Adam. 'Why?'

'Because he currently has a cast-iron alibi. I've checked everyone's statements again, and it's been verified by at least four other people. Harrison's movements are accounted for for the whole period of time during which Miranda could have been killed. He never left the stable. And that's the real crux of the problem here, Adam, because the same is also true for everyone else, Judy included. I still don't believe she's quite as sanguine about having her recipes pinched as she's making out, and Pea's another one who could be harbouring a serious grudge against the woman who stole her limelight all those years ago, but according to what we know, none of them can be our killer.' She paused, studying his face.

'And then there's Midge. Adam, I really hope you can come up with something magical soon because it's not looking good for her. Other people may well have had a motive to kill Miranda, but no one else has motive *and* opportunity.' She sighed. 'I have zero forensics too, nothing to even hint at someone other than Midge being responsible. Miranda's trailer is covered in prints from a number of different people, all of which you would expect to find there. And there was nothing on the murder weapon and no handy trail of blood to follow. Everything we've tested for blood residue has come up negative as well. I've even asked the pathologist several more times if she's absolutely certain about the time of death, and I won't ask her again. I'm skating on perilously thin ice.'

Adam nodded, glum. Perhaps they might have to revise their opinion of Midge after all. Fran wasn't going to like it one little bit, but the facts didn't lie...

'Okay,' he replied, 'message understood. I might go see how Fran is getting on.'

'Oh, she'll be fine,' said Nell airily.

Something about the way in which Nell spoke made him check her comment. 'You seem pretty certain of that and yet after you'd finished with Harrison I bet he wouldn't dare even think about fixing the outcome of the competition.'

Nell actually smirked, something Adam wasn't sure he had ever seen her do before.

'That's absolutely true, but I may have interfered myself. Just a little. I've had quite a busy few hours, in fact, not only talking to Harrison, but having a little chat with Tony.' She smiled. 'And a very satisfactory conversation with Vinny as well.'

'Oh yes? What did you say to *him*?'

'It was a similar conversation to ones you and I have had in the past, Adam. On the occasions when you've been a little... unethical. But, whereas I went easy on you, I'm afraid I gave it to Mr Evans with both barrels. I told him in no uncertain terms that he was not a police officer and I did not appreciate his vigilante-style "help". He wasn't "helping" by trying to uncover people's secrets, he was wasting precious police time and trespassing to boot. I rounded off by saying that he is to keep absolutely quiet about Tony's past and if I ever catch so much as a whiff of him having told anyone about it, I will come after him and throw the full force of the law at him.'

Adam paled. 'Did you really say all that?'

'Pretty much.'

Nell looked away, but not before Adam caught a slight twitch at the corner of her mouth. Was she teasing him? He had no doubt she'd told Vinny what she said – he remembered his past conversations with Nell and if she'd been going easy on him, then—

'I also told him he needed to have a calamitous afternoon in the kitchen,' continued Nell. 'So calamitous, in fact, that Judy will have no choice but to send him home. Because, if he doesn't, I will tell everyone why, and have him thrown out instead.'

Adam grinned. 'And what about Tony?'

'What about him?'

'Will anything happen to him?'

Nell gave him a pointed look. 'Why should it? He's done nothing wrong.'

Adam quickly nodded. 'No, of course not.'

Nell's look softened. 'But you were absolutely right to bring this to me. It's got blown out of proportion, but in essence the fact Tony has a conviction for manslaughter could have had a very real bearing on this case. Information like that would ordinarily have jumped him straight to the top of my suspect list. But, there's nothing to connect him with Miranda, and you might find this hard to believe, Adam...' She broke off to give him a wry smile. 'But over the years I have developed a nose for when someone is telling the truth. And I believe what Tony told me. He made a mistake when he was very young, and while that will never alter the fact that he caused a man's death, Tony has paid his debt. He'll be paying for it every day for the rest of his life, but he *is* one of the success stories. He's trying to turn his life around; in fact, he already has, and I hope his success continues.'

She dropped her head and gave Adam a sideways glance. 'He also has an alibi, as do all the contestants, and until I find out something to the contrary, he's off the hook. Don't go spreading that around, incidentally, you know how I like to keep people on their toes.'

20

'And then there were four,' said Fran, staring morosely at the kitchen window. Another day, another breakfast... She picked up a piece of toast and, with a sigh, bit off a corner. Vinny had indeed left the competition the night before, which just left her, Christine, Tony and Pea fighting for the title. The thought left her cold. Winning was becoming less and less important as time went by, and the trial of another day's competition was almost unbearable.

'At least it's only 'cause people are going home,' said Adam cheerfully. 'I mean, it's not like Agatha Christie, where everyone's being bumped off one by one.'

Nell looked up sharply. 'That's not even funny,' she said. 'Do you want me to give you the statistics for how many murderers go on to kill again? Because if I do, it may put even you off your sausages.'

Adam winced and shook his head, his fork stilled halfway to his mouth. He regarded the piece of sausage it held with a solemn expression before shoving it in his mouth.

'I don't suppose anyone will miss Vinny much,' added Fran. 'Although I'm finding it increasingly hard to understand how

Harrison thinks he can keep the show running. We're constantly being told it's all in the edit, but I'm not sure you can edit something you don't have in the first place. "Cobble together" might be a more accurate description of what Harrison's going to end up with. And if you arrest someone, that's it.'

'Chance would be a fine thing,' muttered Nell. 'I'm falling over people with motives to kill Miranda, and not one of them could have done it. As for Mr Shaw, he gets deeper in doo-doo every day. Nothing would give me greater pleasure than to arrest him right now, the man's really beginning to annoy me.'

Fran snuck Adam a surreptitious look, trying not to laugh. Despite the seriousness of the situation, Nell had such a way with words.

'News about his finances came in late last night,' continued Nell, 'and it doesn't look good. *Country Cooks Cook* is the only show making Harrison's production company any money. And even that isn't what it used to be. Income has fallen year on year, which makes his insistence that the show must go on a little easier to understand, *and* why he was so keen to liven things up a bit. Miranda might have been a massive star, but as far as the TV networks go, everything has its day. Folks around here are very keen to propagate the idea that the show is becoming more successful as each year passes, but the numbers show a very different story. Viewers are turning away, and in quite significant numbers.'

Fran nodded. 'So you think Harrison is simply trying to stay ahead of the curve?'

'Looks like it. And the only person standing in his way was Miranda – ironically, the very person who made him so much money in the first place. Given the argument you overheard, Adam, it's obvious why Harrison was fighting to change the show's direction. He clearly wasn't going to get Miranda's support, and with her gone he thinks he has carte blanche to do what he likes. His company has several outstanding loans, and he personally has an enormous mortgage. If he doesn't make a go of things soon he's going to be on his uppers in a very short space of time.'

She picked up her mug. 'People like Harrison don't do your blood pressure any favours, or your digestion. We're day three now and I don't need to tell you that the pressure for me to make an arrest is rising with...' She paused as a knock sounded at the kitchen door.

It was Clare Palmer. 'Sorry to interrupt, Boss, but you need to see this. Sally Grainger's medical records.'

Nell took the sheet of paper she was being offered and began to read, eyes raking every line of the report. Fran was desperate to know what it said.

After what seemed like an age, Nell looked up. 'Thank you, Clare, excellent work. I think you can guess what my next question will be.'

Clare smiled. 'Already on it, Ma'am. I'll let you know when I find anything.'

A slow smile crept up Nell's face as Clare left the room. 'It seems her name wasn't the only thing Miranda left behind,' she said. 'Because Sally Grainger had a child, when she was only eighteen.'

'But Miranda had no children,' said Adam.

'Exactly. Yet the pregnancy went to full term, so where is the child now?'

'Adopted?' suggested Fran.

Nell nodded. 'That's what Clare has just beetled off to discover. The medical records don't give us any detail, but if the child was adopted, we'll be able to find out.'

Fran stared at her. 'If it's bloody Harrison, I think I might explode.'

'If it's bloody Harrison, I might just explode with you,' said Nell. 'But, unfortunately, or fortunately if your name happens to be Harrison, the child was a girl. Besides, Harrison is too old.

If Miranda was eighteen when she had her baby then she would be—'

'Thirty-four,' answered Adam immediately, before sitting back in his chair at Nell's ferocious look.

'Yes, thank you, Adam. I'm quite capable of mental arithmetic. So, not Judy... or Pea, they're too old.'

'Not Midge,' said Fran, 'she's too young. Nor Hope, she's thirty-six.' She narrowed her eyes. 'Christine maybe?'

'Hmm...' said Nell, taking a drink. 'Christine... now there's a thought.' She drained the rest of her coffee. 'It's a long shot, but in the absence of a confirmed identity, worth following up. I'll check her details.'

'We were beginning to run out of suspects again,' said Adam. 'So, fingers crossed it's her.' He winced. 'Sorry, I didn't mean that the way it sounded.'

Fran smiled. Adam's mouth had a horrible tendency to become disconnected from his brain whenever he was with Nell. 'Yes, but don't forget, Christine has an alibi too. She was with me and all the other contestants at the time of Miranda's death.'

He sighed. 'For God's sake...'

'There is one other line of inquiry I'd like to follow up,' said Nell, getting to her feet. 'So, if you could excuse me.' She checked her watch. 'Good luck with the competition today, Fran.'

Fran groaned. 'Don't remind me.' She looked at Adam. 'What do we do now?' she asked as Nell left the room. 'And don't say eat more breakfast.'

'Actually, I've been thinking,' he said. 'Remember on the day Miranda died when we asked about her next of kin? Midge told us that Miranda was an only child, but she also mentioned that Miranda and her husband had been unable to conceive.'

Fran nodded. 'She said Judy had told her that.'

'Exactly... so I wonder if Judy knows any more about the

relationship and the reasons why it broke up. Miranda *could* have children, clearly, so what went on there?'

'Shall we go find out?' said Fran. 'Good thinking, Batman.' She smiled as the tips of Adam's ears grew pink, and pushed her plate of uneaten toast across the table.

Judy had already finished her breakfast and was busy setting up the stable for the morning's competition. Fran had almost managed to forget she still had to take part, and the sight was an unwelcome reminder.

'Ah, Fran,' said Judy as they approached, 'just the person.' She scuttled across to Fran's workstation. 'I've left you some recipe ideas as per previous days. It's up to you, obviously, but my suggestion would be to go with the top one. It has the wow factor and I'm sure you can pull it off. See what...' She trailed off. 'Is everything okay?'

Fran nodded. 'I'll cook an old leather boot if you want me to,' she replied and then pulled a face. 'Sorry, Judy, I can't say my heart's in this any more.'

Judy frowned. 'Look, I know what you think... Harrison told me he's been in a spot of trouble over the show, and maybe he has been a bit... manipulative over some of the contestants, but that's only because he cares so much. This is still an amazing opportunity, Fran. Just think what winning could do for you.'

Fran smiled. She didn't trust herself to reply, because that was exactly the problem. She *was* thinking what winning could do for her, and it wasn't a happy thought. If she wasn't careful, her business, the one she had lovingly grown over several years, could end up being associated with one of the biggest scandals of recent years – one of the best-loved shows on TV harbouring someone who had deceived the public for years, a cheat, and very possibly a murderer.

'Could we ask you something?' said Fran, changing the

subject. 'Do you know how long ago Miranda and her husband were divorced? Were you working with her then?'

'What, Elliot?' Judy made a dismissive noise. 'Must have been about eight years ago now, maybe longer. But I was with her then, yes. Why do you want to know?'

'Midge mentioned that the marriage broke up because they couldn't have children. She said you told her that.'

'I did, yes. I don't think it was a secret. Or rather the media was kept in the dark, but we all knew about it. It was good riddance as far as Miranda was concerned.'

Fran frowned. 'Oh...?'

'Well, honestly, as if Miranda was going to give up her career to have a child, even if she could, and at her age too. I know lots of people have children later in life these days, but it would have been the worst possible timing for Miranda. Her career would have been over. Show business is a very fickle game, and if you're out of it for any length of time, that's it. People forget you and move on to the next big thing. Miranda wasn't about to take that chance and I can't say I blame her.'

'So, Elliot put pressure on her to have a child?'

'Well, yes, I... At least that's the impression I got.'

Fran exchanged a look with Adam. 'That sounds as if Miranda didn't want children at all?'

'I guess.'

'But, presumably, if Miranda told you they couldn't have children after all, that must mean that at one time she did want to? It's a bit confusing.' Fran cocked her head to one side. 'What was your impression of her husband?'

'Oh, I never actually met him, but Miranda said...' She trailed off when she realised the implications of her words. Did she actually know anything at all or was she simply repeating what Miranda told her? She frowned. 'No, Miranda definitely couldn't have children – I've no reason to doubt what she said. But she never really spoke about it either, not like people do, not like women do with each other. We were friendly, but Miranda wasn't the sort to wear her heart on her sleeve. I always assumed it was the reason why her marriage to Elliot broke up, though. I know he kept wanting her to have tests done, that kind of thing, even when she was approaching an age when having a child wouldn't be all that sensible.'

'Okay,' said Fran lightly. 'Thanks.'

Judy stared at her. 'You're not going, are you? Fran, we start in a few minutes.'

Fran closed her eyes. She really didn't want to do this all over again but she wasn't sure she had any choice. She also didn't know what else she and Adam could do. Until the answers to Nell's inquiries came back they had nothing further to go on. She attempted to find a smile. 'No, all good,' she said. 'I'll have a look through the recipes you've left and we'll take it from there, shall we?'

Judy smiled gratefully and hurried away.

Adam pulled a face. 'Now what? That didn't tell us anything except the fact that Judy knows diddly squat about Miranda's relationship with her husband. She's just repeating what Miranda told her. And Miranda wasn't exactly reliable, was she? She could be pretty economical with the truth when she wanted to be.'

'Hmm... There's something in all of this,' replied Fran. 'But for the life of me I don't know what.'

'Oh dear, someone looks a bit tired this morning.' It was Hope, smiling brightly. 'Shall I liven you up a bit?' she added, brandishing her case.

Fran smiled. 'Can you actually do that? Or have I got to settle for *looking* like I'm wide awake?'

'I wish,' replied Hope, still smiling. 'I could do with a magic wand, I think we're all feeling it a bit.' She pulled a face. 'But I'll see what I can do. Poor Christine has had a huge spot come up on her chin overnight. At least you haven't got that to worry about.'

Fran rolled her eyes at Adam, who grinned. 'I'll catch you later,' he said, mouthing good luck as he melted away.

Fran brightened her face, yet again. 'Right then, let's do this. Work your magic, Hope.'

Try as she might, Fran couldn't get her focus to stay on the competition and she might as well have been cooking an old boot for all the attention she paid her dish. It was a very good job she had Judy's recipe to follow. Her head was filled with questions, all of which went around and around in a loop, never once revealing any answers.

'Cooks, you have ten minutes,' shouted Midge.

Fran stared at her, suddenly hit by the enormity of Midge's predicament. Time was literally running out as far as she was concerned, and Fran knew how that felt.

Nothing had changed since this morning. Nothing which would help Midge, anyway. Miranda might have had a child once upon a time, a child she had very probably put up for adoption, but that didn't have any relevance here. It was something lots of people did. And the chances were that, when Nell found out the identity of the child in question, they'd be living a hundred and fifty miles away, working in a shop, or as an accountant, or head of a school, the possibilities were endless. It would be simply another dead end, a line of inquiry that would fizzle away to nothing, and with it any chance of removing Midge from Nell's suspect list.

'Is everything okay?' It was Pea, waving at her from across the aisle. 'You look as if you're away with the fairies.'

Fran mustered another smile. 'I am. Sorry...'

'Do you need a hand with anything? I'm done... Can't quite understand how it happened but I can help you plate up if you're in a rush?' She threw a furtive look at Judy, who was walking the room with a fixed but expectant smile on her face.

'Are you even allowed to do that?' Fran whispered.

Pea shrugged. 'Who cares?' she said, coming over to Fran's table.

Fran stared at the assortment of food that still lay in pans, oven trays and on chopping boards. 'It's meant to be beef wellington,' she said. 'I was okay while I was cooking, but it suddenly seems to have run away with me.'

Pea gave her a kindly smile. 'No worries. It looks incredible, Fran. Why don't you carve a couple of slices and I'll drain these mangetout?'

Like a camera image suddenly coming back into focus, Fran saw the elements of her dish with fresh eyes, and also what needed to be done. She smiled gratefully. 'Thanks, Pea. I lost it there for a minute.'

'Don't worry about it,' murmured Pea. 'I stood looking at a potato this morning for two whole minutes before I remembered I was meant to be peeling it. How I'm going to get to the end of the week, I don't know. That's *if* I get to the end of the week.'

They worked methodically for a few minutes until Fran was sure everything was back under control. 'Can I check something with you, Pea?' she asked. 'How old were you when you took part in the competition with Miranda?'

Pea screwed up her face. 'Early twenties?'

'And do you know how old Miranda was? Or Sally, as she was back then?'

Pea shrugged. 'About the same age, I guess, why?'

'I was just curious,' Fran replied, wondering if she could ask her next question without causing too much suspicion.

'Fran, we all know you're working with the police,' said Pea, her smile warm. 'Tony told me and Christine last night. And how you stood up for him with that snake, Vinny. He told us about his past too – I think he felt we should know. He seems such a lovely man. He was telling us about the plans for his business, and... Anyway, that doesn't really matter – what I wanted to say was if you need to ask me any questions, just fire away.'

A ripple of shock fired through Fran, which she did her best to hide. After all, at the moment there was nothing to suggest that Christine *did* have any connection to Miranda, and until Nell informed her otherwise, Fran had to assume there wasn't. So what harm could there be in Christine knowing the truth about her and Adam? She looked up at Pea's smiling face and tried to remember what she wanted to ask her.

She leaned in closer. 'I can't say too much, but when you were at the competition, did you see any evidence that Miranda might have had a child with her? You mentioned seeing her parents when we spoke before – could there have been a young child too? Perhaps passed off as a grandchild? Or even a sibling?'

Pea shook her head. 'No, but there couldn't have been. Miranda was an only child. Her mum and dad came to the show, but no one else.'

'Okay, thanks.' Fran thought for a moment. It wasn't conclusive evidence by any means, but perhaps the best they had at present. She stared down at her plate of food. It was as good as it was going to get. 'Sorry, Pea,' she added. 'But I have to dash.'

She found Nell talking to Adam over in the guest wing. They were both sitting in the kitchen, a plate of chocolate Hobnobs between them.

'Well, that's another challenge over,' she said, swiping one. 'Thank heavens for that. God, I'm starving. Anyway, I had a thought, and it's not conclusive, but I've just asked Pea if there was a child with Miranda's family when they were both at that competition. I wondered if they might have been passing her off as a grandchild or something, but Pea said she definitely didn't and—' She looked at Adam, whose gaze immediately dropped away. 'What?' she asked. 'Have you found out who the child is?'

Nell inhaled deeply. 'God, I hate my job sometimes,' she said, pushing the plate of biscuits towards one of the spare chairs. 'Why don't you sit down, Fran?'

'What's happened?' she asked, her heart beginning to thump uncomfortably.

'I've recently had a not particularly pleasant phone call with the district commissioner,' she said. 'I'm sorry, Fran, but I'm going to have to arrest her.'

Fran's eyes widened. 'Midge?' she asked. Although she knew the answer.

'I'm sorry, Fran. She's the only one with motive *and* opportunity. Chasing down potentially adopted children from years ago is all well and good, but even if we find her, there's nothing so far to suggest there's any connection with Miranda's death. If that changes, then great, but at the moment... Midge needs to start answering questions under caution. I wanted you both to know before I speak to her.'

Fran nodded. 'I understand. Thank you.' She bowed her head.

'So, if you've got some new information you think I ought to know about, you'd better tell me quickly.'

Fran shook her head. 'No, only my instincts, which are still telling me Midge had nothing to do with this.' She looked up to see Nell's face full of compassion. She didn't want to do this any more than Fran wanted her to. 'I just can't figure out why Midge didn't lie – if it was her, I mean. If she was the killer and trying to cover her tracks, why didn't she lie about the time she found Miranda? They were the only two not in the stable, so if you think about it, she had all the time in the world to play with. Why say she found Miranda at the only time when everyone else had an alibi apart from her? It makes no sense at all.'

'Maybe she isn't as smart as you think,' Nell replied gently.

'Most people trip themselves up because they make stupid mistakes. Why should Midge be any different?'

'Oh, come on,' argued Fran. 'You surely don't believe that.'

'I don't buy it either,' said Adam. 'Have you seen the timeline she produced? It's a work of art. There's nothing stupid—' He groaned the moment the words left his mouth.

Predictably, Nell's eyes narrowed. 'What timeline?' She looked at Fran, then across at Adam. 'Which one of you has it?' she said. 'Because whoever it is, I want to see it. Now.'

Fran raised her hands. 'Don't look at me,' she said. 'I don't know anything about it either.'

Adam dropped his head. 'I'll go and get it,' he said. 'It's in my room.'

Nell glared at her. 'How many times, Fran? For goodness' sake! I've kept you and Adam in the loop about everything that's been uncovered here. Information that I didn't have to share with you, and now I find out he's been keeping things from me. Again.'

'I'm sure it wasn't intentional,' said Fran. 'Adam will only have been trying to help and—' She stopped abruptly as Nell's eyebrows almost disappeared off the top of her head. She was digging them both an even bigger hole.

Adam returned in short order, laying a line of sellotaped pages in front of Nell without a word. There probably wasn't anything else he could say at this point. She waited while Nell examined the timeline, desperate to have a look at it herself.

'Credit where credit's due,' said Nell a few minutes later. 'This is a very fine piece of work. And one which Midge may well regret spending time on.'

'But that's the point,' argued Adam. 'Don't you see? Why would Midge even think about making something like that if she was guilty? She started it to prove she was innocent.'

Nell rolled up the pages and got to her feet. 'I've been a police officer for a very long time, and I've given up trying to fathom the workings of the criminal mind. The reasons why some people do the things they do are simply baffling and I've learned to accept that. Arresting Midge isn't going to bring me any pleasure at all. I think she's a hardworking, very skilled young lady and I don't want her to be guilty either. But what I want doesn't always fit with what I find, Adam, and I have to make decisions based on hard evidence. People lie, all the time, but time itself never does. If this proves Midge was the only person with opportunity then I have to arrest her.

'However, I hope I don't have to remind either of you that an arrest is simply the first part of a process. Midge will be questioned, under caution, but our investigation will continue. We won't stop exploring every avenue, and if we find anything which even remotely suggests Midge isn't guilty, we'll follow that up too. If you want to help her, I suggest you get your thinking caps on.'

21

'I've got that feeling again,' said Fran, staring at the pile of papers on her bed. 'You know, that one where I think I've seen something really important and for the life of me can't figure out what it is.' She picked up the top sheet, one of the ones Midge had given them on the very first day they arrived.

'I've got it too,' replied Adam. 'I don't have a photographic memory like you, but I'm certain I've missed something so blindingly obvious I'm going to kick myself when I remember.' He almost growled with frustration. 'And now Nell has Midge's timeline and I'm convinced that if I could look at it again, I'd see what's been bothering me.' He peered up at her, a wry expression on his face. 'Sorry,' he added. 'I should have shown it to you, but...'

'Never mind about that now,' replied Fran. 'I understand, and there *was* every likelihood you'd find something. But you didn't, so let's concentrate on what else we have.' She let her eyes run over the information again, but it didn't tell her anything she didn't already know. Names, job titles, how long folks had worked on the show, dates of birth, addresses. And all of it checked by Midge. She stopped, a flicker of something chasing through her head.

'What was it you said when Midge first gave us these?' she asked. 'Something about not taking things at face value?'

Adam frowned. 'Only that we should be wary of accepting information we're given as the absolute truth. When things are written down we tend to view them as accurate, whether they are or not. The difference being that when we hear something verbally we're better able to make a judgement on whether it's true or not.'

'So why do I get the feeling Midge really does have something to do with this, but not in the way we think?'

'Sorry, Fran, you've lost me.'

Fran screwed up her face. 'I've lost myself too. There's something that keeps tripping me up. Something to do with the fact that Midge *is* so reliable – she never gets things wrong. Just now Nell said that maybe Midge isn't as clever as we think she is. But that's just it; I think Midge *is* clever. I think she's accurate and I don't think she tells lies. In fact...' She stared down at the paper in her hand. 'I think we can believe everything she says...'

She ran down the column of names one more time. What was this list telling her? Which of the truths it contained had someone denied...?

And then she saw it.

Handing the sheet to Adam, she tapped her finger against one of the entries. 'Maths was never my strong point,' she said, 'so check for me. Look at that date of birth and tell me how old the person is.'

Adam squinted. 'Born on the fourteenth of January, nineteen eighty-eight, so that makes them... thirty-four.'

'Yet she told us she was thirty-six.'

Adam's eyes grew wide. 'Are you sure about that? Absolutely, positively, one-hundred-per-cent sure?'

Fran nodded. 'But why would you lie about your age? Unless you had something to hide...'

Adam scrambled to his feet, still clutching the sheet of paper. 'We need to speak to the boss.'

Nell was coming down the steps of Harrison's trailer when Fran hailed her, breathless from her and Adam's charge across the car park.

'You need to look at this,' she gasped, thrusting the list of names at Nell.

'Fran, I was just—' Her eyes met Fran's and she stopped. 'What am I looking at?' she said, now utterly focused on the page.

'Hope told me she's thirty-six,' said Fran. 'But she isn't, look. Check her date of birth. She's only thirty-four.'

Nell's eyes widened. 'Okay, but let's not get too excited. Midge might have got it wrong.'

'But she didn't,' insisted Fran. 'That's the whole point. Midge *doesn't* get things wrong and somehow...' She shook her head, tutting in frustration. 'Somehow that's the key to how Miranda was murdered. I don't know the how yet, but I'm certain I'm right.'

Fran willed Nell to believe what she was saying as the detective studied her face.

'Okay,' she said, turning back towards the trailer. 'Come inside for a minute.' Nell directed them towards the rear where Clare Palmer was busy, peering at a laptop screen.

'Have a seat,' said Nell. 'Clare is still looking for the name of our mystery child, but so far we've drawn a blank.' She passed across the piece of paper. 'Clare, can you run the search with this name?'

The detective constable gave a slight nod of her head and began to type. 'The make-up girl?' she asked.

Nell nodded. 'So, let's assume for a minute that Hope is, in fact, Miranda's long-lost daughter. What motive would Hope have for killing her? Wouldn't she be looking for a reunion rather than retribution? The latter seems a little extreme.'

'Not if she were rejected,' said Fran. 'Think about it – if you were a child put up for adoption, wouldn't you already have lived with the thought of rejection your whole life? I imagine it's the main reason many adoptive children never look for their biological parents in the first place – they simply can't get past the fact they weren't wanted. Plus, if they do make contact, there's always the risk they'll be rejected all over again. What if that's what happened to Hope?'

'It's possible,' said Nell. 'But would it be reason enough to kill? And if she did, why now? Hope has worked with Miranda for years. There must be more to it than that.' She suddenly frowned. 'Wait a minute.' She leaned forward to pick up a notebook from the table and began to flip back through the pages. 'When I said I had another line of inquiry to follow up earlier, what I did was ring the district commissioner's wife for a little chat.'

Clare Palmer's head shot up. 'You got a death wish, Boss?'

Nell stuck out her chin. 'I don't like being told what to do,' she replied. 'And it was a legitimate line of inquiry. Bunny was a contact of Miranda's, so—'

'Bunny? Is that her name?' Clare snorted and quickly looked back at her computer screen.

'And when Bunny and I had a chat,' continued Nell, 'she told me quite a different story about Miranda and Elliot. In fact, the picture we've been given, largely painted by Miranda herself, isn't the truth at all. Let's remember that Miranda was a woman who kept everything about herself private. She never let down her guard, even with close colleagues. She gave everyone the impression that *she* divorced her husband, that he was just another in the long line of people not worthy of her. But that wasn't true. According to Bunny, Elliot was the love of Miranda's life, the only person who ever made her happy, in fact. And, moreover, the pain of not being able to have children almost tore her apart. And it succeeded with her marriage. It *was* the reason Elliot divorced *her*, and it left Miranda heartbroken.'

Nell picked up another sheaf of papers from the table. 'These are Miranda's medical records – Miranda's, not Sally's. And there's pages of the stuff – most of it trivial. An appendix scare seven years ago, but other than that, nothing remarkable at all, except for one small series of entries. Entries which are very easy to miss unless you're looking for them. Entries concerning investigations Miranda underwent to see why she couldn't conceive. They were inconclusive, but it was the opinion of the consultant she saw that in all likelihood her infertility had been caused by a previous pregnancy. A pregnancy when Miranda was only eighteen, a pregnancy she tried to hide and never sought proper medical attention for. The child survived, but the trauma of a very difficult birth left her infertile.' Nell threw the report back on the table with a triumphant look in her eye. 'Hope is the reason why Miranda couldn't have children. Hope is the reason why her marriage to the only man she ever loved fell apart.'

'So, when Hope came looking for a happy reunion with her birth mother, you can imagine the reception she got,' said Fran.

Nell nodded. 'Indeed.' She sighed. 'But having said all that, it is, of course, pure speculation at the present time. In the absence of any other leads, however, it's also the best we have. I have to remind you, though, that Hope—'

'Boss?' interrupted Clare. Her eyes were fixed on the screen in front of her. 'It's true. Hope is Miranda's daughter. She was officially adopted by Patricia and Steven Robinson on the seventeenth April nineteen eighty-eight, when Hope was just over three months old. The birth mother is listed as Sally Grainger.'

'Right, let's get her in and see what she has to say. As things stand she has an alibi, so I need two things: the name of whoever's been covering for her, because someone must have been, and evidence of how she killed Miranda. Well done, I think you two might just have bought Midge some time.'

'What did you say?' asked Adam, his head coming up slowly.

'I said you might just have bought Midge some time.'

Adam was staring at a fixed point in the distance but he had that look on his face, the one which could only mean he was on to something.

'What is it?' Fran asked.

'Time...' he muttered. 'We don't have time...' He shook his head. 'No, she had all the time in the world...' He suddenly jumped up, eyes wild. 'Where will Midge be now?'

'In the stable, I expect. Why?'

'Because I know how she did it!' he yelled, already racing for the door.

Fran stared at Nell. 'Does he mean Midge or Hope?'

'I have no idea...'

'Adam, wait!'

But he'd already gone.

'Come and sit down, Hope,' said Nell gently. 'No point making a huge fuss over in the stable, is there? And I suspect you know why you're here.'

Hope nodded, calm and resigned, almost as if she was relieved that things were finally over.

Nell never ceased to surprise Fran; that when sitting in the presence of a murderer she could still act with such humanity. But perhaps that was why she did it. In the face of all that was inhuman, maybe that's all there was left.

'I think you've suffered enough over recent months,' said

Nell as Hope took a seat. 'So, I thought it was kinder all round to simply bring you back here and arrest you quietly. You do know that's about to happen, don't you?'

Another nod.

'You see, I was thinking,' continued Nell. 'I was thinking about Miranda, how she was such a charismatic person in many ways, but also someone who could be cruel and callous when the mood took her. A while ago, Adam mentioned something Betty had said to him, how people like Miranda break hearts and that when people's hearts are broken they do funny things.' She paused a moment. 'Miranda broke your heart too, didn't she, Hope?'

Hope's eyes filled with tears. 'All I wanted was for her to like me, to notice me. But she never really did. I couldn't believe it when I found out she was my mum. Miranda Appleby of all people... stuff like that didn't happen to me. And I know she gave me away when I was born, but I understood that and I didn't really blame her. I mean, she wouldn't have become Miranda Appleby if she had...'

'So, you decided to get a job working on the show?' prompted Nell.

'I didn't set out to, it was just one of those things. But when I saw the job advertised, I wondered if that's why I'd become a make-up artist all along – because I was destined to work with her. And when I got the job, I knew it was meant to be.' She looked down, biting her lip. 'We got on really well, at least I thought we did. I kidded myself we were friends, but we weren't, not really. And even when I started leaving those presents for her, she didn't want to know. I only wanted to be a good friend. I thought if she was scared, and needed someone to turn to, I could be that person. And then, in time, she'd realise how good a daughter I could be too. How much she could depend on me and love me. I asked her over and over again if everything was okay. Each time I left one of the presents for her I made sure I hung around more than usual, asking if she was all right, saying I thought she seemed down or preoccupied, hoping she would confide in me. I knew she was paranoid about her looks and growing old, that's why I chose the things I did. Being a make-up artist, I thought it would make her turn to me, I thought she'd realise how much she needed me. But she never did. She just pushed me away.'

'And what happened then?'

'I got angry. She didn't deserve all her adoring fans. People who worshipped her, who thought she was so lovely. They didn't know what she was really like. She basked in all that attention and it was built on lies.' Hope shook her head. 'And even then, I gave her one last chance. I told her I knew about the presents – that I knew who was sending them and that I could make everything okay.'

Nell flashed a glance at Fran. 'You told Miranda it was you who had sent the presents?'

'Not to start with, but she didn't believe me when I said I knew who it was and could help her. She said I was just a make-up girl, so how could I possibly help? That's when I told her the truth. Told her who I really was – that I wasn't just some silly make-up girl, that I was her daughter, someone she could love...'

Fran closed her eyes, knowing what was coming next. She knew what Hope had done, but her heart still went out to her.

'But she just laughed in my face. Said it was ridiculous, that she could never love someone like me.'

There was an awful silence for a few minutes before Nell leaned forward. 'Did you kill Miranda?' she asked gently.

Hope's mouth hung open as she looked first at Nell and then at Fran. 'No...' She frowned, confusion filling her face. 'Is that what you...?' The frown deepened. 'Oh God, is that what you think? That I killed her?' Tears began to pool at the corners of her eyes and, as Fran watched, one slipped free and trickled down her cheek. 'Why on earth would I have killed Miranda? I didn't hate her... She was my mum... I loved her.'

As Adam launched himself through the stable door, it never even occurred to him that they might be filming and he had just enough presence of mind to catch the door as it swung back. He closed it silently and let his gaze travel the room. Everyone was here, apart from Hope. Everyone, including Midge. But how to talk to her without drawing too much attention to himself? That was the question.

He hovered at the back of the room, watching as Midge noted something on her clipboard before calling out a time check for the contestants. She walked past the empty workstation where Fran ought to have been, but wasn't, and Adam realised that she had given him the perfect excuse to talk to Midge.

Midge had evidently noticed his arrival, because she turned and made a beeline for him. 'Where's Fran?' she said in an urgent whisper. 'She didn't come back after lunch.'

'I'll tell you in a minute,' he replied. 'But first, I need you to come with me.'

'I can't, Adam, I'm needed to keep time.'

He almost laughed at the irony of her statement. Midge, the keeper of time. How true that was.

'You really *do* want to come with me,' he said lightly, but he hoped with just enough of a glint in his eye to make Midge take notice.

She frowned. 'What's the matter?'

'I'll explain on the way. Please, we need to go, only make it look natural, like we're just chatting about something.'

Midge gave an enormous smile. 'What, like this?' she asked.

He smirked. 'That'll do.'

Once outside, he pulled out his phone and sent Fran a quick text before touching Midge's arm. 'We need to hurry,' he said.

'Where are we even going?'

'The cottage. Midge, on the day Miranda was killed, you said you were taking a nap before you went over to her trailer.'

'Yes, that's right.'

'So, what did you do when you woke up? What exactly did you do?'

She paused momentarily. 'I went to get a glass of water from the kitchen, checked the time and dashed back over to Miranda's.'

He nodded. 'Originally, though, you said you thought you'd overslept.'

'That's right. I thought I had. I came to in a bit of a panic, even though I rarely need my alarm. I often wake up just before it goes off – it's like a sixth sense, isn't it?'

'So you weren't actually late?'

'No. When I awoke it was a few minutes before four, so I just glugged down the water and left.'

'Okay,' said Adam slowly. 'I want to get this absolutely straight in my head. When you woke up you thought you were late, but when you checked, you realised you weren't, is that right?'

'That's right.'

'And how did you check the time?'

She frowned, giving him an odd look. 'I looked at the clock. There's one in the kitchen, over the oven.'

They were almost at the guest wing by this stage. 'So why didn't you check the time on your phone first?'

'Because I couldn't find it.'

'You'd dropped it outside, hadn't you? It was in the courtyard and Judy handed it back to you later on. Do you remember?'

She nodded. 'What's going on?' she asked. 'Why are we going to the cottage?'

'There's something I need to check. Something I think might prove to be the key to this whole thing.'

'Adam, you're not making any sense.'

'I will!' He almost ran up the path in his haste to get there. 'Is the back door locked?' he asked, although he was pretty sure he knew the answer.

Midge shook her head. 'No, because of the dogs. Hope lets them out for me sometimes and—' She stopped at the look on his face. 'It's just easier that way,' she finished, confusion furrowing her brow.

He led her straight into the kitchen. There was one final thing he needed to check. From behind the closed door at the far end of the room, he could hear the dogs snuffling, alert and expectant perhaps, but no more than that. The clock was on the wall, right over the cooker where Midge had said it was. 'Is that the right time?' he asked.

Midge checked her phone. 'Yes, it's bang on.'

'And you haven't touched it?'

She shook her head. 'Why, should I have?'

He smiled. 'No, but if I'm not much mistaken, someone else has.'

Midge still looked confused. 'I haven't the foggiest what you're talking about, Adam. What's with the clock? Why is it so important?'

He grinned. 'Because it's going to prove you're innocent of murder,' he said. And then he hugged her.

Fran was practically pacing the floor by the time Adam and Midge arrived at Harrison's trailer, while Nell was standing, hands on her hips, as she stared out of the window. Hope had been allowed to return to her room for the time being, under the careful watch of DC Palmer.

Fran almost fell on Midge the moment she came through the door. 'Thank God, you're okay!' she exclaimed, pulling her into a ferocious hug. 'You *are* okay, aren't you?'

Midge smiled as she pulled away. 'I think so. A bit dazed, actually.'

Fran nodded. 'Adam can do that to people,' she replied. 'He shot off, yelling he knew who did it, and for an awful few minutes, I thought he meant you. I'm so glad he didn't.'

'Me too... although I still don't really understand what he's talking about.'

'Come and sit down,' said Nell, turning around. 'I'm also rather intrigued to hear what Adam has to say.' She gave him a wry smile. 'Let's hear it then.'

Adam grinned. 'I can't believe I didn't spot it before, but Miranda's murder was clever, very clever indeed. It was planned down to the last detail because it relied completely on the fact that one person on set also planned everything down to the last detail. And that person is Midge. Everyone knows how good Midge is with time. She knows where everyone should be at any given moment and she's never late. In fact, everyone else relies on *her* to keep time for *them*. So, when Midge declared that she had found Miranda dead at a very specific time, no one even thought to contradict her. Except that Midge was wrong. Or, rather, it wasn't Midge who was wrong, it was time itself.'

Fran shook her head. 'I'm sorry, I still don't understand.'

'See, what we have to remember is that this is TV and, Fran, you've seen how it works – the show isn't even filmed in chronological order, it's a jumble of scenes which are expertly edited to make it look that way. That's what got me thinking. What if Miranda's death was the same?

'On the day she was killed, Miranda left the stable at a

quarter to four. This time has been corroborated by several people in their statements. She had just finished filming, and any number of people saw her. Then, fifteen minutes later, she was dead. Except that Miranda wasn't discovered bang on four o'clock as Midge said she was, but instead at a quarter past... and in all the kerfuffle and shock of hearing Miranda was dead, who thought to query the fact that Midge didn't appear to raise the alarm until maybe ten minutes later than she should have. Because, let's face it, when that kind of thing happens, who's checking their watch?

'The whole murder relied on the fact that there were two timelines, running in parallel – one outside the stable and one inside. The one inside was running true but the one outside, which only affected Miranda and Midge, was running fifteen minutes behind everyone else's. Someone had deliberately altered time for them by changing the hands on Midge's kitchen clock. Remember how Midge said she thought she'd slept longer than she meant to? She was right, she had. Her judgement, as always, had been spot on. Yet when she checked her clock, lo and behold, she found she wasn't late at all, but instead, perfectly on time. She flew from her cottage, thanking her lucky stars she wouldn't be late for her meeting with Miranda. Yet had Miranda been alive when Midge reached her, she would probably have found her frothing at the mouth on account of her tardiness. Midge *was* late, fifteen minutes late – the clock in her kitchen showed four o'clock when really it was four fifteen.'

'So, the timeline we have here is wrong?' said Nell, looking at the sellotaped sheets of paper Midge had produced.

'Exactly,' said Adam. 'Or rather, it isn't wrong. It is, as Midge intended, a very accurate account of everyone's movements between the two all-important times of a quarter to four and four o'clock. After that time there was no real need to check everyone's movements because we knew that Miranda had been killed some time *before* four o'clock when Midge

supposedly found her. And Midge is never wrong, don't forget.'
Adam tapped the sheets of paper. 'Knowing what we do now,
let's look at the timeline again. See here at three forty-five, this
is when Miranda left the stable to go back to her trailer. In
Midge's altered timeline, however, her clock would have shown
it to be three thirty, but she was asleep, and completely
unaware of this. Then, over in the stable, there's a hive of
activity up until 4 p.m. – the contestants are just finishing their
break; Judy is setting up for the next challenge; Harrison, Sam
and Woody are chatting about the next stage of filming; and
Hope is just about to touch up the faces of anyone who needs
it. Everyone is accounted for and Midge is still blissfully
asleep.

'Now, let's run everything on by a few minutes and, as you
can see, not much has changed – at four o'clock everyone is still
busy and accounted for. Same at five past, same at ten past and,
meanwhile, over in the cottage, Midge is just waking up,
panicking because she thinks she's late. She looks for her phone
to check the time, but she can't because our killer has taken it,
dropping it in the courtyard to be found by Judy later on. So,
Midge checks the clock in her kitchen instead and finds to her
surprise it's still a little *before* four. And it's in these next crucial
few minutes that the murderer's plan comes into its own.

'The timing was tight, very tight, but how long would it take
someone intent on murder to run from the stable to Miranda's
trailer, kill her and run back? A couple of minutes, no more.
And by the time Midge raises the alarm, the murderer is already
back in the stable along with everyone else, safe in the knowledge that because it's now four fifteen, as far as alibis go, it's past
the time anyone will be interested in. Except that when Midge
drew up her timeline, ever diligent, she carried on plotting
people's movements for us, right up until a quarter past four. All
of which means that *we* can now see that, come that time,
everyone is still accounted for. Everyone except for one person.'

Adam pointed to the grid. 'And if we check, that person will be Hope. That's how she did it and I think we already know why.'

Midge's head shot up. She'd been staring at the timeline, trying to make sense of Adam's words. 'Hope?' She shook her head. 'No, it can't be Hope. She's my friend... she would never...' She stared at Fran. 'If what you're saying is true then whoever murdered Miranda knew I'd get the blame for it, they knew I'd be the only one without an alibi. Hope would never do that to me.'

'I'm sorry, Midge,' said Adam. 'I know it's not what you want—' He stopped, looking at the faces around him.

'Adam,' said Fran gently, 'Hope didn't kill Miranda. She confessed to sending those awful gifts. She was angry and desperately hurt by her, but she didn't kill her.'

Adam blinked, looking down at the sheets of paper.

'We obviously need to check out what Hope's told us,' added Nell. 'But I believe her, Adam. I think Hope is guilty of a lot of things, but even after Miranda pushed her away, time and time again, she still believed ultimately that Miranda would grow to love her, as only a mother could. I don't think she had it in her to kill Miranda.'

'Miranda was Hope's mother?' Midge's voice was full of sadness.

Fran nodded. 'She was adopted when she was only a few months old.'

'Oh, poor Hope...'

Adam was still staring at the timeline.

'Hope has an alibi too, Adam, I'm sorry,' said Nell. 'Your idea was a good one but...'

She didn't finish, she didn't need to. And Fran had a horrible feeling she knew what was coming next.

'Midge...' continued Nell. 'I've delayed this as long as I could, while there was still a possibility that someone else—'

'No, wait!' shouted Adam. 'Please... just do as I suggested.

Let's work out the timeline. Let's run everything through with the new timings and check.' He looked at Nell. 'Please.'

The seconds ticked by as all eyes turned on the detective. If ever there was a time for her to give Adam the benefit of the doubt, this was it. She didn't need to, she had more than enough reason to arrest Midge. Fran swallowed. And prayed.

'Okay,' said Nell, rolling her eyes. 'I must be mad. But do it. Quickly.'

22

Time was a funny thing. Fran was often aware of it as she cooked, on occasion running faster than it had any right to, and, at others, dragging interminably. Three days ago, fifteen minutes had been all it had taken to change the course of several lives, and the next fifteen looked set to do the same. Since Adam had explained how Miranda had been murdered, Betty had been called to look after Midge, the full weight of what had happened taking its toll on her. Her tears were a mixture of relief and sadness, and anger too, at Miranda's callous treatment of a friend. Hope was with her, cautioned, chastened, but clearly relieved that Midge was no longer facing the threat of arrest.

In due course, a forensic team would also be arriving to take fingerprints from the clock in Midge's kitchen. Fingerprints which, hopefully, would prove that time had been altered twice – once by winding the hands back by fifteen minutes, and then again when returning them to normal at some point after Miranda's death. Until the results came in, no one would know for certain if Adam's theory was right, but these next few minutes might also prove he was.

Over in the stable, the competitors would be about to finish the afternoon's challenge, oblivious to the drama that had been taking place outside of it. But, then, hadn't that been the key to this whole affair? With the focus so firmly in one place anything could be happening elsewhere.

Checking her watch, Nell nodded. 'Shall we go and wrap this up?' she said.

The mood was sombre as they walked over to the stable, with Fran leading the way. Inside, however, the atmosphere was celebratory. Time had evidently just been called, and Fran caught a round of high fives between Tony, Christine and Pea. They were one day closer to the final. One day closer to winning. It would be hard telling them this was unlikely to happen.

Judy, too, was smiling broadly as she walked down the aisle of workstations. Harrison was waiting for her, ready to add his congratulations and, as Fran watched, they hugged, briefly, but it spoke of the intimacy between them. Pulling away, Judy caught sight of Fran and hurried over.

'Fran! You missed the entire afternoon, we've just finished.' Her expression changed to one of anxiety. 'But we should still be able to let you catch up, just about. We could film it later, couldn't we?' She looked back at Harrison for confirmation.

He nodded, his face falling.

'That's okay,' said Fran. 'Maybe you should just rule me out and let the others go forward to the final. I don't mind.'

'But...' Judy paused, studying her face. 'Is everything okay?'

Fran shook her head. 'Not really, no. Midge has been arrested.'

Judy looked over Fran's shoulder to where Nell was standing with Adam and Clare. 'But surely they don't think...' She looked at Harrison. 'Midge has been arrested,' she said, as if he wasn't capable of hearing it for himself. He looked drawn and anxious.

'I did wonder when I saw her leaving earlier. Hope's gone too,' he said coming forward, his face a picture of concern.

Fran nodded. 'She's also been helping the police with their inquiries.'

'So what have they said?' asked Judy. 'Is Midge okay?'

'Not really. They arrested her for Miranda's murder,' said Fran. She shot a glance at the competitors but they were still in the happy throes of accomplishment and oblivious to her arrival. 'It was horrible. Poor Midge was in a terrible state and for a while it looked as if that was that. Thankfully, some new evidence came in. That's why I've been gone so long. Adam and I have been helping them piece it all together.'

'Oh, thank heavens,' said Harrison. 'Where is Midge now?'

'She's over with Betty. She's a bit upset, as you can imagine. And shocked.'

'I guess it was only a matter of time before she was arrested,' said Judy. 'Given she was the only one among us with no alibi. But, yes, thank heavens. What was the evidence?' she added, adjusting one of the clips in her hair. 'It must be pretty strong if they've released Midge already.'

'It seems she was set up.' Fran looked first at Harrison, then back at Judy, finally turning towards the competitors. 'Isn't that right, Judy?'

Silent seconds ticked past as Fran held her breath, conscious that Nell was standing only a few feet away.

Judy gave a tight smile. 'You know, you do it so well, Fran, the friend-to-all act, when really you're nothing of the sort, are you?'

'I do it almost as well as you plan murders, Judy,' she replied. 'Almost, but not quite.'

Harrison was staring at her, the colour draining rapidly from his face as he took in the meaning of their exchange. 'Would someone like to tell me what's going on?' he said. 'Are you accusing Judy of murdering Miranda?' His head turned, following the line of Judy's gaze as she stared at Nell. 'I've never heard anything so ridiculous. For heaven's sake, why would Judy want to kill Miranda?'

Fran raised her eyebrows. 'I would imagine because Miranda was a big fat fraud and Judy got sick of her taking all the glory for something that was rightfully hers. That's about the size of it, although feel free to correct me if I'm wrong.'

'What?' Harrison was angry now. 'I really hope you know what you're talking about, because that's slander. Miranda might be dead but you can't go around saying things like that.' He swung around to glare at Nell. 'I assume you have some evidence to back up such ludicrous claims.'

'Oh, we do, Mr Shaw, you can be certain of that.'

'Then...?' He stared at Judy, imploring her to contradict what had been said.

'Oh, for goodness' sake, you must have worked it out,' she replied, rolling her eyes at Harrison. 'All those times when Miranda was more than a little vague... when she needed a reminder of a recipe and yours truly came to her rescue. Yes, it's true, I admit it. But so what? Lots of people have ghost writers, in essence that's all I am. In fact, I even volunteered the information to Fran a few days ago. Of course that was when I thought she was writing a book about the show and not in cahoots with you lot. But what's still important here is that I did it because I didn't want Miranda's name to suffer. I did it to protect her. Does that sound like the actions of someone who wanted her dead?'

'Possibly not...' mused Nell. 'Although it also sounds like the actions of a very clever person who knew she might need to justify her innocence at some point. Nice try, Judy, but not enough, sadly.'

'What you've said is pure conjecture. I've made no move to hide my involvement in the show. It's you who are trying to make it into something it isn't.'

'In which case, how about the forensic evidence I'm just waiting to have confirmed? Perhaps that's something which might make you a little more convinced of our case against you. You left fingerprints somewhere you shouldn't, but maybe you have an answer for that too?'

Harrison took a step forward. 'Judy, you don't have to answer any questions, they're just trying to catch you out.' He glared at Nell. 'If you want to ask Judy questions like that then you'll need to arrest her so she can have a solicitor present.'

'I'd be glad to,' replied Nell.

She was about to draw breath when Judy interrupted.

'Oh, for goodness' sake, Harrison, shut up! I'm a big girl, I can look after myself.'

Harrison looked as if he'd been slapped. He stared at her, mouth open, moving ever so slightly backwards. 'Why didn't you tell me about the recipes?' he asked.

'What?' Judy frowned, irritated now.

'The recipes,' he repeated. 'Why didn't you tell me they were yours and not Miranda's?'

'Do I have to tell you everything?' she replied. 'Can't a girl have any secrets?' She smiled, but her attempt at levity fell flat.

'You do when it concerns the show I produce. That isn't something you should have kept to yourself. There are all sorts of implications, contractual ones. Not least of all ones which mean you've fallen foul of the spirit of the show.' He paused, eyes narrowing. 'Oh, now I get it... the way you just happened to have a couple of perfect outfits to present the show. The way you had ideas all planned out and ready to go. The way you got everyone else to convince you to take on Miranda's role in the show and then presented it to me with your simpering smile. "I don't really want to do it, Harrison",' he mimicked, drawing in a deep breath. '"It looks as if I'm using you to feather my own nest, but you know that's not my style." I think maybe that *is* your style, Judy. I think you've been using me, while all the time professing you're not that kind of girl.'

Fran winced. They were pretty much the exact same words Judy had said to her.

'Everything you've done since Miranda died has been to further your own career, hasn't it? Except that you've been masquerading as a selfless, supportive colleague. I don't think you're selfless at all. Instead, I think you're very self*ish*. And if you can use me the way you have, I've no doubt you wouldn't think twice about using Midge, letting her take the rap for something you've done. Wherever your fingerprints are, I hope it's somewhere they really have no place to be.'

'You're pathetic, Harrison, you know that,' retorted Judy. 'No wonder I've had to drive this whole show myself, you wouldn't have had the guts, not really. All mouth and no trousers. But none of that makes me a killer and, besides, I've never been anywhere near Midge's kitchen, why should I have?'

Judy was so busy glaring at Harrison she didn't even realise what she'd said. Until she noticed that everyone was staring at her, one person, in particular, very intently.

'I never mentioned anything about Midge's house,' said Nell, her voice dangerously quiet. 'Let alone her kitchen. Would you like to explain to me why you've just made that assumption?'

Judy's mouth hung open, but no more words came out. They didn't need to – her guilt was plain for all to see.

Nell studied her intently for a few more moments before looking back at Harrison, her expression considerably softer. 'I think perhaps you and I might need to have another chat, if that's okay. In due course...' She nodded towards the show's three remaining contestants, who stood huddled and watchful. 'I think you have enough on your hands right now.'

Then she turned to Clare and smiled. 'DC Palmer, would

you like to inform Ms Mulligan of her rights before I take her away.' She paused for a second, looking as if she was about to laugh. 'You know in America they're known as Miranda rights... How ironic, but quite appropriate, don't you think?'

23

THE NEXT DAY

'So, if you're ready, for one last time... Country cooks, cook!'

Fran grinned as Midge's voice rang out around the stable. Christmas might still be a while away yet but the atmosphere was distinctly festive this morning.

'Wish you were still taking part?' asked Midge, with a gentle nudge to Fran's elbow.

Fran slid her a sideways look. 'No, thank you. I'm much happier on *this* side of the camera.'

The decision to continue with the show had been ridiculously easy in the end. After Judy had been led away the stable had erupted into a flurry of stunned questions, which poor Harrison did his best to answer. At least he, and everyone else, were now in the clear as far as the murder inquiry went, but he had still been left with a show that was floundering on the rocks. Without Judy there was no host, no one to sort out provisions for the competitors and no one to judge it. The mood had quickly turned despondent as everyone realised what that meant until, much to their surprise, Harrison had announced that he was buggered if he was going to let his show be ruined, and asked Fran if she could step into the breach. It had taken

Fran all of two seconds to agree, with the proviso that she stayed categorically *behind* the camera. She couldn't bear the competition to fizzle away to nothing – it seemed the very worst kind of ending.

There were wounds to be licked and a whole gamut of emotions to deal with, but for one last day, all of that would be put aside for the final challenge of the competition – the Christmas centrepiece, a dessert to top all desserts.

'Fran, I can't thank you enough.' It was Harrison, his voice low as he watched the action at the workstations. 'I don't know what we'd have done without your help.'

'You'd have sorted it, one way or another,' she said. 'You're a family and families stick together. We've all had a hand in today.' She paused a moment. 'What will you do now?'

A wry smile crossed Harrison's face. 'Carry on,' he said. 'I'm not sure how, but we'll survive. News about the show will ensure we're plastered across the media for a while yet, but it will pass and we'll soon be old news. It may even do us a few favours and, hopefully, like a phoenix rising from the ashes, a new version of *Country Cooks Cook* will be born.'

'But what will happen about *this* show? Do you know yet?'

Harrison shook his head. 'It's going to be very hard to cobble anything together after what's happened, but I'll give it my best shot. It may turn into a very different kind of programme, but that's no bad thing. Events of the last few days are too important not to acknowledge. Miranda may not have been what I and the nation thought she was, but she was still the face that changed the way millions of people felt about cooking. That can't be allowed to pass by without some sort of tribute.' He smiled at Midge. 'There's still time to reconsider your decision,' he said. 'There'll always be a job here for you if you want it.'

Midge looked much better this morning. There were still a few tell-tale signs of the tears that had been shed, and the weight of anxiety she had carried around for days, but there was a lightness in her eyes now, and a sense of resolve.

'Thank you, that means a lot, but—' She broke off to look at her clipboard. 'I think it's time I put this down for a while.'

'I still can't get my head around what's happened,' said Harrison. 'And the lengths Judy went to, to not only conceal what she'd done, but to leave Midge taking the blame for it. It's the sheer callousness of it I'm struggling with.'

Fran gave him a sympathetic look. 'Judy took all Midge's meticulous attention to detail and used it against her, and it was her clipboard which gave Judy the idea in the first place. Midge had said to her once that there were not enough hours in the day, so Judy simply created a little more time. It was pretty simple in the end, and very effective.'

Beside her, Midge pulled a face. 'She even kept a little dish of chicken in one of the fridges so that she could bribe her way into my cottage – in case Miranda's dogs wouldn't let her in.'

'Adam spotted it, actually, on the day Miranda died,' said Fran. 'Judy asked him to pass her some cream from the fridge to make Miranda a hot chocolate. Of course, he only realised its significance later on. Just like I saw Judy brush dog hairs from her trousers. Inconsequential details when viewed on their own,' she added, 'but which all add up to a much bigger picture.'

'I've been an absolute mug, of course,' replied Harrison, a resigned expression on his face. 'I let Judy's ideas for the show become *my* ideas for the show, never really thinking how much she would profit by them. Once news got out of Miranda's deception, she would have been in the perfect position to take over her empire. In fact, by hosting the show, she already had one foot in the door.'

'Don't be too hard on yourself,' said Fran. 'Judy had everything planned down to the last detail and if it hadn't been for Adam, poor Midge would have been in an awful lot of trouble.'

Midge coloured slightly, her head swinging around. 'Where is Adam anyway?'

'He won't be long,' replied Fran. 'He's helping Nell with a few things.'

Midge nodded as she checked her watch. 'I think we had better do the first of our rounds,' she said to Harrison, nodding at the workstations. 'Or we'll miss the beginning stages.'

Fran smiled as she watched them walk away. Midge was far too conscientious to stay away from her work for long.

Fran couldn't believe what everyone had managed to achieve. Despite all the changes to the schedules, the stress and mayhem, each of the contestants had done themselves proud. She doubted whether she would have been able to produce anything half as remarkable.

Christine's cake may have seemed simple enough, but the sponge was light, moist and packed with flavour. And it was the way she had turned it into Santa's sack, full of toys, which transformed it from the ordinary to an incredible feat of engineering, if nothing else. The presents were each 'wrapped' in brightly coloured fondant paper complete with bows, while the sack was even partially tied at the top with a length of gold braid, made from decorated marzipan.

Pea had opted for a meringue dessert, with no less than fourteen individual layers, sandwiched together with different flavoured creams and decorated with, among other things, a tumble of jewel-like pomegranate seeds down one side.

And last, but by no means least, was Tony. Building a croquembouche was hard enough, making one in the shape of a three-dimensional Christmas tree seemed to defy all the laws of physics. The choux pastry was light and just crisp enough to safely hold its cargo of sweet fillings, from white chocolate and raspberry cream to orange and honey. The whole thing was a triumph, glittering with strands of spun caramel tinsel and tiny baubles on the ends of the branches made from coloured sugar-coated hazelnuts. One or two had fallen off, but Fran could forgive him for that – his hands had been shaking too much to hold them still while the caramel glue around them set.

'I don't know what to say,' said Fran, as she tasted each for about the fifth time. 'I'm just sorry that people won't get to see these on their screens in a few weeks' time. They deserve to be appreciated by the whole country.'

'I'm working on it,' said Harrison. 'I can't promise anything, but I'll do all I can to get out a show of some sort. It may not look much like you thought it would, but I'll do my best. And if I can't, I'll make it up to you all at some point, and that *is* a promise.'

The cameras were still rolling. They had filmed the whole thing as if nothing untoward had happened, maximising the chances of Harrison getting something he could use.

He smiled at Fran. 'So, who's it going to be then?' he asked.

Fran screwed up her face, turning bright red in the process. 'This is so difficult, but it's going to have to be...' – she took in a deep breath – 'Tony. I'm so sorry because you're all incredible. I wish you all could win.'

But Pea and Christine were already busy hugging Tony, who looked stunned, but more than happy.

'Oh, I knew you'd do it,' cried Pea. 'Bloody well done.'

Her words seemed to echo everyone's sentiments and the stable erupted into a noisy round of congratulations, not just for Tony, but for everyone who, despite the odds, had brought the show to an end.

'Oh, I'm going to miss you,' said Fran, throwing her arms around Midge.

'Me too.' Midge squeezed her hard for a second before

pulling away. 'And you,' she added, drawing a very surprised Adam into a hug. Surprised, but really rather pleased, noticed Fran with delight.

'Would now be a good time to add our goodbyes?' said Nell, coming to stand beside them. 'We're just about done here and duty calls back at the station, so...' She beamed at Midge. 'Still got your clipboard then, I see.'

Midge grinned back. 'I do, but look...' She lifted the top page to show the one underneath. It was completely blank. 'That's it,' she said. 'After today, no more lists, no more timings, no more jobs. No more job, in fact.'

Nell raised her eyebrows.

'I've handed in my notice,' Midge added. 'Now that I have my freedom, it felt like something I had to do.'

'Good,' replied Nell. 'I'm glad. It's about time you had a break.'

'Oh yes, I have all the time in the world...'

Nell nodded. 'You have indeed. Do you know what you'll do?'

'Nope. But the dogs and I are going to take some time, relax, have a think and generally decide how the rest of our lives are going to look. Not for too long though, I know what I'm like. I'll probably be bored rigid and desperate to be busy again.'

Nell withdrew a small white card from her pocket. 'Well, when that time comes, give me a call,' she said. 'I have a job coming up in my department soon. For a CIO – that's Civilian Investigation Officer for the uninitiated. It requires someone who's diligent, thorough, with a meticulous eye for detail and who is ruthlessly efficient. I think you'd be perfect.'

Midge took the card with a huge smile on her face. 'Do you really think I could do something like that?'

But Nell just dipped her head. She was never one for being overly demonstrative.

Midge looked down at her hand. 'You will keep in touch, won't you?' she asked.

Fran nodded. 'Of course. We'd both like that, wouldn't we, Adam?'

Adam's beanie was in his hands, the tips of his ears glowing pink again. 'Er, yes. Absolutely.'

Nell was already walking towards the door, a hand raised in a final farewell.

'We'll have to go soon as well,' said Fran. 'And let you get everything *finished*.' She looked around the room, still hung with decorations and full of festive cheer. There was a huge amount of work to be done. 'But perhaps we'll see you soon?'

Midge looked straight at Adam. 'I hope so,' she said.

A LETTER FROM EMMA

Hello, and thank you so much for choosing to read *Death at Beresford Hall*. I hope you've enjoyed reading it as much as I've enjoyed writing it. So, if you'd like to stay updated on what's coming next, please do sign up to my newsletter here and you'll be the first to know!

www.bookouture.com/emma-davies

Time really is the strangest thing, don't you think? As Adam and Fran found out during the course of their latest mystery, sometimes it runs fast and sometimes slow. Sometimes, it can even be manipulated. However, there's no getting away from the fact that time is vitally important to us. We might not like the feeling of living our lives by the clock, often wishing to be set free from it, but it also brings us order and routine and, whether we mark time or not, it still passes. And we must make the most of every second.

To me, time feels very different depending on where I am in the writing process – when I'm writing a first draft, it scurries by as I desperately try to catch more of it. But when I'm editing, with each successive round, going deeper and deeper, line by line, word by word, it slows until it almost feels like treacle. It's something I'm always conscious of and, while there is a rhythm to each book, it's also true that each occupies its own place in time according to whatever else is going on in my life when I'm writing it. So, while each book has a title, in my head it also has a subtitle which reflects what I was doing at the time. This book, for example, is the one I wrote while moving house, or rather preparing to move house – it's not a quick process! But it marks a period of transition and, literally, the ending of a chapter.

My next book, therefore, will be written in a new house, in a new place and, importantly, in a new time. I hope to see you there!

In the writing of my books I'm also incredibly grateful to my wonderful publishers, Bookouture, for enabling me to bring you these stories and for their unfailing support. Thanks also to my wonderful team of editors, in particular, Susannah Hamilton for her sage advice.

And finally, to you, lovely readers, the biggest thanks of them all for continuing to read my books, and without whom none of this would be possible. You really do make everything worthwhile.

Having folks take the time to get in touch really does make my day, and if you'd like to contact me then I'd love to hear from you. The easiest way to do this is by finding me on Twitter and Facebook, or you could also pop by my website, where you can read about my love of Pringles among other things.

I hope to see you again very soon and, in the meantime, if you've enjoyed reading *Death at Beresford Hall*, I would really appreciate a few minutes of your time to leave a review or post on social media. Every single review makes a massive difference and is very much appreciated!

Until next time,

Love, Emma xx

KEEP IN TOUCH WITH EMMA

www.emmadaviesauthor.com

 facebook.com/emmadaviesauthor

twitter.com/EmDaviesAuthor

Made in the USA
Las Vegas, NV
10 February 2023

67268051R00171